Diary of a Mad First Lady

Diary of a Mad First Lady

DiShan Washington

Thanks for your support!

Blessings,

DiShan W.

URBAN
Renaissance

www.urbanbooks.net

Urban Books, LLC
78 East Industry Court
Deer Park, NY 11729

Diary of a Mad First Lady ©copyright 2010 DiShan Washington

ISBN 13: 978-1-60162-206-8
ISBN 10: 1-60162-206-6

First Printing March 2010
Printed in the United States of America

10 9 8 7 6 5 4 3 2 1

This is a work of fiction. Any references or similarities to actual events, real people,
living, or dead, or to real locales are intended to give the novel a sense of reality. Any
similarity in other names, characters, places, and incidents is entirely coincidental.

Distributed by Kensington Publishing Corp.
Submit Wholesale Orders to:
Kensington Publishing Corp.
C/O Penguin Group (USA) Inc.
Attention: Order Processing
405 Murray Hill Parkway
East Rutherford, NJ 07073-2316
Phone: 1-800-526-0275
Fax: 1-800-227-9604

The book is dedicated to my dear grandmother,
Rosia Reese, who has gone on to be with the Lord. I love and
miss you terribly.
April 4, 1937 – February 19, 2009

Acknowledgments

Wow! Where does one begin when attempting such a feat? Being that this is my first work published by a major publishing company, one mind steers me to recognize everyone from my fifth grade teacher, who recognized my writing talent, to the first person who took a chance and bought my first self-published book back in 2004. However, I have learned that when you start thanking people, you always, always forget someone. So, with that being said, I will attempt to just name a few people who I will always be in their debt.

First, to the One who will forever be the visible force behind my success, gifts, and talents, Jesus Christ. It is in Him that I live, I move, and have my being. To Him I owe my life, and it is my vow that He will always have it.

To my king, my husband, my best friend, Myrondous A. Washington: Thank you so much for always being the light in the midst of my darkness, for being the beat of my heart, and for being the melody in the song that our love sings. In spite of all that we have been through, we have overcome. You're the reason I go on, and I will spend my life loving you . . . all of you. Olive Juice. (Our inside joke)

To my parents, Pastor J.C. and Melinda Winters: What a journey we have all had. I want to thank both of you for giving me life. I can truly say that I admire the two of you so much. It

Acknowledgments

is your dedication and faithfulness that has taught me how to persevere. Thank you for being my biggest fans and for being my cheerleaders even when I wasn't in the game. Your unprecedented love will forever live in my heart. I love you both so very much.

To my little brother, Jerrell, and my little sister, Beth: You two are so talented, and I expect nothing from you but greatness. Let them say what they will about us Winters kids, but we are on to bigger and better things. I love you both with all of my heart.

To Detras, Frank, my nieces, and nephews: Much love to all of you.

To my grandfather, Jimmy Reese (Bigdaddy): When MoMo died this year, I saw what manner of a man you were. You have been my strength on so many days, and I admire your courage. You both gave me my foundation in the Lord, and I'm forever grateful. I'm so glad that she had an opportunity to see this book come to fruition, and now that it has gone to the next level, I know she would be even more proud. You just keep the faith, and although our matriarch is gone, I'm the closest thing to her that you've got. (smile) I love you always.

To my grandmother, Sallie Williams: What can I say about such a virtuous woman? A) You're the sharpest dresser I know. B) You're the sharpest dresser I know. C) You're the sharpest dresser I know! But, on a serious note, I think about the many intimate conversations we've had in the past year. And as I reflect, I realize how much you mean to me. You've been through so much, oftentimes giving of yourself so that others can have. I've seen you take a back seat so that others can occupy the front. Well, Grandmama, your labor is not in vain, because the impact you've made in my life is unprecedented. I love you from the bottom of my heart.

To my second mom, Shirley Washington: You're a survivor. I sit in amazement and envy your perseverance. You've beaten the odds and defeated every obstacle that has come your way. Thank you for being my friend and for interceding for me; because I know that if nobody else can get a prayer through, you can! I love you.

To my father-in-law, ML Washington: What a funny man you are. I know that I can always count on you for a moment of humor. Thanks for raising a good man and for accepting me as your daughter. Love you always.

To Melvin, Cornelia, and MJ Washington: You all are more than just in-laws to me. Thank you for your unwavering support of me in everything that I set out to do. I know that if no one else has my back, the both of you do. I will always be grateful for you. Love you both.

To my special cousin, Deborah Ellis: Girl, I love you. Your sweet and humble spirit is what's missing in the world today. Thanks for the level of respect that you give me. It means more than you will ever know. Our bond is unbreakable, and just know that wherever I go, you're going too. I love you, cuz.

To my favorite uncle, Marvin Jackson: Only we know. (smile) You're one in a million, and I thank you for always being there when I need you. Love you forever.

To ALL of my family: It's too many of y'all to name. I heard some of you got mad because I didn't put your name in the other books. Well, to keep that from happening again, I will just say collectively—I love you ALL.

To my literary mother, Victoria Christopher Murray: You believed in me. You never gave up on me. You nursed me back to life in so many ways, and I could NEVER repay you. I pray that God will bless you in ways that you've never known for blessing me in ways that I never knew I could be. I love you so much, and I pray that when my life is over down here on Earth, somebody will be able to say that I'm half the writer that you are. I love you, Mom! (Yes, that's an exclamation point, and I know that I'm past three. Smile.)

To Agape Global Church: You are the best church in the world. Thank you for giving me the privilege of being your first lady. I take that seriously, and while I'm not perfect, I'm striving. I hope that something I've done has been a blessing to you. I look forward to many years to come.

To Shanna Fountain: I miss our friendship. I'm still keeping my fingers crossed that the Iowa snow will deliver you back to the Georgia sun. (smile) Love you, girl.

To my agent, Portia Cannon: Thank you SO much for taking a chance on me when you didn't even know me. I am forever grateful for all that you've done. I look forward to many years of friendship and working together.

To Dr. Bridget Hilliard and the FLN: You all are AMAZING women. Dr. B, words cannot describe the impact you've made in my life. You've been an ear, a shoulder, a confidante. Thank you for everything and for allowing God to use you. I love you.

To all my first ladies on the Network: Much obliged to you for your support and kindness. This book is for you and every first lady across America. We will reshape the way the world sees us. Though the journey gets long, we shall carry on.

To everyone that I did not mention: It doesn't mean that I don't love you. I just can't write a book of acknowledgments—LOL. But, please know that I love you dearly.

To a couple of special people: Regina Crothers and Tara: You were there in a very tough season. Thank you, and I love you both.

Last, to every reader, thank you. It' because of you that we writers have an outlet to express our creativity. I can't speak for anyone else, but as long as you keep reading, I'll keep writing great stories. Much love to you all.

Prologue

Michelle

Things are never what they seem. It matters not that people look at my life and think it's perfect, or that I'm perfect—it's not and I'm not. I've been married for two years and a half, and been a first lady about as long as Barack Obama has been the President, and I'm beginning to wonder if I'm cut out for this. Don't get me wrong; I love my husband and I love our church. But, the drama that I've been though has been unbelievable to say the least. Sitting here in this courtroom waiting for the sentencing of Daphne Carlton, the woman who tried to wreck my life with her devious schemes of harassment, I wondered just how much more I would have to endure as the price of being the first lady.

I never cared about what being the first lady meant. I just happened to fall in love with a man who had a calling on his life to be a pastor. All these women who were wishing they had this "dream" life should take a course on what really goes on behind the scenes before they sign up for the job. The loneliness you encounter because your husband is off somewhere preaching a conference or revival. The bitterness you feel toward people when they mistreat your husband or go against what he feels God is leading him to do with the congregation. The accusations that all preachers are money hungry and only want to ride in fancy cars and live the high life. And, not to mention that it seems to be one judgmental thing after the other.

Darvin was not like that. He really did take what he did seriously, and most times he was not appreciated for it. Sometimes I wished my husband had any other job than that of a pastor— like an engineer, or a teacher. Even being a janitor would sometimes be better. Hell, he was cleaning up people's lives anyway.

I tried to veer my thoughts to something else. Any time expletives started popping into my head, I had to stop and remind myself that I had to keep my cool—my composure. I was a first lady, now. But, the ever so present truth was that I wanted to walk out of this courtroom to the closest bar and grill and order me a shot of Patrón, followed by an Amaretto Sour.

"Will everyone please rise?" the bailiff asked. "The honorable Judge Crothers."

We all rose at the appearance of the judge, who held a manila folder in his hands. This was our third day in court, and even having listened to all of the evidence presented against Daphne, it was still hard to believe that this was really happening to us.

"Ms. Carlton, after reviewing all of the testimony presented against you, it concerns me that a person would go to the levels that you have gone to interfere in someone else's life. I am persuaded that a person with all of their faculties wouldn't concoct the things that you did; which is why I'm ordering you to spend two years in a highly secure mental institution in your hometown of Fort Lauderdale, Florida. In addition to that, I'm ordering a permanent restraining order to be in place. Please take this time, ma'am, to come to your senses." With that, he slammed the gavel.

The heifer was finally getting what she deserved. I hoped with every vengeful nerve in my body that Daphne would rot in that mental institution that the judge had just ordered her behind to for the next two years. Although it was wrong, I prayed that she would spend every minute being tortured by people just like her, in the same way that she had tortured me for the past year.

My husband, Darvin, shook hands with our attorney as I watched the guards take a crazed-looking Daphne out of the courtroom. I shook my head in hopes of shaking away the memory that this woman ever existed. All I had ever wanted since getting into my role as First Lady of Mount Zion Baptist Church was for God to send me a friend, someone I could trust. Being in ministry was not an easy thing; being the pastor's wife was even more difficult.

It was true that I had other friends who were first ladies, but they were all so busy with their own lives that we only had time to see each other once a week.

The day I met Daphne, I had only been a first lady for a few months. I was having brunch at a quaint little diner in midtown. It was one of my favorite little spots to retreat to when I didn't want to be recognized by anyone, be it a church member, or someone who knew me as being the wife of the highly esteemed Pastor Darvin Johnson.

Darvin had become one of the most recognized pastors on T.V., with his sermons being broadcast on stations all over the country. Each broadcast began with him welcoming viewers to the show, and me standing beside him, flashing my 1000-watt smile. So, not only did people recognize him when we were out, they recognized me as well.

Sitting in the rustic restaurant that was popular for its chicken pot pie, I inhaled the fragrance of peace and serenity. I savored the sweet moments of relaxation as I prepared to delve into the lunch portion of the restaurant's special that the maître d' had just placed before me.

As the scent of my lunch tickled my senses, a stylish woman wearing a knee-length red sweater and black fishnet stockings, with thigh-high black patent leather boots, sauntered into the restaurant, commanding the attention of those of us in need of a makeover. Her hair was a brown shade with bronze high-lights, and soft curls framed her face. Her skin was a flawless color of butterscotch, and if her makeup had been any more intact, I would have questioned whether she was real.

The hostess seated the young woman at a small table in the corner. As the woman sat down, she removed a leather portfolio from a black attaché and retrieved some papers that she immediately began to mull over. The woman looked as though something was weighing heavily on her mind.

I soon turned my attention back to my sweet delight, and within thirty minutes was paying for my check and getting ready to head back into the buzz of my reality.

I grabbed my Fendi bag, tossed my leather coat over my arm, and walked toward the front exit.

"Nice purse," I heard a woman say.

I turned to see that it was the woman I'd been admiring earlier from a distance. Up close, she was even more perfect. "Thanks," I said. Darvin had purchased that purse for my birthday and I wore it proudly.

"You're the first woman with such impeccable taste that I've seen since moving here to Atlanta," she continued. She picked up her glass of Pinot Noir and sipped it, leaving a shiny coat of lip gloss on the rim.

"That's hard to believe," I said, laughing, thinking that she had to be joking.

Atlanta was definitely a city chock full of beautiful and nicely dressed women.

"Well, honey, believe it. I've only been here for a few days, and from what I can tell, no one comes close to being suitable for the cover of any magazine," she said, her voice dripping with arrogance.

Taken aback by her load of self-confidence, I said, "Maybe you haven't gone to the right places. I know plenty of women—some being my friends—that would prick the fashion atmosphere they're so sharp."

That garnered a hearty laugh from the woman, who must have thought she had landed on a planet occupied by style disasters.

"Girl, that is too funny. I haven't heard anything that hilarious in a very long time," the woman said.

Not understanding why my words were so funny to her, I decided to move on and let the fashion queen enjoy her lunch. "You have a nice day," I said, trying to force a smile.

She threw her hands up, and the gesture brought attention to the many black and red bracelets dangling from her wrist. "Wait. I'm sorry. But, it's just that your statement reminded me of my family down in Alabama, who I would spend summers with as a child." She dropped her head in more laughter. "They were some extremely polished country bumpkins."

I glared at this woman whose repulsiveness was making me forget all about the nice, peaceful moments I'd just had.

"Mmm. Well, thanks for that, ah, compliment. Enjoy your lunch," I said, and stormed out the door before she had time to continue her insults.

Darvin's nudging brought my mind back to the present. Now, standing in this courtroom, thinking about how much hell Daphne had caused me, I should have known that day that Daphne could have never been my friend.

A month or so later, when she had shown up at the doors of Mount Zion Baptist Church, she'd done everything she could to prove to me that she was nothing like the woman I'd met that day in the diner. She volunteered on several ministries that I was closely involved with, and had many times over proven her competency to be a hard worker. She and I had spent long hours working on church events together; and when everyone would get tired and retreat home, Daphne would always stay behind to help. She soon became the person I turned to for many things.

"Michelle?"

Once again, Darvin interrupted my thoughts. "Yes, baby?"

"Did you hear what I just said?"

"No. I'm sorry. I was just thinking about Daphne," I admitted.

"Honey, there's no need to think about her anymore. This time Daphne is out of our lives for good," he said reassuringly. He put his arm around the small of my back and led me out of the courtroom.

A few reporters had gathered outside to ask a few questions, but it had been already decided that Christopher Tate, Darvin's best friend and our attorney, would make statements on our behalf until we were ready to hold a press conference.

"Are you hungry?" Darvin asked.

"A little. I'm mainly tired. I would prefer to go home and get some rest."

He looked at his watch. "I have a meeting with the new sound technician at the church in two hours. You want to just grab something to go and then head home?"

I glared at him. "How could you set a meeting today? Do you know how taxing this whole thing with Daphne has been on me? I was hoping to enjoy a quiet evening with you free of church business."

He rolled his eyes in frustration. "How many times do we have to go over this, Michelle? I'm sorry, but I can't allow this situation—or should I say this former situation with Daphne—ruin the rest of my day." He looked around and realized that people were beginning to stare at us as we stood on the courthouse steps. He dropped his voice lower. "Look, I promise when I get home tonight, it'll just be me and you."

"Darvin, that's not my issue," I said, frustrated with his failed attempt to pacify me. "Every night when you get home, it's me and you. The baby is already asleep when you arrive. But, once you're there, our routine consists of the same thing every single night. We eat dinner, and then you're off to your office to prepare a sermon. There is hardly ever any intimate time spent between us. When it is, it only involves sex." I felt my eyes get moist. "I just want us to have a day free of anyone else or any other business. I want us to maintain our relationship." I stroked his cheek.

For a minute, I thought he was actually considering my plea. But then, he looked deep into my eyes, and I could tell that he was searching for a way to let me down gently. I had grown to know when I'd actually gotten through to him, and I could feel that this was not one of those times.

"Why don't I call Greg and see if he can meet me right now instead of in two hours? How does that sound? That way, I can take this off of my to-do list and spend the rest of the evening home in bed with you, watching old movies."

I stared holes into him. I concluded that he must have a fever. Either that or he couldn't hear. I didn't want to be brushed off while he scratched off another item on his to-do list. I was always taking a back seat to his stupid list. Matter of fact, at times I felt that if there were ten things on it, I was number ten.

I started walking away. If I spoke right now, I would say the wrong thing. We had only been married for a few years, but I could remember our pre-marital counselor saying, "When you are in a heated moment that's too intense for a response, walk away; for it's better to walk away than to do or say something that you'll later regret."

"Michelle!" he called.

I kept walking.

"Michelle, girl, you know you hear me talking to you." I still kept walking. I crossed the street to the parking lot where I had parked my car. Suddenly, I heard car horns blowing. I turned around to see Darvin's tall behind trying to stop cars by holding his hand up in the stop formation. If I wasn't so frustrated, I would have laughed at his silly self.

He ran up to me. "What are you trying to do? Get me killed?"

"Nobody told you to be deceived into thinking that you

were some type of rubber, able to endure being run over by a car if it should hit you," I said sarcastically.

"Listen, honey," he said as he caressed my arm. "I'm sorry. I know that I've been really busy lately, and maybe you're right; we haven't spent much time together. But, baby—"

"Don't 'but baby' me. I'm tired of the excuses. I've been patient. I knew when I married you that things wouldn't be as they are in normal relationships, but I didn't sign up for this. I don't care who it is; if you don't spend time with your spouse, your marriage will be doomed." I moved away from his touch. "Either we start spending time together, or we're headed for disaster."

"What do you want me to do?" he asked in the tone he used when he was frustrated.

"I don't want you to do anything. I only want you to be my husband. Whatever that means to you," I said.

I turned and walked to my car. As I drove away, I saw that Darvin was still standing frozen in the spot I'd left him. So many thoughts were racing for first place in my mind. This situation with Daphne had certainly taken its toll on me, and ultimately, our marriage. God only knew if we would ever be able to fully recover from it. I knew I'd probably overreacted, but I didn't care right now. After more than a year of battling with the psychotic behavior of Daphne, it was a wonder anyone knew how to act properly.

I hated the day that I had ever allowed her in my home. In my life. In my husband's life. Who could truly blame her for being infatuated with Darvin? After all, I married him. He was a good man—sometimes too good—and it always seemed that some other woman was after him.

But Daphne had taken it too far. Her tactics had gone well beyond the point of admiration and had turned into obsession. Pretending to be Darvin's wife was the final straw. Little did we know this floozy had established her entire life as Mrs. Darvin Johnson. How stupid.

My head ached with the force of a volcano eruption thinking about all that had transpired over the past couple of years. Darvin was right; it was time for me to start moving beyond the past and focus on Michelle.

Chapter One

Michelle
Two years later

I awakened to the rays of sunshine peeking through the bay windows in my bedroom. Had it not been for the rumbling in my stomach, I would have dived deeper into the sheets, even after my alarm clock went off. But the fight going on in my stomach suggested that I better get up before what little was in it came out. This first trimester of pregnancy had been a good one, but every morning I woke up, I felt as though I had not eaten in ages.

I swung my legs over the side of the bed, put my feet in my fluffy hot pink slippers, grabbed the matching pink terrycloth robe that was resting on my chaise, and headed to the kitchen. On my way out of the room, I noticed my husband's empty spot in the bed. Since finding out that I was pregnant, I was no longer able to drag myself out of bed in time to attend the early morning service, and every Sunday at 6:30 A.M., my husband, Darvin Johnson, left the house to go and preach the 7:00 A.M. service.

I pulled open the door to the refrigerator to determine what I would eat. The pineapples and strawberries looked appetizing, but this morning I needed something more than fruit. Being just four months along, I was beginning to show a bulge in my stomach. If I weren't pregnant, I would have rebuked the thought of what was to come next in hopes of getting rid of the "pooch;" but under the circumstances, I decided on beef sausage, two eggs, cheese grits, wheat toast, and some Cran-Grape juice. As I prepared my food, my stomach began dancing from the anticipation of what was to come. Both my stomach and I knew that my hunger troubles were about to be over.

As I sat at the breakfast nook of our kitchen with the plantation shutters open wide, I took in all that God had blessed me with on this beautiful Sunday morning. I hurried to finish eating because it was nearing time for me to start getting dressed. Because I missed going to the first service so often, I was never late for the second. My husband, being the prolific and astounding preacher that he was, enticed the crowd from the first service to stay for the second. He and the board members had been in constant talk about possibly going to a third service, but Darvin wasn't hearing it. He was determined not to let the preaching gift be the cause of his early death.

I finished my food, put the dishes away, and then went into my oversized closet and contemplated what I was going to wear. Thankfully, my clothes were still behaving as they should, in spite of the pregnancy and slightly expanding waistline. I passed a row of St. John knits, a section of Donna Vinci, and stack of Manolo Blahniks to make my way to the "jean section" of my closet. I eyed the jean outfit that I was about to wear and laughed to myself. I was known for not being your traditional first lady, and I couldn't care less that everybody expected me to be sharp every single Sunday. I also laughed because I knew that the deaconess was going to have a natural fit because I wasn't wearing white today. It was first Sunday, communion Sunday, and this first lady was wearing a jean outfit. Like it. Love it. Leave it.

I trucked to the bathroom, took a shower, got dressed in a jean skirt that had a spray of rhinestones cascading down the right side, a black camisole, a matching jean jacket, and applied my makeup. I took one final glance in the full-length mirror next to my vanity, admiring the way the jean skirt tugged at my thighs, just enough for my husband to notice that my shape was still intact, and not enough for the "Mothers in Zion" to start the I-can't-believe-she-calls-herself-a-preacher's-wife gossip. Once again, I laughed to myself, because it wasn't like I cared anyway.

Later on in my car, I opened the sunroof to my Navigator as I merged onto I-75. Spring was definitely in full force. The wind was blowing, the birds were singing, and I felt good.

I turned up my radio to hear the sounds of Kirk Franklin blaring through my radio. "Imagine Me" had become one of my favorite songs, and I couldn't help but reflect over my own life each time I heard it. That song was followed by a song written by the praise and worship maestro in his own right, Mr. Fred Hammond.

I was jamming to the beat of Fred when I pulled into the parking lot of Mount Zion Missionary Baptist Church. By the looks of the already full parking lot, you would have thought that I was a couple of hours late. Parishioners had already filled every empty space, and the parking attendants were directing traffic into the empty lot across the street that was being preserved for the next part of our building phase, the Mount Zion Youth Development Center. I drove to my own reserved parking space, remembering when the parking lot used to be only half full. Those were the beginning days, when we were struggling to keep members.

Darvin's innovative approach to ministry had ruffled more than a few feathers and had ultimately sent people scattering to find a more traditional church. Darvin and I persevered, and two years later, we had the fastest growing ministry in South Atlanta.

The parking attendants greeted me with warmth as I maneuvered my way into the space, and before I could turn off my engine, my armor bearers (known to some as amateur security guards) were already rushing toward me. I smiled, because while most first ladies saw this as an opportunity to take advantage of someone's servanthood, I actually respected my armor bearers as being critical components who ensured that my worship experience was uninterrupted from the time I stepped foot on the grounds.

"Good morning, First Lady," Chanice, my newest assistant, said.

Twylah, my armor bearer for the last two years, came right behind Chanice's greeting.

"Good morning, ladies." I put on my "first lady smile" and exited the truck. Thankfully, today was a good day, and my first lady smile was real.

"First Lady, Pastor is waiting on you in the back. Are you going to need anything before the second service begins?"

I looked at Chanice and admired the beauty of her humbleness. She had only been at the church for six months since moving from New Orleans, but she went to endless measures to make sure I didn't need a single thing. God must have had me in mind when he made her, because she had definitely been a Godsend. However, I didn't miss the disgusted look on Twylah's face.

She and Chanice had been having problems as of late, each trying to vie for my attention.

"No, Chanice. I won't need anything right now." They opened the doors to the sanctuary, and the cool breeze that caressed my face was welcomed, because either the blaring sun was hotter today than usual, or the pregnancy hormones were really kicking in.

My armor bearers and I went to our private area in the back so that I could greet my husband. When he'd left earlier that morning, I'd been so sleepy that I barely heard him leave. Now, I was fresh and in my right mind, and ready to see the man that made my heart skip a beat. Even though I knew that he was getting ready to go into the service, I had to steal a kiss from him.

As we were walking in, he was walking out. His two armor bearers dwarfed him in size and made me and my two assistants appear as midgets.

"Hey, darling," I said in my most cheerful voice, and kissed him dead on the lips.

"Hey, baby," he said in a tone that only I knew and understood. That "hey, baby" was more than just a greeting. It was a promise for later.

I cooed on the inside, and Chanice and Twylah didn't miss a single moment of the passion that passed between us in a simple greeting. I turned to see their reactions, and just as I expected, their smiles were as bright as the sun.

An open display of affection between us was customary around Mount Zion, and my husband always made sure to keep it up. When Darvin first accepted the call to pastor, certain females got a little carried away with their infatuation of the pastor, and Darvin had to set the record straight and let them know who the *only lady* in his life was.

"Are you going into the office to get a bite before you come down to the service?" Darvin asked as Elder Tyrone helped him into his jacket.

"No. I had a big breakfast before I left home, and we are fine." I proudly rubbed my stomach. Once again, my heart warmed, but this time at the thought of bringing our baby into the world in five months.

A couple of years ago, I thought that the Daphne saga would destroy my marriage, but God had turned things around. I was now living my life like it was golden, and savoring every sweet moment of being Mrs. Darvin L. Johnson.

"Okay, baby, I'll see you in service." Darvin kissed me once again before disappearing down the corridor that led to the main sanctuary.

I watched him float away into the harmonious sounds of the praise team, who were getting people into the mind to worship. I strode into the office, took a quick glance into the mirror, and just to make sure that my makeup was still as flawless as it was when I left home, I applied another smooth layer of the M•A•C Studio Fix powder and a fresh coat of Spring Bean lip gloss. After deciding that I was satisfied with my appearance, we went out of the office in the same direction that Darvin had gone just minutes earlier.

I entered the sanctuary to find that we were yet again at seating capacity. As I took my seat next to my husband, I surveyed the audience and noticed that some people were standing with their hands raised, and others just simply bowed their heads as tears flowed from their eyes. The feeling of thanksgiving exuded from the churchgoers, and once again, I felt a peace come over me. I, too, worshipped God in my own way, and concluded that all was truly well with my soul.

As the praise team brought their last song to a close, the crowd was in an uproar, sending praises up to God. But I noticed one lone individual sitting in the back of the church. I could barely believe my eyes. It couldn't be her. Sure, she looked a little different with her hair longer, but even from a distance, I could tell it was her. To those who were unfamiliar with her, she was like any other parishioner coming to the worship service; but to me, she was my worst nightmare.

The glee that had filled my heart just moments before was replaced by a twinge of hatred, just at the sight of her. I knew that it was wrong to feel that way, but nobody understood the hell this woman had put me through—and I was far from forgetting it. As a matter of fact, it might have been safe to say that I was still mad as hell.

My husband's nudging sliced through my thoughts. I turned and glared at him because in that moment, I didn't want to be jolted from my anger. Surely, this woman had come back to terrorize me. But this time, she would meet her match. This time, I wouldn't pray as much as I did before, because when I prayed, God normally spoke some sense into me. I didn't want any sense; I wanted to kick her butt, because I was one mad first lady.

Chapter Two

Michelle

My eyes were so fixed on the woman who had interrupted my flow of worship that my husband practically nudged a hole in my arm, trying to get my attention.

"Michelle," he said as quietly as he could.

I jerked my head around and gave him the coldest stare. "What?" I shouted back through gritted teeth, and this time, a fake smile.

"What are you doing?" The puzzled look on his face matched my own, as I was trying to figure out why he was asking such a stupid question.

"What do you mean?" I asked.

"We are the only ones still standing."

I followed his eyes to the congregation, and sure enough, we were the only ones who were not seated. The announcement clerk was reading today's announcements, and I could hear a few people whispering among themselves, no doubt trying to figure out if something was wrong with us.

My legs were as heavy as steel, but I forced my limbs to slowly move backward as I sat down in my seat with embarrassment all over my face. I turned back to my husband's questioning eyes, and I knew that I had to give some sort of explanation for my behavior.

"I'm sorry, baby. Believe it or not, Daphne is sitting in the back of the church," I managed to get out.

"What? Daphne?" he said as his eyes scanned toward the back of the church. "You must be mistaken. She's in a mental institution, baby. How could she be sitting in the back of the church?"

"I don't know. If I knew that, I wouldn't be so flustered," I said. Suddenly, it came to me. Daphne's two years in the mental institution were up.

"Baby, don't worry about Daphne. Even if it were true that she was here, there's nothing she can do to you here. Before she even gets close, an army of people will be there to stop her."

Did he just hear me? She is here.

And, obviously, she couldn't be stopped, because she was sitting in our church. I wanted to scream this to Darvin, but he had already turned his focus back to the service. I know it had been two years, but was I the only one who remembered just how subtle and conniving this woman could be? It was these traits that landed her directly into our lives.

Her desire to be intricately involved in the ministry matched our own need to have more volunteers. With her passion and willingness to work and make unending sacrifices, she quickly stood out from among the others.

While most were talking, she was busy doing. I had accepted her against my better judgment. As a result, she'd dined with us. She'd shopped with me. She'd spent long hours talking to my husband about various ways she could help us improve the ministry. She'd traveled with me to my speaking engagements and had served me just as if she'd been called by God to do specifically that. And in all of that, I was too blind to see that she wanted to be me. Her plan included taking over my life. As me.

Trying to figure out my next move, I sat looking at Daphne as she swayed softly along with the choir that was now singing J. Moss's "Forgive Me, Oh Lord." I knew that it was wrong to think it, but I just didn't want God to forgive her. I wanted her to pay for every single thing that she had done to try to annihilate my life. Sure, that wasn't the Christian thing, but I was mad. And there weren't too many Christian-like thoughts coming to mind right now.

"Baby, you've got to snap out of it," Darvin said as sweetly as he could. "Don't let the devil steal your joy."

What did he just say? Was he being the husband or the Pastor right now?

If he was being the husband, then that was the wrong thing to say, and if he was being the Pastor, then he'd better find someone else to give a word to, because I didn't need it. Not that one anyway. Because the devil was sitting right in the back of our congregation, and she had already stolen my joy.

The rest of the service went by in a blur. I was extremely agitated that the joy I had when I started the day had been replaced by dreary gloom. My stomach was starting to feel upset, and I felt like I was about to hurl every morsel of my breakfast onto Darvin's tailored suit. He was sitting there looking so good in the charcoal gray suit that he had chosen to complement with a smoky gray shirt, matching tie, and black gators. And if that weren't enough to make him look as if he'd just stepped out of fashion heaven, the salt-'n-pepper hairs that were peeking out of his goatee were sinful enough to drive any woman to hell if she wasn't careful.

Admiring my husband and his delightful taste in clothing took my mind off Daphne, but only for a moment. My pleasure was short-lived, because I returned to my previous thought. Why was Daphne back?

My eyes swerved back to the place where Daphne was sitting, but she was no longer there. I blinked, making sure that my contacts hadn't become dry, thereby giving me the illusion that people were disappearing. What I did see clearly was Darvin taking his place at the wooden podium to deliver his sermon. I turned and saw my two assistants sitting behind me. I saw Mother Hampton dozing off to sleep in the Amen corner, and I saw

Deacon Brown following suit, his snores becoming a part of the amens and hallelujahs.

What I didn't see was the person who had just occupied the last seat on the back row. Beads of sweat began to rise on my face like condensation on the outside of a cold glass of water. I tried to think positive and not believe that something bad was about to happen as Darvin began his sermon on faith.

"Church, we've got to believe that no matter what we go through, no matter what situations we face, God is right there," he said.

Hmph. Where was God when that psycho Daphne was trying to kill me?

Bad memories flooded my mind. Among the many things she'd done to sabotage my life—running my car off of the road and poisoning my food—convincing a locksmith to change all of my locks, leaving me to stand outside in below freezing weather at ten o'clock at night trying to get into my own house, was just low-down and dirty.

God, I know you're always there, but I have to wonder sometimes if you're always looking.

Darvin was deep into his message before I started to listen again.

"When you can't do anything else, put your trust in God! Believe that He will make a way out of no way! Believe that He will turn your darkness into day!" Darvin proclaimed. "Why do I want you to believe today, saints? Because if you believe in God's Word, I'm a witness that it can and will change your very life!"

Darvin spoke with power. He inspired and had people standing on their feet, shouting praises to God. Mother Hampton, who had been asleep just minutes earlier, was now tearing down the "amen corner," stomping her size 13 shoe, and hoisting all of her 325-pounds, six foot three frame up and down. The ushers took their positions behind her as if they were about to go to battle. Getting Mother Hampton under control was no easy task, and it took an army every Sunday to finally calm her down. By the end of her weekly show, her hat always ended up sitting on top of one of the deacon's heads. It was all that I could do not to burst out into laughter, because if no one else thought that Darvin's sermons were rousing, he could always count on Mother Hampton for a little extra affirmation.

Darvin had brought his message to a close and was now, through outstretched arms, extending the offer for anyone who was not saved to come down to the altar. Just as every week, ministers dressed in black suits joined him. They began to walk down the aisles with their arms open wide, as we all stood to our feet and began to pray that someone would give their life to Jesus.

I closed my eyes and remembered the day that I'd made that decision to receive salvation. This element of the service was the most important, because it was always a possibility that someone in the midst was between life and death.

I heard a thunderous applause erupt, symbolizing someone had chosen to take the walk down to the altar. But just as abruptly, it came to a halt. I opened my eyes to see Daphne waltzing to the front of the church. And if looks could have killed, she would have died right before she took the last step that had her facing my husband.

I looked at Darvin because I knew that the sweat on his face had made an appearance for two reasons. One: he was tired from the sermon. Two: he knew that if Daphne couldn't contain herself with the little bit of sense that she had, his pregnant wife would be making the front page of the *Atlanta Journal-Constitution* before the sun could greet the morning.

"Ms. Carlton, is there something that you would like to say to the church this morning?" Darvin asked.

Darvin reluctantly put the microphone closer to her mouth so that everyone could hear her speak. Everybody at Mount

Zion knew how this woman had tried to destroy our lives, and from the looks on their faces, they were wondering why Darvin was even taking a chance on allowing her the opportunity to cause further destruction.

"Yes, Pastor," she said. "I want to first thank the Lord for my being here today, and I want to thank you for giving me this opportunity to say a few words." She looked pointedly at Darvin. "I came up here, Pastor, to ask you and First Lady Johnson for forgiveness. I never would have expected things to get out of hand, but somehow they did. So, on behalf of me and my family, we want to formally ask your forgiveness and the forgiveness of this great church."

Darvin's eyes had reduced to mere slits. He was probably thinking the same thing that I was, which meant she would definitely not get away with this little charade. The nerve of that little heifer! She was good. She thought that she could play the Lord-have-mercy-on-me card, and that everyone would come rushing to her side, praying for her—declaring destiny over her life, casting out all the demons of her past so that she could walk in the newness of life. Well, she was sadly mistaken, because nobody was about to do no praying up in here if I had anything to do with it. And I was fully aware of the nonsense I was thinking, because the church is where you should come to get healing; but she wouldn't find it today, not at Mount Zion Baptist Church. Not at the church where my husband was the pastor. Not at the church where the first lady would tolerate no hussy like Daphne Carlton continuing with this insane woe-is-me act.

I'm glad that Darvin found the words to finally speak before I did.

"Sister Daphne, we—"

She interrupted, but not before I noticed the look of confusion on her face. "Pastor, I'm sorry to interrupt." She hesitantly glanced around the church as if to search for the remainder of her words. "But I'm not Daphne. Daphne is in the care of my mother back home in Florida." She paused before she continued. "I'm Dawn. Dawn Carlton. Daphne's twin sister."

That was the last thing I heard before everything faded to black.

Chapter Three

Michelle

It must have taken all but three minutes for them to get me out of the main sanctuary and into the office where I was now resting on our plush leather couch. I could hear the uneasy chatter of the parishioners outside of the door as I was trying to will myself to open my eyes. I couldn't shake the soft voice that kept reverberating in my mind.

When it finally registered that the soft voice I kept hearing in my mind belonged to Daphne . . . Dawn . . . or whoever she was, my eyes flung open, and I sat up as if I were being raised from the dead.

My head began to throb, and I quickly lay back down. Chanice and Twylah were at my side almost in an instant.

"First Lady, are you all right?" Chanice asked, her voiced laced with concern.

"Yes," I mumbled. The truth was I was not all right. I was a perfect mixture of confusion and disgust. Just as it seemed that my life was starting to take a turn for the better, my worst nightmare seemed to be metamorphosing into a reality.

"Do you need us to get you anything?" Twylah asked with questioning eyes.

"No. Where is Pastor?" I asked. I needed to see my husband because I was sure that he could make me feel better. His positive spirit about everything was contagious.

Twylah and Chanice exchanged glances. "Um . . ." Chanice began, but didn't finish.

here today is to reconcile with me and my wife on behalf of your family." After a brief pause, he continued. "Because, Dawn, I'm having a hard time believing that. You could have easily extended your apologies via phone or e-mail. You didn't have to come here in person. I take it that you know the trauma that your sister caused not only my wife and me, but my church, and it's interesting to me that your step toward reconciliation would be to show up in person. Please, help me understand because right now, I don't."

I could hear the stress in Darvin's voice, and it was making me angrier by the second. How dare this woman come and interrupt our lives?

"Pastor," Dawn pleaded, "you have to believe me. I'm here because my family feels terrible about the trouble that Daphne caused you . . . and your wife. We want to somehow offer restitution to you."

"Why do you care?" I heard Darvin ask. "Your sister has been dealt with. She knows that she cannot come anywhere remotely close to my wife or me, or anyplace that we are, and if she does, she'll be immediately locked up. So, I still don't understand your reasoning."

"Daphne is dying, Pastor," Dawn softly spoke. "One of her wishes includes letting you know how deeply sorry she is for everything she's done."

Dying? Whatever. I had heard enough. It was my time to ask the questions. I barged into the room. Both Darvin's and Dawn's eyes were on me. His was a look of worry, and Dawn's was a look of fear. I, without a word spoken, assured Darvin that I was fine.

"It's Dawn, right?" I asked.

"Yes," she spoke timidly.

Coming face to face with her, I could see that there were more visible differences in their appearance other than Dawn's long hair. Daphne's eyes were hazel; Dawn's were grey. Dawn also had a small mole underneath her nose. And, not to mention she had a lighter voice and timid personality. Daphne was the exact opposite: arrogant, prideful, deceitful.

"I couldn't help but overhear the conversation that you were having with my husband. If I understand you correctly, your sister Daphne is dying and she's sent you hear to clean up her dirty work," I said, not caring to hide my frustration.

"Well, I wouldn't put it like that, First Lady Johnson. She's unable to travel herself because of the stipulations that have been placed on her by the authorities here and for the reason of her illness. So, she asked if I would come in her stead. So I did."

I studied Dawn's look of defeat and was unfazed. "Dawn, no disrespect to you or your family, but your apology is not needed. What Daphne did to me, my husband, and our church was unforgivable. I will not stand here and allow you to think that your coming here today will make me forget it or pretend that it never happened."

"But don't you preach forgiveness? What happened to Christians forgiving one another?" Dawn said with a hint of resentment in her voice.

For a brief second, she reminded me of Daphne with her quick temper.

If I didn't know any better, I would think that Dawn and Daphne were identical in more than one sense of the word.

"Dawn, yes, we do teach and practice forgiveness; however, in this case, I think the choice is ours how we choose to handle what your sister did and now what you are doing. And trust me; it has nothing to do with forgiveness."

Darvin interrupted. "Dawn, my wife and I would like to put all of this behind us as quickly as possible. So, in the effort to move on expeditiously, we accept the apology that your family is offering; however, our stance does not change when it comes to Daphne. I still do not want her near me, my wife, or anyone in my church."

I surveyed him. His tone suggested that I not protest and that Dawn take his comment for what is was worth and go back to wherever she came from. I smiled at the slight gratification that I felt at his dismissing her.

"Pastor, First Lady, there's just one more thing," Dawn said.

Be with me, Jesus.

"I'm moving up here to try and start a new life, and I would very much like . . ."—she paused—"to be a part of your church."

Lord, just take me now.

I knew that at any moment, I would fall into unconsciousness, just as I had less than an hour ago in the sanctuary. This woman was really testing my patience. Did she really think that we would accept her into our church after all that her sister had put us through? She was undoubtedly mistaken. I was not going to tolerate a Daphne-cloned psycho worshipping with me in the same church.

"Dawn, I think what my husband was trying to offer you was an acceptance of your family's apology based on the premise that after that, you leave us alone. And you can't do that if you are attending our church. We would have to be in constant contact with you, and quite frankly, just looking at you reminds me of your sister. And the thoughts that I think when I think of your sister are far from being pleasant. It's just not a good idea," I said matter-of-factly.

"How can you turn someone away from God?" Dawn asked.

"Oh, you must have misunderstood me. I'm not turning you away from God; I'm simply saying that you are going to have to find another church to attend. God is everywhere, Dawn. Did you know that?" She was working my last nerve.

"But I feel so safe here. I feel a connection that I can't explain," she said with her eyes beseeching to Darvin.

I cast a warning glance at Darvin, daring him to accept or buy into what she was saying. "Dawn, the connection that you're feeling is probably one left over by your sister. She may not be here, but I can attest that sometimes her evil spirit can still be felt," I said, hoping to get my point across.

I walked around to the back of my husband's desk. "But I think I have the solution. I know just the place for you." I pulled open a drawer that contained the Yellow Pages. I flipped through a few pages, until I found what I was looking for.

"That's it!" I said, trying to sound excited. "This will be the perfect church for you. The Path to Holiness Christian Church." I turned to my husband. "Honey, don't we know the pastor and his wife over there?" Without giving him time to answer, I continued. "I believe we do. That is a church where the Word is being preached, and I have no doubt that you will be just fine there. Oh, and feel safe, too. They have great ministries to offer, and it's more suitable for someone like you."

"And what kind of someone am I, First Lady?" Dawn asked with indignation.

For a brief moment, I could feel a twinge of guilt; but just as soon as it came, it was gone. I felt nothing toward this woman, and the sooner I could rid myself of her, the better I would feel. She didn't want to start a fight with me, for she wouldn't get near as far as her sister did.

"You're obviously someone who can't recognize when someone is trying to help you. It is my strong suggestion, Dawn, that you take my help to avoid any further disturbance of your or my peace." My glare was now more intense than it was when I first walked in.

Darvin hadn't said anything for a span, but decided now to break his silence.

"Dawn, I think my wife is right. It might be best for you to go to another worship location. I don't think you would grow spiritually here, and beyond that, the people at this church will

never be able to fully embrace you because of your sister's actions. It will be hard enough convincing everybody that you are her sister. I'm sure you saw the skepticism on people's faces when you announced that."

Tears began to form in Dawn's eyes. "I'm shocked, to say the least. I came here hoping to make right what my sister made wrong, and I'm being blamed for her sins. I'm being made to bear a cross that shouldn't be mine to bear." She stood from the leather executive chair that she had been sitting in, and cleared her throat. "Well, I appreciate your time and your willingness to accept my apology. I'll be going now." She grabbed the Coach purse that matched her soft yellow sundress, and headed toward the door. Before walking out, she turned and said, "Oh, and First Lady? I'll look into that church. Thanks for your . . . help." With that, Dawn disappeared to the other side of the door.

Moments passed before Darvin broke the deafening silence in the room.

"Do you think we handled this situation in the right way?"

"What do you mean? Of course we did. What else were we supposed or expected to do?" I felt sweat appearing on the tip of my nose. "This woman waltzed into our church declaring that she was our worst nightmare's twin sister, and we're supposed to shower her with hugs and kisses as if she's the prodigal daughter?" I was getting hotter by the second. I picked up a stack of papers from my husband's inbox tray and begin to fan myself. "I hardly think that God is going to be displeased with the way we chose to deal with this. I think He understands."

I sat down in my husband's oversized burgundy-leather chair behind an oversized, antique wooden desk. I felt myself becoming faint again.

This time, I think it was the guilt of my conscience weighing in on me. I knew that I should have been a little more "Christian-like" with Dawn, but women like her tried the best Christian's religion.

"What if we're wrong about her, baby? What if her heart really is right and she ends up being nothing like Daphne?" he asked as he sat down in the same seat Dawn had just occupied.

All sorts of thoughts were swimming in my head. What if Darvin was right? What if God expected us to show an immeasurable amount of forgiveness, and we shunned His voice due to our own selfish reasons? More like my own selfish reasons.

Once again, resentment rang louder than God's voice, and it didn't sound too bad to me.

Chapter Four

Dawn

I was infuriated as I drove away from Mount Zion Baptist Church. It was bad enough that I had to endure being humiliated in front of the entire congregation, but even worse than that, Michelle Johnson had butchered my pride. With her always put-together persona, she had tried to intimidate me, and as much as I hated to admit it, she had succeeded. I wasn't expecting her to fight back, and her actions caught me off guard.

Earlier that morning, when I'd driven onto the grounds of Mount Zion, I was sure of my plan. I had managed to alter my look enough to be believed that I was "Daphne's" identical twin sister; but after the way it played out, I realized that was the least of my problems. It was not going to go as smoothly as I thought. In my mind, I had seen my apology being accepted by the church, but, most importantly, Pastor Johnson. Once I achieved that, I would be on my way back into his life. Before long, I would be his wife, and not Michelle. It made me sick to my stomach to refer to her as his wife, because she didn't deserve the role. She was as much qualified to be the wife of Pastor Darvin Johnson as Snoop Dogg was for the presidential office.

My ringing cell phone brought me back into the present moment. I glanced at the caller ID and smiled to myself. My mother had been trying to contact me for several days now. I knew that eventually my avoiding her would probably lead to a massive search for me, and I didn't have space for that in my plan. I answered.

"Hello?"

"Hey, baby," Mom said.

"Hi, Mom," I replied dryly.

"That's certainly not happiness to hear from me, dear." Mother was already jumping up and down on my last nerve, and the conversation had only been going for ten seconds. "Mother, what is it that you want?"

"Why can't I call to check on my daughter? After the way you left here, it would only be right to be concerned." She paused. "Baby, why don't you consider coming back home? You have no business in Atlanta. Florida is your home. You hadn't been out of that institution long enough to be out on your own again. You need to be close to family. Besides, what if they find out what you're up to? What if those people hurt you?" Her voice started to crack.

"What if I never see you again?"

For a quick moment, I wanted to run the rest of the way to my house, purchase an airline ticket back to Ft. Lauderdale, and go home and run into my mother's arms. It bothered me that she was so upset; but I was on a mission, and I couldn't let anyone deter me from that, not even her.

I made up in my mind a long time ago that I would not end up like my mother. She was a good woman, but she had nothing to show for it. My father walked out on us when I was twelve years old, and she never picked up the pieces. Up until that point, I thought my father was a superhero. He was always supportive of us, and made it his business to make sure we never went without anything, but one job layoff changed our entire lives.

Soon after losing his job, he became an alcoholic and would roam the streets all night. I watched my mother leave my brother and I many nights to search the corners for my dad. Each time she would drag him back into the house a few hours later, clean him up, and nurse him back to health. She would

always tell us that it was better to have him home drunk than to not have him home at all.

Finally, one day, he left for a trip to the store, and that trip turned into an eternal vacation. I never saw him again. Truth is, my father left a long time before he left and never came back. Nonetheless, my mother felt she had let us down, and slowly her heart turned to iron, and the only thing she concerned herself with was making sure our needs were provided.

She did the best she could trying to be the mother and the father, but no matter what people might say, you can't be both. There's no substitution for a man. She could never give me the life I felt I deserved. So, it was paramount that I didn't fall into the same pattern. God forbid any man leave me, which was why I had to make sure I chose a good man. A man that would love me all the days of my life. A man who would not walk out on me and my kids. A man like Darvin Johnson.

Listening to my mother's plea made me curse the day I told her of my plans and reason for moving back to Atlanta.

"Mom, I'm sorry that I've had you worried, but trust me; I'm fine. All is well. Pastor and First Lady Johnson, along with their church family, have accepted the apology, and we've moved on to reconciling." I hoped that my chipper tone was enough to convince my mother. I was wrong.

"Baby, but it's just not right. You have to think of someone other than yourself. I know you have your reasons for being there, but, baby, you've got to know that God ain't pleased. What are you gonna do when you reap what you've sown? Child, the tables will turn, and you're going to wish that you'd thought better of what you're trying to do."

Sometimes I wondered whose child I was. I never knew my father, but it was in times like these that I wondered if I knew my mother. She had no backbone and obviously didn't know the definition of persistence.

I concluded that this conversation wasn't going any-

where. "Mother, we're going to have to discuss this later. I've been busy trying to get settled and today I got up early for church. I'm tired. I'll have to call you back later." Before she had the opportunity to protest, I closed my pink RAZR flip phone.

I drove up to my driveway, clicked the button that opened and closed the massive gates, pulled into the garage, and turned off the ignition of my blue BMW 750Li.

The cost of living in Florida was astronomical compared to the suburbs of Atlanta, and three months ago, I didn't think that I would ever be able to make Atlanta my permanent residence again. But I was here to stay. Nothing would stop me. My brilliant plan, which would assure me of my dreams, was already working.

Granted, I'd had somewhat of a minor setback with Michelle, but she could be handled. Before long, I would be where I belonged—in the arms of Pastor Darvin Johnson. This time, I wasn't going to stop until I reached my destination. And my final stop would be in the role of Darvin's wife and the First Lady of Mount Zion Baptist Church.

The excitement of that thought caused me to practically jump out my car and run into my house, where I kicked off my three-inch white sandals and fell back onto my couch. I smiled as I looked at the dry-erase board that I'd hung on the wall in the kitchen next to the refrigerator, and I made a mental note to cross out the first step to becoming Darvin Johnson's wife. It was now time for me to get to work on step number two.

Glee filled my heart because I could smell the fragrance of victory and it hadn't even come yet. One thing I'd learned from growing up in church was that you didn't have to wait until the battle was won, but you could shout right now. And that is what I did. I stood up and gave God praise for giving me the luminous mind that He did. Because it was nobody but Him who'd spoken to me this plan, and the least I could do was obey. Some would classify me as crazy for even thinking that God would outline a plan to me that would take another woman's husband—but He did.

Although the homes on my street were guarded by gates, the view of each home was obtainable from certain rooms in my house. I ran to an upstairs bedroom to see if the Johnsons had made it home. It was perfect timing. Their armor bearers were helping them into the house, and Michelle was slowly moving toward the front door. Looking at her, I was quickly reminded that I had another problem.

Before returning to Atlanta, an inside source from the church had kept me abreast of all the happenings of the Johnsons. Just before I was released, I received the letter that drove me back to crazy land. The letter informed me that Michelle was expecting. Now, watching her from across the street, I could see the tiny bulge in her stomach that was peeking out from under her shirt. That tramp was pregnant with my man's baby.

I was suddenly outraged and wanted nothing more than to go and push her down onto the concrete driveway. But as soon as the thought came, I dismissed it, because her pregnancy may actually work to my benefit. Yes, I would use her pregnancy to my advantage, and by the time I was through, she wouldn't know what hit her.

Feeling a slight sense of achievement, I slipp-ed out of my yellow sundress right in the middle of the guest bedroom, and I let it pool around my feet. I stepped over it and headed to my bathroom to take a long soak in some Sun-Ripened bath bubbles while I focused on my next course of action.

Going into the bathroom, I glanced at the picture of Darvin sitting on my nightstand. He was so handsome and so innocent. I knew after leaving him today that I'd left him thinking. I always had that effect on people, especially him.

I picked up the picture frame and kissed the image of the man who was soon going to be mine. If I stayed on course, by this time next year, the AJC would be doing an article on me

and my husband. I could imagine the headline in bold letters:
FLORIDA NATIVE WEDS RENOWNED PASTOR DARVIN JOHNSON.

I placed the picture back into its place, and caught a
glimpse of the worn piece of paper that first held my plan before
I transferred it to the dry-erase board in the kitchen. One day, I
would share with our children how God told me exactly what to
do to get their father to see we were meant to be together.

I could only pray that they would be as bless-ed.

The little paper was crinkled to say the least, but I unfolded it and looked at my first two steps. 1. Introduce myself as
Dawn Carlton; 2. Befriend First Lady Johnson . . . again.

Starting off, my plan looked simple. But it wasn't. For
the rest of my life, I was going to have to remind myself every day
that I was no longer Daphne Carlton, the person that I was born
as, but Dawn Carlton. Not only that, but I had to keep what
little family I had away from Atlanta. Since no one understood
how important this was to me, they were sure to sabotage everything that I was working so hard for. Many people didn't get the
option to start all over in life, but I'd created my own destiny.

It had been a little easier that I'd imagined convincing
Darvin, Michelle, and the church that I was my own twin. Oh,
and I couldn't leave out my little informant that I had been paying generously to give me whatever information I needed—when
I needed it.

After leaving town as Daphne, I served my two years in
that god-awful hell hole. When I first arrived, I thought all hope
was lost. But after hearing my story one day, my roommate reminded me that I could have easily been sentenced to do some
jail time. That's when I realized that God had looked out for me
and was giving me this opportunity to regroup.

An investment I made with an old friend and business
associate, Steven Chiles, just prior to being locked away, materi-
alized and produced a sizeable return. Oh, what a happy day it
was when Steven called me and told me the good news. My third

stop after being released was to his office to pick up my check. The first was home to change into some decent clothes, and the second was at Krispy Kreme Doughnuts. God knows I had an obsession with glazed doughnuts. So, I picked up the check, cashed in, and was now sitting in a very comfortable financial position. I could pretty much buy anything I wanted—including happiness.

By the time this was over, everyone but Michelle was going to love me.

Chapter Five

Michelle

It had been a very long day, and the tranquility that I'd experienced when the day began had long been replaced with fatigue, stress, and anxiety.

Dawn Carlton's appearance had shifted my mood for the entire day, and all I wanted to do was get inside of my house and go to bed.

Chanice, who decided to ride home with me today, noticed everything. She said, "First Lady, would you like for us to order dinner in for you? I know that you normally cook on Sundays, but I think it will be best if you ordered out today."

I continued to look out of the window as we were driving down our street, hoping to find my thoughts on one of the street signs. The signs failed to yield any answers to the many questions running rapidly through my mind.

Why was Dawn Carlton really here?

"First Lady?" Chanice repeated. "Do you . . ."

Her voice trailed off as I put my hand up to interrupt the rest of her statement. I didn't want to be asked any more questions. I had enough of my own. I turned to face Chanice, who was sitting in the back of my Navigator.

"I'll be fine." I looked at Twylah, who was driving, and said, "You guys are great, and I don't want you to think that I'm being unappreciative of what you're trying to do, but I just want to get into my own space and sort through the events of the day."

Exhausted by that one statement, I turned back around to continue the search for answers outside of the window.

As we pulled into our driveway, I looked at the house across the street. It had been for sale for some time now, but the FOR SALE sign had been taken down earlier in the week. I made a mental note to introduce myself to our new neighbors, something that was often unheard of anymore.

We drove through the gates that led to my own safe haven, and no sooner than the automatic locks could free me from my current prison, I was opening the door. Darvin, who pulled right behind us in his black Mercedes S550, saw the swiftness in me trying to get out of the truck, and rushed to my side to help me out. I glanced quickly into his eyes and pleaded with him not to ask the same question people had been asking me since I'd left the church. I was fine, and would be better if I could just get to my king-sized bed, dive underneath the same covers that had engulfed me earlier that morning, and drift away into an ocean of deep sleep, leaving all of my troubles behind.

I walked into my doorway and kicked off my shoes. My house still smelled of the breakfast that I'd eaten just hours before, and unexpectedly I found myself in the guest bathroom emptying my stomach of all that I'd delighted in that morning. I seldom had morning or anytime sickness, but today was an exception. Considering the turn of events, I was almost expectant that the day would only continue to get worse.

I found the strength to get to my bedroom, shed my clothes, and climb into my green sea of Egyptian cotton high thread count sheets. I heard Chanice and Twylah discussing with Darvin the dinner plans before I drifted off into unconsciousness.

***

As I drove up to my house, I noticed that it was unusually dark. I tried to always leave a light on, especially when I knew that I would be out late. In spite of the nervousness that I felt, I got out of my car and went toward the door. No sooner than I could step over the threshold, I saw her. Even in the piercing black, I could see the anger in her eyes. Fear had me frozen in place, paralyzing all of my rationale and my ability to decipher what my next move should be.

"So, Michelle, you've made it home." I could hear the sarcasm dripping from her tone. "Why don't you turn on the lights? Let's talk."

"Dawn?" I asked, trying to grasp that she had somehow gotten into my house.

"No, Michelle. You're mistaken. I'm Daphne," she said with a smirk.

I could feel my throat getting tight. How had she gotten in? Wasn't she supposed to be in Florida?

"Daphne, please, whatever you've planned, don't do it," I pleaded.

"Michelle, don't give me that pathetic plea. It's not going to work. I've waited a very long time for this day, and you aren't going to destroy this moment by attempting to make me feel guilty. Nope. Not gonna work." I felt an eerie feeling that I was desperately trying to ignore.

"Now, Michelle, I'll ask you again. Turn on the lights," she said through what sounded like clenched teeth.

I hesitantly, by memory, moved to the small table that held the antique lamp. I switched on the light and jumped at the sight of Daphne standing next to the staircase dressed in one of my Donna Vinci suits and wearing my matching J.Reneé shoes. My diamonds flanked her neck as if they belonged there, and my grandmother's earrings clung to her ears as if she were the owner of them. Looking at Daphne Carlton was like looking at my own image. Her makeup was absolutely flawless, and a waft of my perfume, Angel, slid across my nostrils. Her outfit was near perfect, except for the 9mm accessory in her hand.

"Michelle, lock the door," she commanded.

"Daphne . . ."

"Michelle!" she interrupted. "Stop it! I'm the one doing the talking. Just do what I tell you to do!"

I turned back to the door. For a split second, I thought of running out, but I knew a bullet would be in my back before I could get two feet. I had to figure out a way to buy myself time.

"Michelle, I know what you're doing. And trust me; you're not going to find a plan to escape engraved in the door, so turn back around," she demanded.

I slowly turned around. The slight flutter in my stomach was the reminding force that propelled me. I became like a wild lioness whose sole objective was to protect her cub. The thought of my unborn baby and its safety was enough to develop the strength I needed to conquer this giant.

"Daphne, I don't know what you think you're doing, but you are not going to get away with it. You will not come into my home and take over while I sit back and watch you do it."

Her laughter sounded like something from a horror movie.

"Michelle, you never cease to amaze me. Just when I think I've got you all figured out, you surprise me. You actually have a spine." She began to walk closer to me. "What am I going to do with you?" She paused and turned serious again, and was now standing directly in my face. "After I kill you." She grazed the tip of my nose with the gun.

Those four words were like death to the confidence I possessed moments earlier. The strength that exuded from me minutes before had been drained like a pool at the end of the summer. It never occurred to me that Daphne wanted me dead. Sure, I knew she was crazy and wanted to take over my life—but death? Was she really crazy enough to go through with it? Could this actually be the end of my life?

The constant flutter in my stomach didn't have the same effect or purpose that it had the first time. It was my nerves, and they were getting the best of me. I was too afraid to even breathe. Breathing was a sign of hope, a sign of life, and I didn't feel as if I had either right now.

"Michelle, go into the living room and sit down on the couch," Daphne said as she waved the gun.

I did as she directed, trying desperately to think of a way to get help, but I could hardly think. I surveyed the room, trying to find any logical escape route. I could make a run for the kitchen, but once again I would be gunned down. Along with my baby.

Tears silently streamed down my face, and a PowerPoint presentation of my otherwise happy life began to flash before eyes. I was thirty-two years old, pregnant with my first child, happily married to the man of my dreams, living in the home I'd always wanted, and this time tomorrow it would all be over. Just like that. No warning. No nothing.

You shall live and not die.

God's voice came rushing into my ears like waves on the bank of an ocean, and again, I gained strength. I smiled at this small feat of victory. I knew in my heart that this was not my battle. It was the Lord's, and He would fight it.

"Are you smiling?" Daphne asked, interrupting my thoughts.

I turned to face an irritated Daphne, who was hoping to keep her game of scare tactics going. But that was unfortunate, because I felt a peace in my heart that superseded the capability of any weapon. Or any devil.

"Do you think I'm something to laugh at, Michelle? Do you think I'm some sort of joke?" My silence aggravated her more, and her evil laugh returned. "You know what?" She didn't wait for me to answer. "I see that you're going to make this difficult. I was actually going to let you write some sort of goodbye note. I see my kindness is not appreciated."

I dropped my head. The anger I felt was gone, and in its place, sadness.

Daphne needed help. She needed to know and experience the love of God, for if she knew like I knew how God's love could transform your life and fill any void that one could have, she wouldn't be holding me hostage in my own home.

Before I could lift my head, I heard the click of the trigger; then, the loud noise that drowned out all sounds of normalcy. The sound that would always live throughout the crevices of the walls.

"Michelle! Michelle!"

I opened my eyes to a very worried Darvin shaking me into reality. My hair was matted to my head by the sweat that was pouring from my body, and my clothes were equally soaked.

"Baby, you had a bad dream." He sighed in relief. He pulled me into his arms and held on to me as if tomorrow would never come. "I've got you now, and I'm not going to let anything happen to you. Ever."

He scooped me into his arms and held on to me as if I would vanish any second. I laid my head on his shoulder and couldn't help but wonder if I had just experienced a warning for what was to come. Sure, it was a dream this time, but would Darvin really be able to protect me if this dream ever came true?

Chapter Six

Michelle

After waking up from my dream, I knew that if I was going to survive whatever Dawn Carlton was up to, I was going to have to think. And I was going to have to think much harder than I did with Daphne.

My mind drifted back to the night that Daphne appeared at Mount Zion's door a few years ago. She appeared to be a sweet little lamb not possessing the ability to harm a fly, but from our encounter at the diner, I knew better. So, my thoughts of her were much like our first meeting—I was intimidated.

She was attractive, with long legs, a figure that would get the attention of any man, a gorgeous smile, and her wardrobe choice had made mine look as if I'd gotten dressed with my eyes closed. Worse than that, she'd been in the car with my husband that same day. What a strange coincidence that had been.

Darvin had called me from the grocery store, telling me that he was giving a ride home to a lady whose car had broken down in the parking lot, but he failed to mention that she was a beauty queen. Little did I know that it was the beauty queen from the restaurant.

He introduced us, and the look in her eyes told me that he had failed to mention at least two things to her: one, he was a pastor, and two, he was a married pastor.

I plastered on the best smile I could. "Baby, we've already met," I said.

I surveyed her. She certainly didn't look like the type of

woman who would be riding in a broke-down car. Nonetheless, she apparently was, and my husband had come to her rescue.

I don't know if that was what made me mad, or the fact that after his introductions, he held a private conversation with her over to the side.

Later that evening while driving home, I took the opportunity to find out what they had been discussing.

"What do you think about Daphne?"

He purposefully kept his focus on the road. "I don't think anything about her. She's a lady whom I gave a ride home and who visited our church tonight."

My calmness was leaving me. He knew what I meant. "What were the two of you talking about so long?"

He laughed. "Michelle, I can't believe you. What do you think I was talking to her about?"

"What's so funny, and what can't you believe?"

"This is funny. You. This whole conversation. It's like I can't win with you. Are you going to be intimidated by every woman I meet?"

If he had not been driving, I would have knocked him straight into heaven—partly because he always had a way of reading between my lines.

"Intimidated? Do you think I was intimidated by her?" I said, trying to hide the apparent truth.

"It seems that way to me. I mean, out of all of the women that I talked to tonight—and some longer than I talked to her, might I add—you only asked about her," he said in frustration.

"For God's sake, you gave her a ride home. Why can't I ask you about her? So, the question remains the same. What were you two talking about? And don't lie to me, Darvin. I know that whatever it was, she was upset with you."

He paused, obviously trying to come up with another clever remark. Finding none, he said, "She was mad because I didn't tell her I was a pastor."

"And why didn't you?"

"She asked the same thing." He paused. "I don't know, Michelle. It's not like I go around telling people that."

"But didn't you invite her to church? Why didn't you tell her then?"

"Think about it. If I invited her to church, don't you think I knew she would find out that I was the pastor? Shouldn't that count for something?"

I thought for a minute. He did have a point. However, I was still not satisfied. "Did you tell her that you were married?" I asked, hoping he would say he did.

"No, but I knew that if she came to church, she would find that out too."

Wrong answer. "What! Are you serious? What if she had not come to church? How would she have found out then? Is there any particular reason why you didn't want this woman to know that you were married?" By this time, I was fuming.

"I was only trying to help her out. She never asked me, and I never told her. Simple as that."

"Oh, it's not that simple, Pastor Johnson. It is so not that simple. You led this woman on. You made her believe that she had a chance with a married man."

This time he turned toward me. "How did you get all of that from what I just said?"

"Because I'm a woman, and I know how women think. You are so naïve until it sickens me. One day, you are going to wish you had listened to me. That woman was upset tonight because I bet you any amount of money that she came to that church with the intentions of leaving with you."

"You need some help. You really need some help. Granted, she was upset because I didn't tell her that I was a pastor or married, but she made no insinuations that she was in the least bit interested in me." He sighed heavily.

I sighed equally as heavy. I put my face into the palms of my hands. "Darvin, Darvin, Darvin. If she didn't have any other motives, why did she even care if you were married or not? I can understand being upset about the fact that you didn't tell her you were a pastor, but explain to me why she was upset because you didn't tell her you were married." I sighed again. "Never mind. Don't answer that. It doesn't matter anyway."

Darvin clicked the button that opened the gates, and drove into our driveway. Before getting out of the car, he turned to look at me. "Don't talk like that. Listen, I didn't mean anything by it."

I looked into the eyes of the man I was deeply in love with. With tears threatening to fall, I said, "It will never stop, will it, Darvin? It will always be somebody trying to come between us, won't it?" I dropped my head just as a tear escaped. "I don't know if I can handle it. I was just not ready for this.

And you know what? Even if Daphne meant nothing by it, I'm too paranoid not to think otherwise."

He leaned over and stroked my cheek with his forefinger. "Baby, you've got to stop taking things so personal. Every woman doesn't want me. I know we've had our share of women at the church trying to come between us, but I'm not going to let that happen." He paused and lifted my chin. "I love you and only you."

"I've never doubted your love. It just seems that every woman who looks at you only sees the power, money, and fame. They don't seem to want you for who you are. They don't seem to care about your virtues and your vices. All they see is the 'Pastor.' I just can't seem to shake this feeling that one day somebody will take it too far. And I know you may think I'm being over emotional, but this is so frustrating sometimes. I'm always faced with women that can't accept that you're taken, which leads to their own agenda to have you for themselves."

"And you think that's Daphne's agenda? Me? Because I can't do anything about anyone else's agenda. I can only control what I do."

Silence permeated the car. I knew that Daphne was probably like all the rest of the women, smitten with a good-looking, wealthy black man, but I was always on watch. Maybe it was time for me to let my guard down. Maybe she wasn't after my man.

"That's not fair to her, honey. I can't really say that's her agenda." I turned to look out of my window. "But if it is, who could blame her?" I focused my attention back to Darvin. "You are a good catch."

He leaned in for a kiss and I met him halfway. Darvin was a good man, and sometimes I wished I was the only one who knew it.

Thinking back, that was the night that I decided to give Daphne a chance. I didn't know if I'd ever see her again, but had decided that if I did, I would try to at least be nice to her. At that time, Darvin appeared to be right. I needed to stop thinking that every woman was out to destroy my relationship. But had I known what the days, weeks, and months would bring, I would have never trusted that two-faced snake. I wouldn't have trusted her any further than I could see her.

That's why Dawn wasn't going to get past me. She would not come in here and deceive me like her twisted twin sister. I would be ready for battle this time, and I wasn't planning on walking away a loser. She'd better bring it, as they say, because as far as I was concerned, it had already been brought.

Chapter Seven

Daphne

I woke up to the birds singing melodiously in my ear. As the sun was softly kissing the earth, my alarm clock was invading my peaceful calm, signaling the start of a new work day.

I groaned, turned to stop the annoying sound, and rolled onto my other side to catch a few more minutes of sleep. Before I could drift completely into unconsciousness, the picture of Darvin's broad smile greeted me good morning. There he was, encased in a chrome frame, dressed in black Armani slacks and a red LaCoste shirt, looking as good as the day that I laid eyes on him.

It had been a smoldering summer day when I first met him. Having just moved to Atlanta from Florida, my car chose the hottest day of the year to break down in the parking lot of the Whole Foods Market. Not having any roadside assistance, coupled with the dilemma of not knowing anyone to call, I leaned against the trunk of my beat-up Honda Accord and sighed in frustration. I'd known when I arrived in Atlanta that the car was rolling on fumes and worn rubber, and the first thing that had been on my agenda was to buy a new car. But my agenda and my finances failed to meet, so I was stuck barely getting around. I'd taken a position making nearly six figures, but it was taking me a while to get caught up.

After a brief moment of sulking, I decided that the sun wasn't getting any cooler, and if I didn't want to be stranded all day, I'd better figure out something.

And then it happened.

My angel came walking out of the store. He was the most perfect man I'd ever seen. With his broad shoulders and a strut that would make any woman weak in the knees, I knew in an instant I'd fallen in love.

The man continued to stroll with groceries in one hand and his cell phone in the other. I plastered my best look of despair on my face, and all but fainted when he started walking my way. The moment reminded me of one of those scenes in a movie when the woman in distress was broken down beside a long, dusty road, fanning away the heat with her wide-brim hat, her dress clinging to her body like the wrappings of a Christmas gift, and just enough leg showing to get the first man's attention. With that thought, I unbuttoned the top two buttons of my white cotton blouse, signaling that at any moment I would just melt from sunburn.

The closer he got to me, the more the scent of his cologne, Cool Water, filled my nostrils. He had a perfect blend of cologne and body chemistry, and a gorgeous smile that sent me into a whirlwind of emotions leaving me with flushed cheeks.

Suddenly, the man whose attention I was desperate to get, had stopped and was facing me.

"Ma'am, I'm headed to my car, but I can't help but notice that you appear a little flustered. Do you need some help?" he asked.

I laughed gently. Who did he think he was fooling? He couldn't help but notice all right. "I guess I do look a bit of a mess out here in this hot sun, huh?"

"No, ma'am. I didn't say that." He returned the smile. "Oh, you said it all when you called me ma'am," I teased back.

He laughed. "You know, people are always telling me that I have a tendency to put my foot in my mouth."

If only he knew what all I wanted him to do with his delicious mouth. His lips were perfectly curved, made perfect for soft kisses.

"Well, we'll call it even if you can somehow help me get my jalopy back rolling." I patted the old beat-up Honda.

"What seems to be the problem?"

"I don't know. I've been having several problems out of this antique."

That was true, but I lowered my eyelashes so that he wouldn't be able to see the lack of innocence I possessed at the moment. And when I raised them again, his smile was even wider.

"I'm sorry; I didn't get your name." His intense stare almost made me crumble into pieces.

Somehow I managed to think of my name. "Daphne. I'm Daphne Carlton."

Even though I couldn't see the smile plastered on my face, I was sure that it would have intimidated the most photogenic model.

"It's a pleasure to meet you, Daphne Carlton."

The way he said my name was as smooth as silk. Who was this man?

Why did he unnerve me?

"And you are?"

"Oh, I'm Darvin Johnson."

He was looking so deeply into my eyes that I could have sworn he saw past my little attempt to seduce him. Obviously, he was enjoying this moment of flirting, because he allowed it to linger.

"So, Mr. Darvin Johnson, you've come to save the day. My day." I flashed another smile before lowering my lashes once more.

"That's me. Darvin Johnson, Superman here to the rescue," he joked.

What I wanted to ask was if he'd been rescued by some lucky woman, but I didn't want to seem too desperate. I made a mental note that he was not wearing a wedding ring. "So, you know much about cars?"

"Not really, but I know enough to stay rolling. Why don't you raise your hood and let me take a look."

He shifted the bag he held to his other arm and walked to the front of my car. He set the groceries down on the ground as I released the latch to the hood. When I did, smoke almost suffocated the poor man. I hurriedly jumped out of the car to find him coughing and gagging, trying to catch a breath.

"Are you all right?" I asked.

Still coughing profusely, "Yes" was all he said. He slammed the hood of the car back down, wiped away the sweat from his forehead, and walked back to where I was sitting in the driver's seat.

"Daphne, as I said, I can't say that I know a lot about cars. But I know enough to know that something is terribly wrong with yours." His gaze shifted back to the hood of the car. "I think that it may have run hot, but I don't want to take a chance that the problem may not be a more serious one." He turned his piercing gaze back to me. "Do you have someone you can call to come and get you? I wouldn't trust this thing even if it was running."

It was at that moment that it hit me. I knew how I was going to learn more about the man who had silently, and without knowing, seduced me.

"No, Darvin, I'm afraid I don't. I just recently moved from Florida and I have no relatives here. Matter of fact, I haven't even started my new job, so I don't even have friends." I put on my most somber face. "I guess I will just have to call a wrecker and then maybe call for a cab."

Darvin studied me intensely. I could almost see the battle going on in his mind. He was trying to determine if he should trust my story and offer additional assistance, or walk away in approval of my own solution. He looked as if he'd been in this very predicament before.

His conscience and better judgment must have given way to his heart.

"The wrecker is going to cost you a fortune." He paused. "The cab, too." He paused again. "Do you think you can afford that?"

There it was again, the battle. Little did he know, I didn't pick fights I couldn't win. And this was one that I intended to win. "Mr. Johnson, I know that I must appear to be in bad shape here, but I'm not destitute." I pretended to cast angry eyes at him. "Thanks for your help." I got out of the driver's seat, closed the door, maneuvered my way around his muscular body, and proceeded to walk back in the direction of the store.

As I walked away, I made sure to add a little extra sway to my hips. If he was like any other man, he couldn't resist a shapely body and feet clad in three-inch heels.

Just as I expected, he called out, "Ms. Carlton!" I wanted to allow his voice to bounce off my back for added drama, but I couldn't resist him. I stopped in my tracks and hesitated to turn around, so he would think that I was really upset. When I did swirl around, I was facing a very apologetic-looking Darvin.

"Ms. or Mrs. Carlton," he said more in a question form, "I'm sorry. I didn't mean for it to seem as if you couldn't afford to handle your business. As I said before, I always have a way of putting my foot in my mouth."

And if it weren't for those cute little puppy dog eyes, I wouldn't have broken my resolve so soon. A smile curved the corners of my lips.

"That's okay. The truth is I can't afford it right now. I mean, I can, but . . ." I paused. "Anyway, don't let me trouble you with my problems. I've already held up too much of your time." I touched his arm gently. "Thanks again for your help, and oh, I'm sorry about my attitude back there." I pointed in the direction of my car. "I'm just so frustrated."

"I understand." He lowered his head and cast his eyes toward the ground as if it would somehow show what his next words should be. His head slowly came back up.

"Daphne, why don't I give you a ride? I can take you wherever you need to go."

Yes! The scent of victory was a sweet-smelling fragrance in my nostrils.

"I really don't want you going out of your way for me, Mr. Johnson."

"Daphne, please, call me Darvin."

Another victory. "Darvin, I couldn't ask you to do that. I'm sure you were on your way someplace." I fanned away heat as if I had a built-in fan on my hand.

Darvin looked at the diamond Rolex flanking his arm. "I have a couple of hours to spare before my meeting. I could at least take you home so your groceries won't spoil."

I hadn't even thought of that. That would be even better. Taking me to my home signaled that he trusted me. And that meant that I could invite him in for lunch to thank him for his kindness. Once again, a wide grin spread across my face. "That would be great. I'd forgotten all about my groceries."

We both turned and went back to my car. I grabbed my bags and purse, and turned to thank him again, but he was making a call from his cell. He moved over a couple of feet to get some privacy, and I did everything I could to distract myself so that I wouldn't eavesdrop. After a couple of seconds, he ended his call and came back toward me.

"So, Daphne, where to?"

"Home," I said with meaning behind it. Darvin must have felt it, because he shifted uncomfortably on his feet. "To my house," I corrected quickly.

"All right, Miss Daisy," he teased, "to your house it is. That's my horse and buggy over there."

The horse and buggy that he referred to was a shiny black Mercedes S500 parked a couple of spaces over. Some horse and buggy. I sashayed over to his car, and being the perfect gentleman, he opened the passenger's door for me as I got in, and then he dipped to his side of the car.

"This is a really nice car." I admired the smo-oth gray leather interior.

"Thanks. It'll do," he said, obviously trying to show his humbleness.

He started the engine, and if I didn't know any better, I wouldn't have known that the car was even on. The quiet purr of the luxury car was soothing, and the air that was blowing generously from the vents surrounded by cherry wood grain was like water in the desert. I leaned back to fully enjoy the comfort and allowed my body to sink into the plush leather.

"So, which way?" he asked.

I adjusted myself in the seat. "I live in Atlantic Station."

He jerked his head in my direction. "Atlantic Station?" he said in surprise. "No wonder you don't have any money."

I glared at him. I knew that he would think that as soon as I told him where I lived. But I was always ready for a comeback. "It's not like what you think. I'm subleasing from a friend who relocated to Texas. She's allowing me to stay there until my house is finished. I bought a place over in South Atlanta."

"Really?" he said in even more surprise. "What a coincidence. I live in South Atlanta."

This must be fate. "Really?" I said in astonishment. "What part?"

"Fayette County."

"Me too!" I said with a little too much excitement.

Darvin looked at me as if I were growing a second head.

"I'm just excited because at least I know one person in Atlanta," I explained to help reduce his concern.

"Oh, I wouldn't worry about not knowing anybody," he said as he drove onto the interstate. "Do you go to church?"

Wow. Was he inviting me to his church already? This was going better than I could imagine. I couldn't contain my excitement. "Of course I go to church." I looked over to him. "Do I look like I need to be saved or something?" I said sheepishly.

His laughter returned. "No, I was asking because I was going to invite you to my church tonight." He paused. "Tonight is our midweek service."

Who would've known that my old beat-up Honda would prove to be a blessing in disguise? "Sure. I would love to go to your church. Only thing is,"—I bowed my head to my lap for added measure—"I don't have transportation, remember?"

"I'll handle that. You just be ready at six-thirty."

This man was a godsend. My mother had always told me that God will give you the desires of your heart. Darvin Johnson was certainly becoming a desire of my heart, and my moving to Atlanta was starting to be one of the best decisions of my life.

Chapter Eight

Daphne

I got out of bed still thinking about that day. The smile on my face quickly faded as I remembered how the remainder of the evening had played out.

I strolled into the bathroom and snatched a towel from the linen closet. That stunt Darvin pulled that night still had a way of upsetting me to this day.

I sat on the edge of my oversized Jacuzzi and allowed my mind to once again drift back to that day.

Finding an outfit for church had been like finding the perfect dress for the red carpet. That night was about more than just going to church; it was about making a statement. I'd already thought of the women that I would have to impress because I was sure that Darvin was a highly sought-after bachelor. My thoughts for the men included leaving a hint of jealousy behind, so that they would envy Darvin and the new woman-to-be in his life.

Finally, I selected a black Chanel suit that my ex-boyfriend had purchased for me. The skirt stopped flirtatiously above the knee, and the four- inch heels that I selected to accompany the suit were the perfect item to accentuate my long, mocha-colored legs. I got dressed, dug through a plethora of unpacked boxes to find my jewelry box that contained my diamond necklace and earrings, took one final look in the mirror, and went to the living room to wait for Darvin.

After a few times of going back and forth to the mirror to assure myself that I still approved of my look, I glanced at the clock sitting on the bar that separated the living room from the kitchen, and noticed that Darvin was late.

It suddenly dawned on me that he and I had not exchanged phone numbers, so even if something had come up, he wouldn't have a way to contact me.

The clock now read 6:45, and that meant he was fifteen minutes late. He struck me as the type to be prompt, but maybe I was mistaken. My thoughts drifted to the many possibilities that would cause him to be late or not show up at all, and I suddenly felt a wave of sadness come over me. Maybe he'd known the entire time that my intentions had more to do with him than going to church, and he had decided not to be bothered with me. I could have kicked myself. I should have never been so aggressive.

My thoughts were interrupted by the sound of the doorbell. My heart and stomach simultaneously did somersaults and my palms became sweaty. I calmly walked to the front, and with my award-winning smile of the day shining brightly on my face, I opened the door.

Immediately, my enthusiasm was drained out of me, and without having to look, I'm sure that my color followed close behind it.

"Can I help you?" I asked, not disguising my disgust.

The man at the door was dressed in a dusty black suit, a white shirt that held a crooked black tie, and had two gold teeth in the center of his mouth.

The '80s-old Jheri curl had strands of his hair stuck to his face, causing his skin to shine from the grease. He had a wide smile, and was looking at a piece of wrinkled paper in his hand. Then, he allowed his eyes to do a once over of me.

"Are you Ms. Daphne Carlton?"

"Who wants to know?" I said with my attitude still intact.

His smile no longer there, he said, "Ma'am, I've been sent here to take you to Mount Zion Missionary Baptist Church." The man grew impatient. "Are you planning to go or not?"

A slight grin turned the corner of my mouth at the thought of Darvin sending a driver for me. I realized that I'd struck gold—literally—and hadn't even been in the Peach State for an entire week. I looked up to the invisible heavens and gave God thanks for hooking a sister up!

"Forgive me. Let me get my purse." I grabbed my Prada bag from the couch, and turned to meet my driver. "Ready?"

"Yes, ma'am."

"Well, let's go then." I locked the door to my apartment and could hardly wait to see what type of car Darvin had sent for me.

As I walked gleefully down the corridor to the elevator, the man must have noticed my sudden excitement.

"It's been a while since I've picked up anyone that's been this excited about going to church." He pressed the down arrow on the elevator control panel. "I can't wait to tell Pastor. He'll be glad to know that."

"I must admit, God has certainly been good to me, and I'm thrilled to be standing in the direct flow of his blessings."

The man just smiled as the elevator door opened and we stepped inside.

I could hardly contain my excitement on the short elevator ride to the first floor. I was completely consumed by my thoughts of Darvin. He barely knew me, and already he was making some impressive moves. His interest in me must have been just as intense as mine was in him.

We stepped off of the elevator and walked through the revolving doors that led from the lobby to outside. Had it not been for the van that was blocking my view of the car Darvin had sent for me, I probably would have floated right to it.

The man in the dusty suit stepped up to the van, opened

the door, and extended his hand toward me. I looked at him with eyes of confusion, and the smile on his face suddenly looked sickening to me.

"Ms. Carlton, your chariot awaits," he said as he pointed to the vehicle.

The big white blob parked in front of me was in no way a chariot. The oversized red letters boldly displayed on the side of it read: MOUNT ZION BAPTIST CHURCH . . . A CHURCH WITH A VISION.

I blinked my eyes over and over in hopes of making the van and the man disappear. I simply could not believe that Darvin would send this man, who looked as if he had just stepped out of the *Soul Train* line, to give me a ride to church. The nerve of him.

"Ms.," he said impatiently, "I wish I could stand here all night, but I have other people to pick up. Are you going or not?"

If visions of Darvin and his kindness earlier in the day hadn't suddenly come to mind, I would have marched through the same doors that I'd just exited, and gone back to my apartment. But I figured that the least I could do was go to his church to pay him back for giving me a ride home. And besides, he was as fine as the day was long. Surely, there was a good explanation behind this whole thing.

So, I reluctantly entered the van and was immediately greeted by an elderly woman wearing a dress that looked as if it dated back to the '70s, and a small boy who appeared to be her grandson.

I returned the greeting with a simple nod of my head. Had it not been for the fear of wrinkling the expensive suit that I was wearing, I would have sunk deep into the seat with no regard for anyone noticing that I existed.

I was so grateful that no one knew me in Atlanta, because I wouldn't have been caught riding in a van to church.

I survived the ride and was in awe when we drove up to

the massive edifice. I don't know why I was expecting anything less, because Darvin didn't seem to be the type to be affiliated with anything other than the best. On the other hand, I didn't think he would send the church bus to pick me up, but he did. I thanked God that the ride home would be different, and it was that thought that brought the sunshine back into my day.

The driver came around and opened the door for all of the passengers and I carefully stepped out. Since it was my first time attending, I had no clue where to go. The other passengers seemed to be so familiar with what to do, so I followed everyone else.

I walked into the spacious foyer of the sanctuary and beheld the expensive chandelier hanging from the ceiling. I admired the marble tile that appeared to have been flown in from another country, as well as the life-size statues of lions that were protected by chain ropes. I was more than impressed with what I saw, and I was eagerly looking forward to the service that was yet to begin. I'd been in church all of my life, but had never really gotten involved. I felt a change coming on, and from the looks of it, Mount Zion Baptist Church would benefit from my plethora of talents. My mother used to always tell me that if I didn't start using the gifts God gave me, He would eventually take them away. Now that I was about to have me a churchgoing man, I certainly didn't need that to happen.

I followed the signs that led to the sanctuary and walked inside. If the foyer wasn't enough to capture your attention, the sanctuary didn't disappoint.

With T.V. cameras, special lights, and the plush carpet, the atmosphere was breathtaking. Mount Zion was definitely the opposite of what I was accustomed to seeing at home in Florida. The church that I grew up in was a small white church that had wooden floors and pews, yellow jackets buzzing in the summer, and the smell of fried chicken in every room. So, this was a new perspective of church, and I was enjoying it already.

I took a seat in the back of the third section about mid-way down the row, hoping to catch a glimpse of Darvin before the worship service began.

I also took a moment to survey the environment. There were women pacing the floor, microphones in hand, praying for the pastor and his wife, praying for the flow of the service, and for all of the souls that would soon come to Christ. Admiration filled my eyes at the sight of those women, and hope filled my heart, that maybe one day I could pray with such power and conviction.

Other parishioners filed into the sanctuary as the service prepared to start. The musicians took their places on the instruments, and before long, we were all standing and swaying to the sounds of rich gospel music. I kept scanning the audience for Darvin, but he was nowhere in sight. I'd purposely sat in the back so that I could get a good look at everyone who came in, but even after twenty minutes, Darvin was not one of the ones sitting amongst the worshipers.

I was frustrated, to say the least. Not only had he invited me to his church and failed to pick me up, it looked as though he'd decided not to attend. That meant I would have to ride that silly van back home. All of a sudden, neither the service nor the appealing features of the sanctuary were enough to calm my nerves. Darvin had lost major points in my book, and I intended to let him know if I ever saw him again.

I tried to assure myself that since the church was so large, maybe I'd missed seeing him come in.

Before long, the entire sanctuary had filled to capacity, and it was getting harder and harder to maintain my view of the front. Lost in my thoughts, I heard a man come to the microphone and call everyone to attention.

"Brothers and sisters of Mount Zion, we want to thank you for coming out tonight to our weekly worship service. We certainly hope that something has been said or done thus far that will richly bless your life in the days to come, and for those of you visiting, we pray that you will come back to worship with us again." He took a brief pause as members began to respond to his comment with hand claps. After things had calmed down, he resumed speaking.

"Well, saints, it's time." The church erupted in shouts and screams as the musicians played louder than they had previously. I hated to admit that their outburst scared me half to death.

The man continued. "It's time to hear a Word from the Lord! It's time for your breakthrough! It's time for your healing! Now, are you ready?"

People all over the building stood, shouted, and applauded their agreement.

"Let's prepare to receive the man of God who's been sent to Mount Zion to lead us and deliver this life-changing Word."

Everybody stood to their feet and I followed suit.

"Let's give it up for our pastor, Pastor Darvin Johnson!" Before he could get the words out of his mouth, the screams erupted again. Except mine.

I was convinced that the Earth had ceased turning on its axis and that I was in one of those nightmares that went in slow motion. Did he just say Pastor Darvin Johnson?

As Darvin approached the podium, the scre-ams got louder. And as for me, I wanted to reduce myself to a liquid and pour myself down the nearest drain. *Shock* was not the word to describe my emotions. As a matter of fact, there were no words in the English language to describe how I felt. Why didn't Darvin tell me that he was a pastor?

I tried to shake away all of this newfound information with a motion of my head, but it didn't work. Darvin was still standing in the pulpit in what appeared to be a tailor-made suit, and he was preparing to speak. Lord knows he looked good;

however, it was no excuse not to enlighten me on his occupation.

Would this change anything for us? I had never met a pastor other than the one who'd baptized me when I was nine years old. But wait a minute; didn't every pastor have a first lady?

My heart started skipping beats. Was he married? Sure, he wasn't wearing a ring earlier, but was that because he forgot it at home?

Once again, with a motion of my head, I tried to dismiss the thought of him being married. He couldn't be. He was supposed to be my man, not anyone else's.

"First, I give honor to God, who's the head of my life," he spoke. "And second, I give honor to my beautiful wife, Michelle, who's the love of my life."

The remainder of what he said, as well as the service, whizzed by in a blur. All I could think about was the fact that some woman named Michelle was married to my man. God, this was so unfair. If this was God's idea of a joke, I didn't find it funny at all.

Somehow, when the service was over, I managed to unglue myself from my seat and exit the sanctuary as everyone else. Still in a daze, I bumped into a man who I didn't have to see to know who he was. By the smell of his cologne, I knew that it was Darvin. Pastor Darvin.

Realizing that it was me who'd bumped into him, he said, "Sister Daphne, I'm glad that you made it." He then nudged his wife, who was greeting other parishioners, and said, "Honey, this is Sister Daphne Carlton. She's the woman I told you I gave a ride home today."

She turned, and immediately my eyes grew big. It was the woman from the diner! Looking like she'd just come back from shopping at a yard sale, her smile vanished.

Michelle extended her hand, and if it weren't for all the eyes on me, I would have tried to break it off and slap her with it. Instead, I extended my hand to her as well. However, my handshake didn't symbolize a greeting; my handshake was a sign of battle.

And secretly, with my eyes, I told her that the best woman would win.

Most women were intimidated by me; she was no different. I could feel it, and it showed in her eyes. My smile returned because getting my man from her would more than likely be a breeze.

"It's nice to see you again, and don't you look . . ." I took a moment to scan the likes of the yard-sale outfit. "Lovely. You look lovely."

Her nose flared. "You look rather, um, nice yourself," she said, trying to mask her apparent irritation.

I guess Darvin could feel the tension brewing between us and decided to intervene. "Ladies, I'm going to step over here and finish greeting the others. Daphne, please don't leave until I speak with you further."

Michelle could have choked on her tongue.

"Sure, Pastor. I would love to speak with you in private," I said, hoping to irritate Michelle even more.

It seemed to work. The fire in her eyes would have consumed me if the water of my confidence hadn't put it out.

Chapter Nine

Daphne

I had been waiting to speak with Darvin for more than ten minutes, and my patience was wearing thin.

No longer able to hide my frustration, I wheeled around on my feet in the direction of the door through which I'd entered, and after tonight, the door I planned to never use again.

As I walked away, Darvin called, "Sister Daphne!"

I whirled around with images of fire in my eyes, and through gritted teeth, said, "I am not your sister!"

He stopped in front of me. "I know that. It's just a term we use in church."

"You know, contrary to your belief, I know a little something about church. It's not like this is the first time I've stepped foot in one." I shifted my weight to my right side and placed my hand on my hip. "Who do you think I am? Some hopeless woman in need of saving and sanctifying?"

Darvin looked apologetically into my eyes. "No. I don't think that at all." He paused. "Daphne," he said, intentionally not placing the word *sister* before my name. "Thank you for coming tonight. How did you enjoy the service?"

What! Did he really think I was able to focus on a service? "It was nice, Darvin." I released a sigh. "However, I just have one question."

"Shoot."

"Why didn't you tell me you were a pastor?"

He cast his eyes to the floor and then returned my gaze. "Because I didn't want you to think that I was being nice to you simply because I was a pastor."

"Then why were you nice to me?"

I looked around his back and noticed that Michelle was watching us even as she was talking to another churchgoer. "You still should have said something. I mean, I was totally blown away when they announced you as the pastor tonight." Michelle was staring at us so intently; I shifted my body more to the left so that Darvin's body would shield mine.

"Maybe I should have. But . . ." He paused.

"But you wanted to flirt with me," I finished his statement. "Not to mention that you never said anything about being married."

His eyes told me the truth, but his mouth said, "No. I was not intentionally flirting with you." He looked at the floor once more. "Daphne, there's something special about you. I really think that you have great things in store for you, and hopefully I can assist in that."

What the heck was he talking about? Was he a prophet too? Or was Darvin trying to send me a coded message? Little butterflies began to flutter inside of my stomach. For whatever reason, my hope had returned. I continued to gaze into his eyes, and for a moment, neither of us said anything.

"Darvin, sweetie, are you ready to go?" Michelle's voice interrupted my bliss. Little did she know that I had enough to last me through the night.

"Pastor and First Lady, it was a pleasure meeting you." I put on the best smile I could muster and moved to walk away.

"Daphne?" Michelle called.

"Yes?"

"Don't forget to stop by the visitor's information desk on your way out to get your complimentary gift and information about our church."

"I'll do that." I turned again and followed the signs that led to the area that Michelle spoke of, as a new plan was already forming in my mind.

I arrived at the desk, where volunteers dressed in black were smiling and greeting the visitors. I filled out an information card and exchanged it for my gift bag with the volunteer.

I took my bag and went out the door, dreading the return trip on that dreadful church bus. But I was so excited to get home to further devise my plan that I didn't mind being temporarily inconvenienced.

Twenty minutes later, I walked into my apartment, kicked off my shoes, threw my purse on the couch, and headed to my room to get my pen and paper. I needed to write down all of my ideas and place them in order so that I could get to work immediately. I took a notepad and pen from the nightstand and began making notes.

Number 1 - Find out more about Darvin and Michelle (i.e. his and her background, how long they've been married, any kids, etc.)

Number 2 - Call the church office and set up an appointment with Michelle.

Number 3 - Get a new car.

Chapter Ten

Michelle

Since Dawn had shown up, it was difficult not to spend my extra time thinking about both her and Daphne. The two of them were so much alike, in that they were both persistent.

Dawn, just as her sister, was obviously determined to show us that she would be a part of Mount Zion whether or not we wanted her to.

As I entered through the doors that led to the administrative wing of the church, I thought back to a rainy day similar to this one, when I'd walked into my office to find one of our newest members. It had been Daphne.

I had been ready to start the new work week, glad that our Annual Empowerment Revival was finally over. It had been a lot of work leading up to the revival and I, for one, was glad that it was over. It had proven to be a successful event, and more than forty people had given their lives to Christ. Daphne Carlton had been one of them. Up until the revival, she'd been doing everything that she could to arrange a meeting with me, but I would always conveniently find something to do. That day, I'd run out of excuses. It was either me or Darvin.

"Good morning, First Lady," Sabrina, my executive assistant said.

When Sabrina said that, I had a déjà vu moment. My thoughts escaped back to that day in my office.

"Good morning, Sabrina. How's Caleb?" I said, referring

to her two-year-old son, who'd recently been sick with chicken pox.

"He's fine. Just as hyper as usual." She beamed.

I returned the smile. "Well, that's good to hear. Any calls for me yet?"

"No, ma'am. No calls. Um, Daphne Carlton did arrive early, and I seated her in your office. I hope you don't mind, but all of the conference rooms are being used at the moment, and Pastor said that he would sit in there with her until you arrived." She must have detected my confusion. "You know, for extra precaution. You can never be too careful these days," she clarified.

Hmph. Extra precaution, all right. "Of course," was all said. I grabbed a stack of books that Sabrina had ordered for me and had not yet taken to my office, and walked one door down from the reception area where Sabrina sat, in the direction of my husband and Daphne. Lord knows I didn't want to have this meeting with her. I agreed to give her a chance, but I certainly didn't want to know anything more than I had to know about her.

I opened the door to my office and was greeted with laughter echoing from both Darvin and Daphne. Daphne sat on my cream-colored leather couch, dressed to kill in a turquoise St. John knit suit, and Darvin was next to her, looking equally as delectable in a black linen pantsuit. If I didn't know any better, I would have thought they were a happy couple, waiting to share some important news with me.

I cleared my throat because obviously my presence was not felt, and they both turned toward me. Darvin was the first to stumble to his feet. He greeted me with a kiss on the cheek.

"Hey, sweetheart. You look gorgeous today," he said.

I half-heartedly smiled. Any other day that compliment would have meant the world to me, but not today, as I stood in the room with America's Next Top Model. "Thanks, baby," I managed to say.

"Daphne was just sharing with me some of the different, creative ways, I should say, that the men here at Mount Zion are using to try to get her attention. I tell you, I'm going to have to do a better job at teaching the brothers on how to attract a woman like Daphne. Those played-out lines they're using have been reduced to mere quotes in a joke book."

Darvin looked over at Daphne and they both laughed. I didn't find anything that he said funny. Did he say, "a woman like Daphne"? And since when was it the pastor's job to do a men's Bible study on how to attract a woman in the first place? It was hard not to start a verbal war, but I held my peace.

"Yeah, you're just going to have to do that." I shifted the focus back to why we were here. "Daphne, Sabrina said you have been trying to meet with me for the longest." I walked past them and to my chair behind my mahogany desk. "I apologize, but I've been extremely busy with the revival, and had no free time. It was always this meeting and that meeting." I exaggerated the statement with a circular movement of my hands.

"But I'm sure you enjoy every minute of it." She looked at Darvin before looking back at me. "I know that I would."

The little skeezer. I was no model, and in my opinion, I wasn't above average in the looks department, but I had plenty of common sense. I knew enough to know that she didn't come here to simply meet with me and share what the Lord had been speaking to her lately.

"Looks can be deceiving, Ms. Carlton. If, and I do mean if, you are ever to be in a position such as mine, you'll understand why I say what I say." I sat down in my chair. "The life of a pastor or his wife is not all glitz and glam," I said, satisfied with my comeback.

"Life is what you make it, First Lady. I've come to know that it can be whatever you want it to be," she slammed back.

Darvin decided that it was a good enough time for him to escape.

"Baby, Daphne, it's been real, ladies, but I've got to get to my own pastoral duties."

He turned toward Daphne. "Daphne, we're glad to have you as a part of Mount Zion, and if there's anything that we can do for you, just let us know." He then walked over to my desk and once again kissed me on the cheek. "See you for lunch, baby." He turned and walked out the door.

As he walked out, the residue of the smile that he left on my face vanished when I saw the same smile on Daphne's face. If I didn't have Jesus all over me, through me, and around me, I swear I would have slapped that silly grin off her face.

She detected my annoyance with her. "First Lady, let me say that I'm so glad to be a part of the ministry here. I've been visiting here for almost three months, and it was past time that I made that next step."

Feeling my "first lady mode" coming on, I said, "As Pastor has stated, we are glad that you chose Mount Zion to be your church home."

"I really appreciate that." She lowered her eyes. "I know you're wondering why I wanted to meet with you." Finally. The reason why we were here. I couldn't wait to find out, because the sooner I knew what she wanted, the sooner we could be done.

"I must say that I have been interested to know why you've been so persistent."

She looked pointedly in my eyes. "First Lady, I believe that God has sent me here. To this church. For you."

"He has?" I said, trying to contain the laughter that was threatening to erupt. I seriously doubted that God had told her anything close to that.

"Yes. I believe that I've been sent here to serve you. I as well as anybody know that you can't lead where you can't first serve."

"Oh." It was starting to make more sense. "So, you're expecting to be in my shoes one day?"

"I don't know about your shoes, First Lady," she said. "But maybe some similar."

I ignored that comment because its sarcasm was filled with the potential to start World War III. "And how similar?"

"I really believe in my heart that one day I will be a pastor's wife. And since I've watched you for the past three months, I can't think of anyone else I would rather learn from. You are the epitome of what a first lady should be."

I looked deep into her eyes, trying to find any trace of deceit, but I found none. She seemed innocent enough.

"That's an honor. I appreciate your kind words; however, I don't know what you can learn from me. I've never had a request such as yours. Outside of that, I'm not sure that you can ever really learn how to be a first lady. There's not a step-by-step guide out there."

"I can learn a lot from you. I already have. I've paid attention to your temperament. Your dislikes and likes. How you respond to difficult people such as myself."

She let that comment linger, and I pounced on the opportunity to respond. "What do you mean by that?"

"I know that I can be difficult to deal with sometimes. My personality is strong, and I can come across in the wrong way. I can be very intimidating, but I really don't mean to be. And—"

I interrupted her with the wave of my hand. "Do you think that you've somehow offended me with your 'intimidation,' as you call it?"

"No, not at all. Although I must admit that I did recognize a little apprehension between us, and I assumed that it was because of my aggressive nature."

"No, Daphne, it was because of your not-so-subtle flirtatious gestures toward my husband and your pastor."

She folded her hands, placed them in her lap, and then sighed. "I've done it again," she said softly.

"Done what?"

With her left hand, she massaged her right shoulder and said, "I always seem to give people the wrong impression. I didn't mean any harm by any of the remarks or comments that I've made to Pastor Johnson. True, I'm a single woman looking to find a good Christian man, so my desires sometimes override my better judgment to pay more attention to what I do and say when I'm around the type of man that I want to marry. But I certainly have better sense than to hit on my pastor." Her eyes softened. "You all are my spiritual parents. I would never do anything like that."

Once again, I felt reduced to my shoe size. I vowed that I would give the poor woman a chance. She genuinely wanted to get to know me, and I had almost pushed her away.

"Daphne, I'm sorry." This time I dropped my head. "It's just that it's so hard to trust people when you're in ministry. It seems that everyone has a motive and an agenda, and good, honest people are hard to come by."

"I understand."

"No, you don't. But if you feel God is leading you to walk in this same anointing one day, then you will understand. Until then, you can never understand."

The atmosphere grew still, and I was eager to change the subject to a lighter one. "So, you want to serve me, huh?"

She smiled. "Yes. I do."

I returned the smile. "I must say, I haven't heard that one before. I've had a lot of people offer many things, but never to be my servant."

"Well, I'm not sure if *servant* is the word."

"I'm only kidding. I know what you meant. You're asking if you can be my armor bearer?"

"Is that what you call it?"

"That's what we call it in the church. Many people desire the title, but hardly anyone understands the work. It's more than what it seems. I don't just need somebody following me all over the place and carrying my bag; I need someone who is going to have my best interests in mind. I need someone who is going to pray for me when times are tough and even in times when it's not, so that I'm prepared for when it does get tough. I need someone who's just as spiritually sound as I am, so that if I'm ever not where I need to be, I can be reminded of where God is taking me."

By the time I was done explaining what it meant to be an armor bearer, she was sitting with her mouth open.

"That's a serious job description. I don't know if I qualify for that."

I stood and walked over to sit next to her.

"Daphne, do I look as if I'm qualified for this position? Do I look as if I have all of the answers or that I know exactly what I'm doing?" I gave her a moment to think about it before I continued. "No matter what it looks like, as I said before, looks can be deceiving. The truth is, I don't know it all, and I don't have it all together. Ministry is a journey, and understanding ministry is a process. You will never understand it completely. You just have to trust God that He will lead you in the right direction."

"And what if He doesn't?"

"What do you mean?"

"What if God doesn't lead you in the right direction? What do you do then?"

"Daphne, God always leads you in the right direction. We just don't always follow his instructions."

She nodded. "So, do you think I can be your armor bearer?"

I was silent for a moment. "I don't know. I know nothing about you. You wouldn't believe how many women would die to be my armor bearer at this church. None of them have ever had the boldness to ask, but I have my way of knowing."

The noticeable look of shock on her face told me that Daphne had just realized she was just one in the number trying to get close to me.

"My intentions are good and my heart is pure. I don't want to hurt you, and I hope that one day you will be able to trust me."

Once again, I studied her intently. "Maybe one day I will. Right now, let's get you through new members' orientation and we'll see where it goes from there."

"In the meantime, do you mind if I help you out in any way that I can? I mean, I don't have to do any major stuff, but just if you need help with something, I would like it if you gave me a call." She paused. "I really want to help."

"I'll do that, Daphne."

She leaned over and gave me a hug. I got an eerie feeling on the inside, but I ignored it and embraced her as well.

We both stood and I walked her to the door.

"Thanks for meeting with me," she said.

"The pleasure has been all mine." I opened the door. "Have a good afternoon."

"You do the same, First Lady."

She walked out the door and I stood staring at her.

I couldn't help but wonder who Daphne Carlton really was. And only time would tell.

Chapter Eleven

Michelle

    That day in the office was one of the few light moments Daphne and I shared. It, among others, were moments I would later live to regret. She'd somehow deceived me into believing that she was concerned about my best interests, when all of the time she'd been thinking only of herself.

    As I drove downtown, I tried to temporarily escape my thoughts of Daphne, and not let any thoughts of Dawn appear. It was a crisp evening, and the stars were peeking delicately out of the black silk of the sky. The beautiful scene created a peaceful calm in my spirit as I drove to my weekly meeting. The meeting was a gathering of the minds; specifically, the minds of other first ladies.

    A few of us got together and decided that it was in the best interests of our sometimes demanding congregations and even more demanding husbands that we take one night a week and vent to each other the frustration that came along with this much-desired-by-women-who-didn't-know-any-better position. Our husbands were affluent and highly respected men in the community, and it would not look too good if each of their wives slowly lost their minds. So, our group met for the purpose of supporting each other, because we all understood pointedly what the other was going through. Therefore, the men never complained about our weekly gathering at Houston's.

The first ladies who had children left their husbands to fend for themselves at precisely 6:30 P.M. every single Thursday night. Some left even earlier than that, depending on their drive time. But none of us ever missed a meeting. I didn't have kids yet, so my desire to escape wasn't fueled by the need to have an adult conversation instead of one that included SpongeBob and popsicles. My driving force was to get around a group of women who had no expectations of me, and who knew all too well the challenges I faced from day to day.

I drove into the parking lot of Houston's just off Peachtree, silently wishing that they had a valet. The parking lot was already full, and I knew that I would have to walk a short distance from my parking space to the door.

It was getting harder by the day to do things that I did pre-pregnancy with little to no effort. A few months ago, I would have appreciated the walk, but tonight, my feet were swollen and I was almost out of breath at the very idea of walking.

I managed to make it inside the restaurant without collapsing in fatigue.

I glanced around, hoping to get a glimpse of the other ladies, but apparently I was the first one to arrive. I looked down at my watch and noticed that I was a few minutes early. I stepped to the hostess' station and gave her the information she needed to secure our table, and went to sit on the bricks they referred to as the waiting area. Once again, I noticed a pre-pregnancy vice. Before tonight, I never paid attention to how hard the bricks were, but tonight my butt was already starting to become numb and my back was sending pain signals straight to the numbness, creating an uncomfortable mixture of annoyance and aggravation.

Just as the hostess was motioning to me that the table was ready, all five of the first ladies, my girls, were walking in at the same time. Each of them was clad in outfits to kill, diamonds that would catch the attention of anybody, and bright, confident smiles that would intimidate the sun. They strutted over to me and did their usual; they each tried to measure my stomach to see if I had gotten any bigger since the week before.

"Ladies," I said, "hello to you too." Since announcing to them my impending arrival, they no longer cared how I was doing; their only concern was the baby and if I was taking care of myself. For the sake of the baby, of course.

"Michelle, girl, you know you looking good," Marjorie, the next to the youngest first lady and my best friend, said. Her husband was the pastor at Renewed Faith Christian Fellowship out in Stone Mountain. They had only been married for a year. Her ride to the "front row seat," as we called it, was packed full of drama. Before she and her husband Stephen met, his church was filled to capacity every week, with women hopeful of being the first lady seated in the front row. Marjorie told us hilarious stories about the weekly shenanigans the women underwent to get Stephen's attention, even after he'd announced their engagement to the congregation. She told of one woman who had a crying fit one Sunday during altar call, exasperatedly proclaiming that she was supposed to be First Lady Thompson and not Marjorie. She proclaimed that Stephen was going to cause the church to suffer because he was disobeying God.

During this time, Marjorie informed us that her only tactic was to stay controlled and poised—two attributes that landed her the marriage proposal in the first place—until she became Mrs. Stephen Thompson. Then, and only then, would she deal with those man-stealing, low-down, dirty women whose motives were to destroy relationships.

I continued to beam as the ladies complimented me on how well I was carrying the pregnancy and how gorgeous I looked in my green apple sundress with an embroidered green-and-gold jacket to match. Darvin had bought it for me while away on one of his preaching engagements in Virginia. It was customary for him to bring me expensive gifts from his out-of-town trips.

The rumble in my stomach immediately brought to my attention that we'd done enough greeting one another, and it was time to eat. I was starved, or at least I felt that I was.

We walked to our table, which was situated in its own little corner in the back—just as we preferred. We never wanted to take a chance on having one of the members of our congregations listening in on our conversation.

We sat down, and before long, had ordered our drinks, appetizers, and entrees. None of us needed to look at a menu, seeing that each of us had tried everything on the menu at least once.

"So, Michelle, I hear that it was you who had the most interesting week of us all," Pamela House said. She was the oldest among us, and had been married to Bishop William House for more than twenty-three years. Together they served as pastors and founders of New Light International Fellowship Church, in Decatur.

"Yes. To say that it was interesting is definitely an understatement." I told them the entire story that I was sure Marjorie must have already told, but my version was much more dramatic. If I had not lived it, I wouldn't have believed it myself. I had been asking myself all week the likelihood that the sister of my former terrorist had not only appeared at my church, but had appeared with the desire to become a permanent part of my life. It was ridiculous. The more I tried to understand it, the less I understood.

"So, what I want to know is, did you knock her into her eternity, or at least her teeth down her throat?" That was spoken by the youngest member of our group, Shaunie Anderson, a first lady for a good three months. She was also the rebel of the group. She couldn't understand that our position required us all to try to remain dignified, regardless of how many irate members we encountered.

After we silently bored holes into her, she shrugged her

shoulders and said, "What? I'm just being real; something that all of you chicks need to try at least one time in your life." She took a swallow of her water. "Because I'm going to tell you like this: if that broad had walked up in my church, her true intentions would have been revealed based on where she woke up."

"Woke up?" I asked in confusion.

"Yeah. If she woke up in hell, then her motives weren't right. If she woke up in heaven, then she was sincere. Either way, she would have died and went somewhere. My objective would have been to protect myself, my husband, and our congregation. Because I swear to y'all, I would have killed her." She rolled her eyes as she picked up a piece of garlic cheese toast.

"Shaunie, you have a lot to learn. You can't go around killing everybody that poses a threat to you," I said. "You've got to learn how to strategize without compromising your position as a first lady, or the reputation of your husband."

"Strategize my you-know-what! Are you expected to let some floozy come into your church that you helped your man build, and mumble out a string of apologies while you walk away as dumb as a doorknob, only to find yourself in another precarious situation with an off-the-rocker Carlton sister?

"Honey, please. You need to wake up, Michelle. These sisters are out to get you," she said as she dipped a tortilla chip into the spinach dip.

Taking a calmer approach, Lisa Hodges, the most shy of us all, who often got trampled over by the women in her congregation, said, "Michelle, I think that you are handling this well. There's no need to get all in a frenzy. Especially with your being pregnant. I think you handled it with the class and poise that you should have."

Shaunie, by this point, was irritated with the little-miss-perfect demeanor of Lisa. Lisa had been married for twelve years and had four children by her husband, Charles. Charles was the pastor of a very traditional Pilgrim Hall Baptist Church, where the members staunchly believed in the first lady claiming no authority, except as the president of the youth choir. Other times, she was to sit on the front row, wearing wide-brim hats the size of UFO saucers, and never mumble a word contrary to anything or anybody at Pilgrim. Lisa often went home in tears, wishing she had the nerve to stand up for herself, but the older members loved her passive personality. They thought it was fitting for what a first lady should be. She was scoring points with them, but losing the game with herself.

"Well, since none of y'all have asked my opinion, I figure I'd better chime in before we move on to something else," said Delisa Promise, who we referred to as Dee-Dee. Dee-Dee was married to a very fine, smooth-talking, charming man, Stanley Promise. As a result, she had more trouble out of conniving women than any of us. Her battle to keep her sanity was ongoing, and a couple of times over the five years that they'd been married, she'd almost lost it. But her advice to us all, including Pam, was priceless. She had the man with the power, the extraordinary talents, pre-pastorate wealth, and the good looks in one combined package. She had dealt with females on every level.

Delisa continued on. "I just want to say this: Dawn Carlton is definitely up to something. She has to be. Why else would she be here? I wouldn't be surprised if her sister sent her here and is planning to make a return so that they can double-team you." She looked at me to see if I'd considered that as an option. I had not. "Michelle, you can't underestimate anybody that's willing to do anything to walk in the position that you walk in. If you do that, you'll end up dead or behind bars."

She took a bite of the Hawaiian rib eye the server had just placed in front of her. Between bites and enjoyment of pure culinary pleasure, she pointed her fork toward me. "This is a serious one. Don't play with this one, Michelle." She then dug the fork into her loaded baked potato. "That's all I have to say."

"Delisa, you can't just leave it like that. What do you

mean by what you just said? Do you think I'm in danger? Do you think this Dawn woman would go as far as to try and kill me or something?" I asked.

"I don't know," Delisa said as she continued to eat. "I'm simply saying don't take a relaxed approach to this. You have a baby on the way that you have to protect. Because I think by the time this is over, none of us would have ever imagined the outcome."

That statement sent chills through all of us, and the rest of the evening was spent with each woman talking about what she'd gone through since the week before. I wasn't able to concentrate on what they were saying or the oven roasted chicken I'd ordered. What if Delisa was right? What if Dawn Carlton came here to finish me off as some sort of revenge for her sister? What if Daphne was secretly conversing with Dawn to concoct a sure plan that would not only end my marriage, but my life? I thought about that dream I'd had. I couldn't help but wonder if it really was a sign to come or if I was, in Darvin's words, just being paranoid.

Again.

Chapter Twelve

Michelle

I walked in the house from my weekly meeting still consumed in my thoughts from the conversation with the ladies. Delisa's comment bothered me most, and no matter how hard I tried, I just could not stop hearing her words over and over.

I placed my purse in its usual place by the phone in the kitchen, took my shoes off, and headed to my bedroom to change into something more comfortable. I'd called Darvin on my way home, and we had decided to watch some old movies together.

Once in my bedroom, I glanced at the clock sitting in total darkness on the nightstand, and the bold red numbers that showed it was eleven o'clock.

I flipped on the lights and groaned because I was tired, worn out, and no longer felt that I could watch previews, let alone an entire movie. My eyes were practically closing as it was.

I walked into the closet and placed the shoe-curses that I'd been wearing back in their respective box. As I took off my dress, I noticed a sound coming from upstairs. I knew that I was sleepy and all, but it seemed as if the sound kept getting louder and louder. I froze in a silent panic, because Darvin wasn't supposed to be home for another thirty minutes.

The bumping was getting louder. For a second, I debated whether I'd fallen asleep and was going into another nightmare, or if I was awake and somebody was really in my house.

I quietly walked out of my closet and back toward my bedroom when the bumping turned into a crashing sound. Somebody was definitely in the house and was obviously vandalizing it.

Paralyzed by fear and not knowing what to do next, I walked to my bedroom and prayed that Darvin had left the cordless phone on the charger. He had a habit of walking around the house on the phone and leaving the phone in whatever room he was last in.

Thankfully, the phone was indeed on the charger. As I moved toward it, I heard footsteps coming down the stairs. Afraid that the intruder might try to come into the room next, I quickly grabbed the cordless phone from my reading table and made a dash back to the closet. My heart was pounding at a rate that was causing my breathing to be labored, and beads of sweat rolled down my face faster than a New York minute. I pressed the TALK button and dialed 911.

"Nine-one-one, what is your emergency?" the nonchalant woman on the other end said.

"Yes, someone has broken into my home, and they're still here."

Silence.

"Hello!" I said as loudly as I could, without being heard.

"Ma'am, I'm here. Can you confirm your address?" "Twenty thirty-five Country Lake Drive."

Crash!

I jumped at the sound of glass breaking into pieces. "Ma'am, can you please tell them to hurry?" I was practically hyperventilating.

"Do you believe that the intruder is still in the home?" the woman asked.

"What, are you deaf and dumb? I already said that!" I yelled.

"Ma'am, just calm down."

"Don't tell me to calm down! You try having someone break into your house, being four months pregnant and don't know if you're going to make it out alive, and then tell me to calm down! Lady, you just don't know."

"I can understand your frustration. I have a team on their way to your location right now. Just try to remain calm and make sure you stay on the phone with me until the police arrive."

If I could somehow reach through the phone and strangle the woman on the other end for acting as though my situation was just a number of many, I would have done so with joy. I'd only had to dial 911 a few times in all of my life, and each and every single time, the attendants were less than attending. They were almost downright rude. No sympathy or concern was laced in their voices, only impatience and aggravation.

Just as I was about to respond to the woman, the doorbell rang. Despite my disbelief that they would arrive before the intruder had a chance to get away or kill me, they made it in what seemed like record time.

"Ma'am," the woman said, "the police should be there. Do you hear your doorbell yet?"

"I just heard it."

"Okay, I need you to go to the door and let the police in."

"Are you insane?" I questioned, hardly believing that she would even suggest I come out of hiding. "Do you really think that I'm about to go out there and face the intruder? Woman, please. I've seen plenty of movies where the police were able to break a door down, so if they want to get in tonight, they better give that door one hell of a kick."

The woman sighed in frustration. "Okay. Let me try to reach the police on the radio. Hold one moment, please."

I heard her mumble to the police officer something about having a difficult pregnant woman on the phone that was refusing to leave her hiding place in order to let them in. Well, I didn't care one way or the other what she or the police officers thought about me. I was not about to leave my closet for all of the diamonds in Tiffany's.

The woman came back on the phone. "Ma'am, is there any other way that the officers can gain entry to your home without having to kick down your door?"

I thought for a moment. "Yes. I can give you the garage door code and they can come in that way."

"That would be great. May I have that code, please?"

"Two-nine-seven."

"Okay. One moment while I relay that information to the officer."

Once again, I heard her tell the officer the information that he needed to come in and arrest my intruder.

By this point, my head was spinning. Reality had finally set in that somebody had actually broken into my home. Could that somebody be Dawn? If so, how did she get into my house? Was she here to kill me? Look for something? Destroy my property? My thoughts were interrupted by the voices of the police officers, who had now gotten in and were taking down the intruder. All I could manage to hear one of them say was, "Stop right there!"

After a couple more minutes of me straining to hear what the officers were saying, the 911 attendant came back to the phone and said, "Ma'am, they've caught the intruder. Can you please tell me your location in the home? The police would like to speak to you."

"I'm in the closet inside of the master bedroom just off of the kitchen."

My voice was trembling. It was over.

She relayed the information to the police.

"Okay. Someone is on the way to your location."

Sure enough, an officer shined a flashlight inside of the closet and saw me hiding behind several pieces of luggage.

"Mrs. Johnson? Are you all right?"

A single tear slid down my cheek in relief. "Yes. I'm fine. Did you catch them?"

"Yes, ma'am, we did. We have the intruder in the patrol car. If you're up to it, we would like to see if you can identify this person and then help us complete a police report for what happened here tonight."

At that moment, Darvin came rushing into the closet.

"Baby! Are you okay? The police told me what happened," he said, sounding extremely worried. "I didn't even stop to notice who it was. I wanted to get in here to you."

I immediately came out of my hiding place and leaped into Darvin's arms, the place where I felt most safe in the entire world. "Yes. I'm fine."

The tears that came rushing down my cheeks proved otherwise. I released all of the terror, fear, and trauma that I had experienced since coming home.

Darvin held me until I had no more tears to cry, and the police officer, definitely being more sensitive than the woman I'd spoken to on the phone, simply just walked away and gave us our space.

I pulled myself together. I wanted to—no, needed to—know who had broken into our home, the place that was supposed to be my refuge. The place that was meant to keep me safe from harm.

Darvin smoothed a loose strand of hair away from my face and brushed away the residue of the tears with the back of his finger. "Baby, are you sure that you're ready to go out there?" He paused and turned my face so that I could look him directly in the eyes. "Because you don't have to do this now. We can go down to the police station a little later."

I looked in the depths of Darvin's eyes, trying to find the strength I so desperately needed. I looked away. "No, I'm fine. I would rather get this over with now so that I can go to bed and relax."

We walked into the kitchen and found glass sprawled all over the floor. The crystal frame that was given to us as a wedding gift and that once held one of our honeymoon photos, was now broken into several tiny pieces.

That explained at least one of the crashes I'd heard. Why would somebody break a frame? The police motioned for us to step outside to try to identify our uninvited guest. The more steps I took toward the police car, the more weak my legs became. My feet froze like the ice in Alaska when I got close enough to see who was sitting in the back seat.

With her head held down, it wasn't the woman I was expecting to see. It wasn't one of the Carlton sisters, as my gut had anticipated. I closed my eyes and opened them again and again, greatly wanting to make the image of the woman vanish. No matter how much I tried to will her away, the woman sitting in the back seat of the police car was still there.

I looked over at Darvin, who was standing in disbelief. We were both thinking the same thing: Why would Twylah Andrews, my armor bearer of the last two years, break into our house?

Chapter Thirteen

Michelle

It was well after 2 A.M. before I was finally able to even think about getting into bed. After accepting the fact that Twylah had broken into our house, and going to the police station to give a formal statement, I was beyond the normal level of exhaustion. I was still in a state of shock, and no matter how hard I tried, I couldn't understand why Twylah would invade our home when she could come in whenever she got ready.

Twylah had moved to Atlanta a few years ago, and we'd met in one of the aerobics classes in the gym. We'd hit it off instantly. We became friends and spent almost every Saturday shopping, getting manicures and pedicures, and eating Mexican food until heartburn forced us to stop. She had grown up as an only child, just as I had, and in our minds, we were to each other the sister that neither of us had.

We would spend countless hours talking about Rodney Landers, the man who had stolen and broken her heart all in the span of one year. She'd waited all twenty-three years of her life to give her virginity to a man, and when she decided to take that step (against her moral beliefs), she did so with the wrong man. Rodney had chased her, wined and dined her, wooed her, and everything else that would make a woman fall in love. And Twylah had fallen hard. Real hard. She became so depressed when their relationship ended that not only did she have to leave Charlotte, her birthplace, but North Carolina altogether.

She couldn't even bear to be in the same state with him. Especially not with him and his new wife—a white woman.

So, initially all of our conversations were about the life and death of Rodney Landers and Twylah Andrews.

Finally, one day over cheesecake, she swore to never let another day go by crying over a man who didn't care about her in the first place. She decided to move on with her life and on to better things.

Reflecting back on all of the things that we'd shared, it was hard to imagine, yet alone grasp, Twylah doing something like this. She was the prime example of what my grandmother used to refer to as a wolf in sheep's clothing. No matter how hard I tried, I could not think of anything that she ever did that would point to her doing something like this. Sure, she had little bouts of jealousy when it came to me asking Chanice for more than I asked her, but that certainly was not enough to justify this behavior. But one thing I'd learned in my thirty-one years of living: it's common conduct for the devil to sneak up and catch you off guard. First, Daphne. Second, Dawn. Now, Twylah. Who and what was next?

Shortly after we acknowledged to the police that we knew who she was, I'd gone upstairs to survey the damage. Just as I'd imagined, she'd broken several of my crystal vases. Not just any vases, those vases had been heirlooms in my family, and Twylah knew that they were dear to my heart.

Tears had slowly begun to fall as I surveyed what used to be my great-grandmother's fiftieth wedding anniversary vase and the matching diamond-encrusted plate that it sat on, broken into pieces finer than sand and strewn on the floor of my office. In searching the other rooms, I found one crystal heirloom after the other, demolished from the brutal attack of Twylah. The thing that baffled me most was that she had also broken every frame that held a picture of Darvin and me.

I was too tired to put any more effort into thinking about

it. I resigned to deal with it later, and headed to the bedroom. Shortly after, Darvin walked into the room with the evidence of stress residing underneath his eyes and fatigue claiming his body. Darvin was unlike most men. He had a heart for people and a genuine concern for even those who abused him. I knew that he would wrestle for the remainder of the night, trying to determine what was going on in Twylah's mind when she decided to raid our privacy.

Unlike me, he'd been leery of her from the beginning because of her baggage, but, I'd reassured him that her baggage was going to remain with her and would not have any bearings on me. After some time, he began to trust her, and his initial suspicions had been replaced with an authentic love for her and her well-being.

As much as I didn't want to, I knew that I had to talk to her in order to get some answers. Something had to be wrong. The woman that I'd grown to know was not the woman who would do something like this. There had to be some sort of explanation.

"Baby, you still awake?" Darvin asked as he began to shed what was once a neatly starched shirt and creased dress slacks.

"Yes, honey. Can't seem to fall asleep."

He sighed. "I feel you. I don't know how I will sleep tonight myself." An understood silence lurked in the room as Darvin took his place next to me in our bed. It wasn't long before he broke it. "Baby, I'm going to look into hiring twenty-four hour security for you. I know that's not something that you're fond of, but I just can't trust anybody anymore. You could have been hurt tonight, and considering all that we've been through, I think it's time to take another approach to our safety."

I didn't even have the energy to fight him, even though I'd always said that pastors with security were just going overboard.

Before marrying Darvin, I'd had my share of gossiping with my fellow hair salon associates about pastors and their wives and how arrogant—not to mention, unreachable—they were. I'd always complained about how you had to go through a secretary to get to talk to a pastor, when in the old days, it was common to see a pastor hanging out and having dinner at a member's house on any given day. But things had changed, and it took me wearing the shoes to understand. After stretching ourselves from one end to the other trying to get around to every dinner, every funeral, every hospital, every birth, every family reunion, and every other social event in the lives of our congregation, we soon realized that we couldn't do it all. We realized that if we wanted to live long, productive lives and see our children grow up, we'd better slow down and allow some things to be delegated. Now, every appearance request for us had to go through our respective assistants, and "our" time was "our" time. No matter what. Darvin called it "First Church." After all, God created the institution of marriage before the church was created.

So, regardless of what I previously thought about pastors, their wives, and their methods of doing things, here I was staring their same mountains in the face. And like it or not, this was the life we had to live.

"Darvin?"

"Yes, baby?" From the sound of his voice, it was obvious that sleep was trying to settle in.

"Do you think that God is trying to tell us something with all of these things happening to us?"

"I don't know. Why do you think that?"

"Well, I can't help but wonder why it seems that we can never just find peace. It's like when we get over one thing, something else comes along." I paused. "It's like we're cursed."

Darvin rolled over onto his side to face me. "Michelle, you know that if the devil isn't after us, then that means we are no threat to him." He sat up on his elbows to further drive in his point. "He knows where God is taking us, and he has waged war on us. We've just got to be strong and weather this storm."

I released a deep sigh. "But I'm tired of weathering storms. Every time I turn around, I'm hearing the same thing. You're coming out. This is your year for a breakthrough. And to be honest, I'm sick of coming out. I want to be out."

"Baby, do you think that we're exempt from trials?" He didn't wait for my response. "Because we are not. We are just like every other Christian, but because of who we are, the warfare is stronger. Because we are called by God for His work, the devil's assignment is to take us out, and if he can't do that, he will try to get us to take ourselves out." He rested on his back.

"The worst thing we can do is give up now. You don't have to tell me that you're tired. I know that you are. I'm tired. But I have to keep pressing. I have to be determined to press on, no matter how much I don't want to." He touched my hand. "I need to know that I can count on you, Michelle. I need to know that you aren't going to throw in the towel."

Darvin was unaware of the tears streaming down my face. Some of my tears were for Twylah. Some were for my own situation and fatigue. And some were for my husband, who sometimes didn't know how to stop being the pastor. I knew that he was exhausted, yet he was preaching to me.

As he kept talking, I closed my eyes and partially listened. There was one part of me that wanted to get excited about the trials we were going through because I knew that after every great storm, there is a great calm, a season of peace. A season of tranquility. But the other part of me was raging at the havoc in my life, wondering when it would all end. Just when I thought things were looking up, situations sent me downhill again.

And the new issue with Twylah was an entirely different problem. It wasn't so much that Twylah had broken into our house. My concern was if someone as close to me as Twylah could cause such devastation, what could someone who wasn't as close do? People didn't understand how hard it was for pastors to trust people. It was hard to discern when someone had your best interests in mind, or when they were just trying to get in your business in hopes of getting some dirt on you to expose.

For Twylah to do this meant that I'd missed something. As hard as it was for me to trust people, somehow she'd gotten past my spiritual radar. I shuddered at the thought. Here I was focused on the enemy outside of the camp, when there was a mole inside of the camp all along. And God only knew how much damage she'd really done.

"Babe, are you asleep?" Darvin asked.

"No. I don't think I'll be getting too much sleep tonight."

He leaned over and put his hand on my stomach. "Listen, I know it's hard for you to do, but I don't want you to worry. I'm going to take care of this and make sure that you don't ever have to go through anything like this again." He rubbed my stomach gently. "We have a baby on the way, and I need you to make sure that you stay as stress-free as possible. I want you to get some rest. It's not good for you or the baby."

I put my hand on top of his. "I know, sweetie. I'm trying. I don't want to do anything to hurt the baby." I allowed my eyes to close, and imagined our little one. "I've wanted this baby for so long, and I just can't do anything to jeopardize this." At that moment, the floodgates reopened.

As if he could see in the dark, Darvin gently smoothed away my waterfall with the stroke of his finger. I savored his touch and allowed myself to rest in the comfort of the moment. For a split second, I allowed myself to forget about the drama and embrace the blessings that God had given on us.

Yes, things were a little bleak in our lives, but God had still been good.

And no matter what, I knew I had to survive this.

Chapter Fourteen

Michelle

The Fulton County Jail was overcrowded with inmates and baby mamas. Staff members were trying to get a handle on the multiple situations that were going on. I felt a twinge of apprehension as I was being escorted to the room where Twylah was waiting for me.

Darvin was livid the next morning when I'd told him that I wanted to see Twylah. But I explained to him that my need to speak to her to attain closure was something that I had to do. I had to try to get some sort of explanation to make sense of it all.

The guard led me into a room where several inmates sat and talked to their respective family members, friends, and attorneys. Some inmates sat with looks of regret on their faces, and others with demeanors that could not be interpreted.

My attention suddenly focused on a young woman sitting in the back of the room with a shred of light beaming on her sandy-colored hair from the slit in the wall too small to be considered a window. Twylah seemed so downtrodden, I'd almost forgotten the reason she was incarcerated in the first place.

I squirmed as I felt my heart experiencing a tug of war. One side was pulling against her, almost happy to see her miserable in a place filled with criminals such as herself. The other side was pulling for her, silently wondering how she could be helped and released. The battle continued as I got closer to the table where she was sitting. The closer I got, the more I felt that my feet were in chains, making each step harder and harder to take.

Once at the table, I nodded to the guard, thanking him, and slowly took my seat across from Twylah. She sat with her head down.

"Twylah?" I spoke softly. She kept her head down with no response. "I know that you're probably embarrassed by your actions, but I just want to talk to you." I wrung my hands together as if I were squeezing water from a sponge. Realizing that Twylah wasn't about to offer any words, I continued.

"I'm not sure what happened last night, but I'm here to talk to you as your friend, not as your first lady." I shifted in the metal chair that was provided for visitors to sit in. "I know that the person who broke into my home last night was not the person who I've come to know. So I guess what I want to know is . . . why did you do it?"

Twylah lifted her head with not a single tear in her eyes or an ounce of remorse on her face. Without having to check my compact mirror, I knew that confusion was etched on my face. Here I was, sitting across from a woman who'd nearly tried to destroy my house, and she had the audacity to sit in my presence and show no sorrow?

"Michelle—and I do hope that you don't mind me calling you Michelle, especially since you came as my friend and all," she said mockingly. "Matter of fact, I'm sure it hurt your Gucci-clad feet to even step into a place like this." Each word was dripping with sarcasm.

I was beyond appalled, and if it weren't for fear of something in the trash-filled room flying into my mouth, it would have been gaping open. Did she just get sassy with me? I know this little heifer didn't. "Excuse me, Twylah, but I really don't think you're in a position to take that tone with me. Have you forgotten what you've done? Who do you think you are?"

"No, who do you think you are? Have you ever stopped

to think that it's not all about you? The sun doesn't rise and set around what you want and when you want it. For more than two years now, I've been at your every call, doing this and doing that for you. And quite frankly, it's gotten old," she said as she gazed deeply into my eyes.

Anger flared my nostrils. "Nobody told you that you had to do anything for me. You were the one who came to me and suggested you serve in that position when I was searching for some help. So whatever you did was done on your own accord, and not because you were asked," I countered.

"But the point is I did it," she countered back. "I've been like your slave, and I've watched you live the life of the rich and famous, while I go home to my peasant lifestyle."

"What!"

I hadn't realized the inflection of my own voice. The sudden quietness of the other people sharing the space with us made me look around, only to notice that people were starting to stare at us.

"Peasant lifestyle? Twylah Andrews, I made you! I introduced you to some of the finest things in life, and you consider it peasant? Do you know how many women would love to be in your shoes? Would love to be close to me for the perks and the benefits?" I asked.

"Until they realize that it's just a bunch of hog wash," she sneered. "I realized that I would never be you or have your life. I realized that all people would ever see me as is your adjutant. Your gopher. Your servant, as you love to call it," she said mordantly.

If I didn't know better, I would have thought I was smack dead in the middle of a dream. Surely this woman was not sitting here acting as if she were the victim. "I don't mean to add insult to injury, but when you moved to Atlanta, you didn't have anything or anybody. I befriended you, helped you find a place to stay, had an associate employ you, gave you an extreme makeover, and then taught you everything you know about being a lady. And on top of that, I listened to those long, tired stories about your heart being broken.

"And yet you twist your mouth to hurl insults at me? Tell me again how you are tired of not being able to be me?" The way I was rolling my neck, it's a wonder it didn't get dislocated. And I wasn't finished. "Oh, silly woman, let me tell you something. You could never be me. All of the training in the world couldn't have trained your polished country behind to be on the level that I'm on." The remnants of my first lady demeanor vanished.

"Polished country!" she shouted. "Who are you calling polished country? Without that M•A•C, those fake eyelashes, that expensive weave, and that Hooked on Phonics vocabulary, no one would want to know your name. On top of that, it's because of Pastor Johnson that people even tolerate you."

I was laughing now. "Is that what you think?"

"Oh, that's what I know. Nobody likes you, Michelle. People think you're conceited. And before you try to defend that, please let us not forget that I've been on both sides. I know the 'real' you." She accentuated her point with her fingers symbolizing quotation marks.

"And just what is that supposed to mean?"

"Don't play dumb with me. You ain't the little miss perfect that Darvin and the church think you are. Truth is you don't even want to be a first lady.

Think about how much you talk about how unhappy you are."

I interjected. "Twylah, you know that's not true. Okay, so I get frustrated sometimes. But who doesn't?"

"Yeah, but every time we're together, all you talk about is how this woman gets on your nerves, and how this member makes you sick."

"I've never said those words."

"Maybe not, but that's what you meant. Nobody at Mount Zion or anywhere else will be good enough to meet the Michelle Johnson up-to-par list. And you know what? I'm tired of trying to live up to your expectations. I'm tired of living your lie."

"Living a lie? What are you talking about? I've never asked you to be something that you're not." She was obviously deranged.

"But when I wasn't what you thought I should be, you tried to fix me. I eventually forgot who I was."

"That is a cop-out. You didn't know who you were when I met you. It was all I could do to convince you that you your life was even worth living. When you left North Carolina, you were dried-up and your man didn't want you."

It was her turn to have the gaping mouth. I had not intended to bring that up, but she had pissed me off. Without knowing it, she was less than a minute away from having everything but blessings coming out of my mouth. True, I was a first lady, but I don't know how many times I had to tell people that being a first lady didn't mean you had supernatural powers, feelings, and emotions.

"How could you?" Twylah said as she jumped out of her chair. The guard started toward our direction, and I motioned to him that all was well. I wasn't worried about Twylah doing anything but posing idol threats. She was trying to boast a tough appearance, but she knew that hitting a pregnant woman in the presence of security guards would earn her more time in the pen than she'd bought herself last night by breaking into my home.

"No, how could you? Did you forget that you broke into my home, destroyed priceless heirlooms, and are sitting here as if you did nothing wrong?"

I gave my words a second to soak in. "How could you pretend to be my friend, when all the time you were jealous of me? Because if the truth be told, that's what this is about. You're jealous of me, and you're blaming me for being privileged to have a blessed life."

Her irritation was obvious. "Why don't you just leave? I don't know why you came here in the first place." This time, it was Twylah who shifted in the metal chair. "You want to know why I broke into your home, destroyed your prized possessions, and now sit here as if I don't give a damn?"

I jerked my head back once again, astonished at the actions of the woman before me. The Twylah who I'd come to know would have never so much as uttered profanity in my sight, even if she was thinking it. But the Twylah I knew would have never broken into my house, either.

"It was quite amusing to have the upper hand on you for a change." She smirked.

Tears began to well in my eyes. I had no idea that Twylah felt like this. I really counted her as a friend. I thought about the many times that I'd helped her financially. I stood up for her when some of the members at church didn't understand, and were hesitant about accepting her neo-soul style with the dyed afro and ethnic wardrobe. I even went against my mom, who would have preferred me to choose a more "suitable" assistant. I'd gone against all of my first lady friends, who tried to warn me that I was walking into a trap by allowing a friend-turned-church-member to be so close to me. I'd gone against the grain, and to hear these words from her now made me feel even more betrayed than I already did.

"The tears . . . they aren't cute. Besides, your makeup will smear, and Lord knows we don't want that." The words she spoke were as cold as a winter day.

But my tears remained, and hurt was the force causing them to flow.

"Why do you think I'm superficial, as you call it? Out of all of the first ladies that you've been introduced to by being in my circle, you know that I try with every fiber of my being to

uphold my reputation, and maintain integrity in my position."
God knows that I'd done everything in my power to remain
humble, even in the face of adversity.

"Yes, you have. I'll give you that."

"You know the expectations that are placed on first ladies to always have a flawless appearance, inside and out. But
you've seen me on all levels, and you of all people should know
that there are some things that penetrate deeply, with few people
to understand. But again, you know this. How many times have
we talked about this? How many times have I confided in you
personal fears and failures? And now, you throw it back up in
my face?"

I noticed that the guard was approaching us. "Ma'am,"
he said to me, "your visitation time is up. I'm sorry, but you have
to prepare to leave now."

I looked up at the more than six foot guard and obliged
his command with a nod of my head. I turned my gaze back to
an unapologetic Twylah, gave up my efforts to get a better understanding of her behavior, picked up my purse, and stood to
my feet. I took one final look at her, and when I concluded that
I would never understand, I turned to walk away.

"Oh, and Michelle?" she called out.

I whirled around to face her.

"What?"

"Can you please tell Pastor Johnson that I'm sorry and
really didn't want him to get hurt in all of this?"

This woman had some serious nerve! She was concerned
about my husband's feelings and not mine? If it weren't for the
vision of choking her, I might have seen the flicker of remorse
before it was erased.

I started to just walk away without even responding, but
I had one more question. "Twylah, why did you break all of the
frames that held pictures of me and Darvin?"

She laughed, and smoothed her tiny fro. "Because, what

you and Pastor have together is as fragile as those frames I busted up. And just like the glass from those frames burst into tiny pieces, so will your marriage."

She smiled a smile that said more than her statement.

I was fuming, and didn't care to know what she meant. "Let me get something straight with you," I said through clenched teeth. "I want you to know that no weapon formed against me, my husband, our baby, our ministry, or our marriage will prosper. So, while you're getting to know your new neighbors in here, just think on that. And for the record, your threats don't scare me, because God has not given me the spirit of fear, and, baby, when it is all said and done, I will be the one laughing." I put on my first lady smile just for the heck of it, and proceeded to march out of the place of bondage—back into the free world.

Once outside, I put on my Versace sunglasses and headed to my car more determined than ever to take control of my life. I didn't know who the devil thought he was messing with, but if he thought I was going down without a fight, he was sadly mistaken. Raindrops would fall on his head first.

It was time for me to dry the tears and put on my war clothes. The only way I would lose this fight is if they buried me.

Chapter Fifteen

Michelle

Praise and worship always had a way of taking my mind off of the things that I was going through. After my visit with Twylah, I'd been somewhat on a mission to take control of my life. I'd started reading my Bible again every day, praying harder than usual, and had started trying to figure out how I was going to move beyond my current circumstances.

Being here in church, I was totally relieved of everything. I was in a place of total worship, and had no concern for what was going on around me.

Most of the members had heard about what Twylah had done, and had been asking me questions all morning. So getting into my "secret place" with the Most High God was refreshing and renewing.

As praise and worship came to an end, the Spirit of God was high in the place. I opened my eyes to see worshippers crying, and some had come to kneel at the altar.

I looked over at Darvin, who had been relatively quiet the entire morning, but was now crying himself. I didn't know if they were tears of joy and adoration to God, or if they were tears of sorrow for the drama we'd been experiencing lately.

I placed a reassuring hand on his shoulder and felt his body tense underneath my touch. That was unusual and disconcerting to me, because I wanted my touch to be soothing. Calming. Encouraging.

I tried to search his face for answers but found none. Immediately, the bliss I felt in worship was starting to fade. I shook my head, knowing that this was the devil's way of stealing my focus and taking my mind off of Jesus. But I was determined not to let anything rob me of my joy.

No sooner than I could think those thoughts, Darvin moved to the pulpit to deliver his weekly Sunday morning message. I was a little taken aback because it wasn't time for the sermon; yet, he walked toward the podium in a zombie-like state, and took the microphone from its stand.

"Children of God, I stand here today thanking God for His presence. Thanking God for His anointing. Thanking Him for making a way out of no way and being a light to my path when I couldn't even see."

People were shouting their amens and hallelujahs, and Darvin seemed to escalate higher and higher with each one.

"We need to know today, church, that God is a good God and worthy to be praised! We need to know that in the time of battle, we can hide in Him. We need to know that in the midnight hour, when we are tossing and turning, not knowing what to do, He'll be there! Can I get a witness?"

People shouted in agreement. Some members had caught the Holy Ghost and were shouting all up and down the aisles. The Mothers in Zion were not standing to their feet, but were raising their fans in the air, signaling their own agreement. The deacons were shouting, "Preach, Pastor Johnson," and the musicians were backing him on the B-3 organs and Triton keyboards, sending an electrifying feeling through everyone in the building.

I felt myself getting tingly, and was trying hard to contain my emotions. I didn't want to break my neck and hurt the baby by dancing all over the stage.

But I sure wanted to join in with my own shout.

I looked around and didn't see Chanice standing in her usual place behind me, but instead saw a gatekeeper headed in my direction with a note in her hand. Sister Betty Fields walked up to me with a smile as big as ever and handed me a small piece of paper that read: *Please give to First Lady Johnson immediately.*

A creepy feeling traveled the length of my spine, and without having to open it, I knew that its contents were nothing less than upsetting.

I slowly opened the note that said:

YOUR HUSBAND IS SUCH A GOOD FRIEND TO ME. THANKS FOR SHARING HIM.

Waves of anger permeated through me. What woman had sent this? It had been a while since we'd heard from Dawn. She'd not been at church in a few weeks, and had she been there, I would have presumed that the letter came from her.

Since she wasn't, I continued on in worship and turned my attention to what Darvin was saying. I was not about to let some woman who was too coward to identify herself interrupt my flow. I was learning more and more about being a first lady, and one thing I'd learned quickly: I would always have to deal with some woman proclaiming her admiration and love for Darvin. I made a mental note to alert the president of the usher board to not give me any more notes that had not been checked first.

"Folks, we need to know that the enemy has come to destroy us, but I declare right now that no weapon formed against you, your family, your marriage, your finances, or your health will be able to prosper. I need for those of you who believe that to give God a thunderous praise!"

Once again the shouts erupted, the screams were released, and the people who had sat down from shouting were back up again.

I smiled because it was good to see people praising God in the manner in which they were praising. In a time when people were turning their backs on God and were being consumed by material possessions, it was awesome to see a remnant still thankful for what God was doing in all of our lives—even in the midst of turmoil.

I felt a tap on my shoulder and turned around to see that Chanice had returned to her seat. The smile that I wore was erased by the look of shock on her face. My heart started skipping beats and the palms of my hands began to sweat. I started to wonder if I was a magnet for trouble. A target for pain. In a line for sorrow. It seemed that every time I turned around, evil was always present.

I leaned back. "What is it, Chanice?"

"First Lady, I don't want to upset you right now. I'll wait until service is over. I just wanted to let you know that I was back. I'm sure you noticed that I was gone for quite some time."

I leaned forward again to steady myself better on my feet. I'd chosen to wear some three-inch heels, and a pregnant woman leaning back on three inches wasn't good. Glancing at Darvin, I noticed that he was in the throes of his message. Some called it whooping. Some called it hollering. Whatever it was, it had everybody in the building on their feet, praising God.

I turned back to Chanice and whispered, "Pastor is almost done. When he finishes, we'll go to the back."

Darvin's sermon went on for about another fifteen minutes. By the time he was done, he was sweating profusely. His dry cleaning bill was something serious every other week. His suits, shirts, and ties did good to survive six months. Preachers often got a bad rap about their tailored suits, but if only people understood the need for them. Style wasn't the only factor, but quality certainly was. It wasn't anything for him to spend a couple of hundred dollars or more every week or so on dry cleaning. He was one of those pastors who dressed up every day in full attire, whether he was preaching or not.

As soon as the altar invitation for salvation had been closed, Chanice and I slipped out the side door that led to the private entrance to our wing.

Once inside my office, I kicked off the BCBG heels that I was wearing, and moved to my chair behind the desk.

"Chanice, what's going on?"

She searched the floor for apparent ways to say whatever she wanted to say. "First Lady, I'm sorry to have to be the one to tell you this, but something terrible has happened."

Always the one to respond at a glacial pace, she dropped her head as tears flowed down her face.

"Are you all right? What happened?" I asked. The impatience was replaced with fear. I got up and went to sit by her on the couch.

She looked into my eyes. "I don't know how to tell you this."

"Whatever it is, just say it."

"First Lady, Twylah is missing and is presumed dead."

The shock paralyzed me. She had to have that wrong. "Ch-Chanice," I stuttered, "are you sure?"

"Yes. They found a suicide note, and a pool of blood on the bathroom floor."

"What? Are you—wait just a minute. You're saying that Twylah killed herself?"

Chanice lowered her eyes again. "That's what they believe. But the startling thing is they can't find her body."

That made no sense. "What do you mean they can't find her body? How can a person kill themselves and then dispose of their own remains?"

"I don't know."

My spirit leaned against the walls of shock, and my heart was consumed with sadness. Why in the world would Twylah kill herself? Sure, she'd broken into our house, but was that the reason?

"Who gave you this information?"

"One of the elders notified me that the police were here looking for you just as service was starting. You were so consumed in praise and worship that I didn't want to disturb you, so I took the call at the door for you." She reached over to the cherry wood table sitting next to the couch and pulled a couple of tissues from a box. "The officer said they wanted to ask you a couple of questions because you were one of the last ones to visit her in prison."

"Me? They want to ask me questions? What would I know about Twylah killing herself?" I started to get really confused. "When I last saw her, she didn't even hint that she was thinking about ending her life."

"First Lady, don't worry about it. I'm sure it's just standard procedure, considering the break-in." She patted my hands that were folded tightly in my lap. "It's going to be fine."

I physically allowed myself to be drunk in by the plush leather of the couch, and I wished I could stay there until I was totally away from reality. The up-and-down roller coaster of one thing behind the other was taking its toll on me. Tears raced down my cheeks and onto the Louise Ricci suit I was wearing. The soft, expensive fabric of the suit didn't deserve to be drowned in my tears, but I didn't deserve to have this much drama happening around me. My grandmother would tell me right about now that there was a brighter day ahead, but I was beginning to wonder if such a day existed.

I sat there and wept until my makeup had smeared lines on my face. Until my eyes burned from the mixture of the pain and mascara that had found its way into my eyes. And it was at that moment that I realized that, although her death was tragic, Twylah was in a much better state than me. If only I had the nerve to do what she'd done. If only I could muster up the strength to go against everything that I was taught; I, too, would rid myself of this never ending saga. I knew I shouldn't have been thinking that way, especially being the Christian that I was, but I couldn't help it. The strength I once had was all gone.

I wondered if all this drama was really worth it, and if one day it would be a distant memory hidden in the crevices of our minds. Or perhaps, someone would finally pinch me and wake me up from this long string of nightmares.

I don't care what anybody says, the glitz and glamour of being in ministry was not worth the pain that you sometimes had to encounter. It was not worth moments like this, when you didn't know whether to turn to the right or to the left. It was not worth having to bear the burdens of everyone else, while your own remained uncarried.

"First Lady, would you like me to get you a glass of water?"

"No," I said simply.

"Would you like some fruit or some crackers?" she said, speaking in reference to the food trays arranged on the table adjacent to me.

"No."

"Would you—"

This time I interrupted her. "Do you want to know what you can get me?"

Eager to help, she said, "Just tell me whatever you need."

I sat up and replied sarcastically, "I need a new life. Can you get that for me? Huh? Because if you can get it, a new life is exactly what I need."

Chapter Sixteen

Michelle

Things hadn't been completely the same since learning of Twylah's apparent suicide. I'd been in a somber disposition, and hadn't had much to say to anyone. Including Darvin.

I guess none of us would ever know why Twylah chose to end her life. It had been a couple of months, and her body had still not been found. We later learned that coincidentally, some men had broken into her home that same night. It was believed that during the robbery, they removed her body so it wouldn't appear they were the killers.

They confessed to dragging her out of the house and dumping her in a lake somewhere in northern Georgia. Much to our dismay, and in spite of the search efforts, her remains were yet to be found.

Twylah's mother didn't want to give up so easily the hope of finding her, but with the coaching of the lead detective, she decided to anyway. He had advised that the quicker the case was closed, the sooner we would all begin to heal. I wanted to object, but I had no right to do so. I had to respect her mother's wishes.

At the memorial service, Darvin had preached a "We all must die" message, ultimately asking those who were not saved to accept Jesus as their Savior.

Twylah's few family members had shown up, and much to my surprise, Twylah's ex-boyfriend, Rodney. I couldn't believe that he had the nerve to show his silly face at her memorial after the way he'd broken her heart. He'd come in there wearing blue jeans, a white shirt, dark blazer, and accompanying dark sunglasses, and had approached the table that held a collage of Twylah's photographs in a dramatic way.

Once there, he stroked the frames tenderly and allowed tears to freely fall as he pretended to be devastated by her death. After he held up the line for a few minutes, the funeral home attendants assisted him in moving on so that other people could pay their respects. As they tried to drag him away, he openly and loudly began to profess his undying love for her. What a nice to time to do it when she couldn't hear a word that he was saying. If it had not been for my own sorrow, I would have put a stop to his charade.

Twylah's mother seemed to be the most hurt of all. She and Twylah had been very close, and losing her was traumatic to the fragile woman who'd sat in the front row of the church, mourning her daughter. Dressed in a black dress with a white lace collar, the woman was poised and controlled, unlike others in her family that were behaving in typical fashion at an African-American funeral. Most of them kept fainting and feigning death, while others just screamed Twylah's name over and over, asking why she had to leave them on Earth to live without her.

The whole thing was draining. After the service, I'd personally gone to each of her family members and introduced myself. I told them how she and I had become good friends, and that I would greatly miss her.

And the truth was I would miss her. Twylah had been a good friend to me; at least that's what I thought. Something still didn't seem right with the attitude that she'd had the last day that I saw her, but I'd learned to accept what she said and count it as a loss. My memories of her were not all bad; some were good and would never be forgotten.

In the meantime, Darvin's and my relationship was getting worse. We would practically go a week sometimes without much conversation—only saying what was necessary to say. I guess our troubles were starting to get the best of us. He went about his normal routine, and so did I. All of our talks turned into arguments, and it seemed that every night he had a meeting to attend, which, in my mind, was just another excuse to keep from coming home. He once even told me that he found more peace away from me.

So, instead of meeting the ladies for our Thursday night dinner, tonight, I decided to stay home, cook, and wait for Darvin to come. We needed to talk, and I didn't want to wait another day. Besides the tension between us, there seemed to be something else looming above us.

Before I knew it, steam from the pot that held my rice was burning my arm. I quickly moved my hand, but the damage was already done. I rushed to the sink to put some cold water on my arm, but it did no good. After a few moments of allowing the cool liquid to soothe the burn, I went to the oven to remove the chicken. I'd made one of Darvin's favorite dinners: cream of mushroom chicken with seasoned rice, broccoli and cheese, and dinner rolls.

All I had to do was make the lemonade and everything would be ready.

The phone ringing interrupted the thoughts I had of Darvin's would-be appreciation for the home-cooked meal.

"Hello?"

"Hey, baby, how are you?"

I glanced at the clock on the wall. It read nine o' clock. "I'm good, baby. How are you?"

"I'm okay." Silence. "Um, listen, I'm not going to be home for at least another couple of hours, and I didn't want you to feel that you had to wait up on me."

Not able to hide my disappointment, I said, "Darvin, I thought you told me earlier today that you would be home by nine-thirty."

He sighed. "I know, baby. I did. I just had a couple of things come up unexpectedly, and so, like I said, it will be another couple of hours."

I was fuming inside as I looked at all of the hard work I'd gone through to make him a special dinner. "But, Darvin, I cooked one of your favorite meals tonight," I whined. "I thought we could sit down and have a real conversation—without arguing. You know, like old times." A smile turned the corners of my mouth as I said that, reminiscing about the conversations that we used to have until the wee hours in the morning.

"Baby, I would love to, but you know what I do. I'm a—"

"Pastor," I said, finishing his sentence. "The whole world knows it."

I slammed the pot's lid down on the counter loud enough for him to hear.

He ignored my frustration and continued. "When things come up at the church or with the church members, it's my responsibility to make sure that they are taken care of." He paused. "Look, I will make it up to you, okay?"

"No, it's not okay, Darvin. I'm tired of your excuses. It seems that when your own home needs tending to, you find another one to upkeep."

"What's that supposed to mean?" Darvin said with anger evident in his voice.

"It's not supposed to mean anything. It means what it means. While you are off seeing to the needs of the church, the needs of your wife aren't being met," I huffed.

"Well, if my wife would take an interest in someone other than herself and her problems, then just maybe she would see that she isn't the only one dealing with something," he said.

"And what is that supposed to mean?"

"In your words, it means what it means."

I hated when Darvin used my own words back at me. "In case you haven't noticed, I've been dealing with a lot lately, and so what if I've only been concentrating on myself? Shoot, after all I've been through, I deserve to act how I want to act. So what if my attitude was less than pleasant? What do you expect out of me? Do you expect me to always have it together and never get off track?"

"I just expect you to be you," he stated simply.

Just as I was about to say something, I heard a female voice in the background on his end. Silence permeated through the phone lines as quickly as a virus could spread.

"Who was that?" I asked as anger began to swell up in me. I knew the voice of Darvin's assistant, Felicia, and that was not her voice.

"What voice?" he said, sounding clearly disturbed.

"Please don't play games with me. Now, I know I heard a female's voice, so whose was it?"

"I don't know what you're talking about, Michelle."

"So, now it's Michelle? What happened to baby? You've been referring to me as baby this entire conversation, but now I'm Michelle to you?" I was clearly agitated. "Who's there with you? And I want to know right now."

"Listen, I don't have time for this. Like I said, I'll be home in a couple of hours, and if you need to get me, just call me on my cell."

"Are you dismissing me?" I shrieked.

"Calm down. It can't be healthy for you. Please. Let's just drop this and finish it later. We've been arguing too much lately, and to be honest, I just don't feel like it anymore. I'm tired. I don't care where I go; I don't fight with anyone else nearly as much as I do with you."

"What does that mean?"

He sighed. "It means I need to hang up now. This is going in the wrong direction."

"No, the only things going in the wrong direction are you and your secrets. Just simply tell me who she is and I'll drop it."

Darvin didn't offer any more information as to where he was going or who he was going with, so I was left to assume that the woman that I heard was the woman who would be accompanying him.

"Okay. Have it your way. Matter of fact, don't even worry about trying to get home in a couple of hours. Stay as long as you like. Dinner will be in the refrigerator, and I will be in the bed. Please don't wake me."

"Michelle, if you want me to come home, I will," he said as if he were about to lose his best friend.

"I want you to do whatever makes you feel good. That's what everybody else seems to be doing lately."

He was quiet for a moment. "Look, we are both tense right now. Let's not say anything that will further agitate the situation. And how will it look for the pastor to be agitated, especially while on duty?"

"Do you expect me to care about your agitation? You are purposely avoiding my questions, causing more agitation than you'll ever know." I paused for a second. "I don't understand you. It's like you'll forsake everything, including me, for the sake of the church and for the sake of how people perceive you as the pastor," I shouted.

"How many times do I have to explain to you the seriousness of what I do? I know that you don't understand, but you need to figure out a way to deal with it. I'm a pastor, and I'm going to be until the day I die, so if you don't like it, you might need to consider some other options," he said coldly.

The eye wells had opened back up and were dousing my face.

"Be careful what you say, Pastor Johnson. While I know that you're the pastor, you have an obligation to your home too. And when the needs of the home aren't being met, the home might have to relocate and allow someone else to take care of it."

Darvin's laughter infuriated me the more. "Where are you going to go? Your mother's house?"

If I could have reached through the receiver and socked him in the mouth, I would have knocked all of his teeth down his throat. How dare he insult me? "I don't know who you think you are or what type of woman you think I am, but please know that my mother's house isn't my only option. Don't you ever underestimate me, Darvin Johnson."

His cell phone died after my statement, and after trying for several more minutes to reach him back, I finally decided to go to bed. But I had no plans to sleep. I watched several reruns of the *Cosby Show*. I had a doctor's appointment early the next morning, but I was determined to stay up until Darvin came home. I was not done with what I had to say, and regardless of how tired he was when he got home, I was going to make him hear me out.

I heard the sound of the alarm and prayed that it was Darvin coming through the door. I glanced at the clock on the nightstand; it read 2:06 A.M.

I felt my blood pressure rising as I looked from the clock to Darvin.

"Hey," Darvin mumbled after seeing that I was awake.

"Hello," I said cautiously, trying not to show my anger before giving him an opportunity to explain why his behind had been out until after two in the morning.

"I know you're wondering why I'm just now getting home. And let me just say that you have every right to be."

It was good that he was cutting straight to the chase; however, he was still going too slowly for me.

"Why haven't I been able to get you on your cell phone? And please tell me where in the world you've been until this time of the morning."

"First, my cell phone battery went dead right while I was talking to you, so—"

I interrupted. "And what was wrong with the car charger, might I ask?"

"I didn't have it with me."

I rolled my eyes in exaggeration. "I'm finding that hard to believe. You take that thing with you everywhere, especially since we found out that I was pregnant."

Darvin cast his eyes to the floor. He knew that what he was saying didn't make any sense. All of a sudden, I started getting this gut-wrenching feeling in the pit of my stomach. I had never considered that Darvin might have been staying out and acting out of character because . . .

"Michelle," he said, interrupting my thoughts. "Before you allow your imagination to get the best of you, let me just say that I'm sorry for how I acted earlier."

"So, what did you do?" I asked impatiently, not caring to know anything more than that.

He sat down on the bed and dropped his head. I prepared myself for the worst. I had never been concerned as to whether he'd ever cheated on me, but tonight I was beginning to wonder. I didn't have any idea what he was about to say to me.

"The reason I didn't answer you earlier on the phone when you asked me who was in the background was because I didn't know how to tell you."

I was sure that my heart was skipping several beats.

"It was a woman by the name of Alexandria." He hesitated before he continued on. "I've been helping her through some things."

It was my turn to say something. "Things like what?"

"Well, I met her a few weeks ago when she dropped by the church office. She'd never visited the church before, and was coming in to inquire about the church and service times."

"What?" He was impossible. "She didn't see the huge sign in the church's yard listing the service times, website information, so on and so forth?"

He released a breath. "I don't know. Anyway, she came

in, we started talking about the church, and immediately she was excited about what we had to offer. She then began to share with me some things that she was going through in her personal life, and I agreed to help her. It wasn't until tonight that I realized at what cost."

Clearly disturbed, I said, "Darvin, you have a big sign on your head that reads *stupid, stupid, stupid*. How many times do I have to tell you to stop being so naïve? You always fall in the same trap with the same type of women, who play the 'woman in distress' role, and it's like you lose your head. I don't understand you."

"Michelle, it wasn't like that. I really wanted to help her. It wasn't until tonight that I realized that she didn't want or need my help."

"Why?"

"Why what?" he asked, confused.

"Why didn't you tell me about her if it was so innocent?" I paused.

"Here I was dealing with all the mess I've had to deal with—needing help myself—and you, my husband, were off helping someone else."

"Michelle . . ." he said, moving toward me.

"Don't you dare touch me! I don't want you to come near me," I said, my breath so hot it could've been mistaken for fiery flames.

He looked defeated. Out of all the things I'd had to endure, never would I have imagined this. True, we had our struggles; we had our days of breaking up. Now, the man of my dreams, who I thought could do no wrong, was standing before me talking about the "other woman."

"So, tell me, what did you do?" The next words were hard to squeeze out. It was like trying to get the last of the toothpaste out of an empty tube. "Did you sleep with her?"

"No," he said somberly.

I exhaled a sigh of relief.

"But I'll be honest. I can't say that I didn't want that at some point."

This time, I held my breath, and it was filled with anger. In this case, the truth was better left untold.

"That's why I got so defensive with you on the phone. We went out to dinner, talked for hours, and she talked to me about how she was just getting over a bad relationship. I've been counseling her for weeks—trying to be a true friend—but she wanted more than that. It was something about her that was intriguing, and my sin nature wanted to give in, but when we drove up to her house, I realized I was making a mistake."

It seemed that lately shock was the only emotion that applied to me. I didn't even know what to say. My husband was sitting on our bed, telling me that he'd almost had an affair. Some would say almost didn't count, but it did to me.

"Darvin, I'm sorry, but I don't understand. I know that the past few weeks—maybe months—haven't been good. Is that just cause for you to go out and start having an affair on me? What did I do to deserve that? Or should I say the thought of it?"

"Nothing. I'm just going through some things within myself. Michelle, in my heart, I didn't want to do it. I just wanted to escape reality. I wanted to go to a place where my reality was somehow different. Where it seemed as if I could escape and where our problems didn't exist."

Jesus, keep me near the cross. Did he just say escape? Who didn't want an escape?

"Did you ever stop to think that the place you were trying to escape to was a place that I'd love to go myself? Did you ever stop to think that I've been hurting too?" The thought of his selfishness made me angrier. "How do you think I cope? I would like to take a vacation to la-la land, but I can't, because I know you're counting on me. Our baby is counting on me."

Darvin allowed the tears to flow freely. He looked as

if he'd aged several years. I'd never seen him so broken about something, and while I knew that he wasn't perfect, I never thought that we would be having this discussion.

He shook his head. "I will never be able to make this make sense. I've made a terrible mistake. I should have never entered into any type of relationship with this woman without you knowing it. For any reason. Ever."

"So, is she the person you've been spending your evenings with?"

He looked up at me as if he feared for his life. "Yes."

I suddenly remembered the note that I'd gotten in church that Sunday. My instincts told me that the woman must have been there, and it was evident that she wanted me to know it. Didn't men know that the other woman would never be completely satisfied with just being the other woman? Females like her wanted to be the one and only. Women like her made me think of Daphne and Dawn.

"But what did I do? Why didn't you come and talk to me?" I questioned.

I didn't understand this. Couldn't understand it. Wouldn't understand it.

"And say what? That I met another woman that I'm attracted to? A woman who validates me and is just as passionate and understanding of ministry as I am? Another woman who seems to understand what I go through—all while helping me to forget what I'm going through?" He turned around on the bed. "You know that I couldn't have told you that."

He sure in a devil's hell couldn't. He was already about to get his head knocked off had he said one more thing about this woman.

"But we could have talked about it nonetheless. We could have communicated about what the other was feeling. If you had voids, you should have come to me. I'm your wife and you're my husband. That's what married people do. They work through their problems."

"Those are the politically correct answers, Michelle, but until you're faced with temptation, you don't know how you will respond." He stood and began unbuttoning his shirt. He took it off and tossed it on the nearby chair.

"I don't know what to say, and I know that saying I'm sorry is not enough. You don't deserve this, especially with all that you've had to deal with lately. For some strange reason, I felt that all of what's been happening was my fault. I told myself that you were disappointed in the life you had to live because of being married to me, so instead of facing you, I ran. It seemed as if one thing after the other was happening, and because I couldn't do a single thing about it, I took off my Superman cape. I retreated into the false safety of Delilah's lap."

He took my hands into his own. "I can never make up for this, Michelle. I won't even try. I won't lie to you anymore and try to pretend that I'm perfect and that I have it all together. I thought I was above reproach and falling down, but this has taught me that I'm just as vulnerable as anyone else. I went seeking someone to validate me and to reaffirm that I was a good man, something that I felt I wasn't being to you anymore."

Once again, tears were flowing; this time from both of our eyes. The enemy had tried once again to destroy me, Darvin, and our home. He gave it his best shot to take us under. But every time, we came out stronger. I didn't know what the future held, but one thing I did know was who held the future. And my life was in His hands.

Darvin slid over to my side of the bed—slowly crossing the emotional borders that I'd created in response to his confession. When he reached for me, I allowed myself to fall into what seemed like unfamiliar arms. Had she also been in his arms? It was a question I was too afraid to ask.

The assurance I once had in our tight-knit bond had slowly faded into the night, and dark clouds loomed over it.

He stroked my face with the tip of his thumbs and allowed the trail to continue down my bare forearm. The heat from his touch made me want to loosen my resolve, but the memory of his actions made me resist the temptation.

"Darvin," I said between kisses he was now placing on my neck.

"Yes," he replied seductively.

Mmm . . . the rich sounds of his baritone voice always made me weak.

Not tonight.

"Your blanket is already in there on the couch."

He came to an abrupt halt. "Excuse me?"

I eased off the bed, grabbed the pillow I kept on the chaise for extra back support, and gave it to him.

"And here's a pillow."

He looked into my eyes—his own confused.

"What are you saying, baby?"

"What I'm saying is you're sleeping on the couch. Now, will it be one pillow or two?"

Without saying a word, he reluctantly took the pillow, and I watched him and his entire make-me-wanna-throw-him-down-and-make-love-to-him body walk out of our bedroom. I was pissed at what he'd done, but was also grateful that he'd come to his senses before it was too late.

However . . . his behind was still sleeping on the couch tonight.

Chapter Seventeen

Daphne

The drive to church made me nervous. It had been a few months since I'd shown up again at Mount Zion. I had to be careful not to blow my cover as Dawn, so I decided to lurk in the shadows. I wanted them—specifically Michelle—to think she'd somehow gotten rid of me. Since Twylah's death, I felt showing up at church would have been just a little too risky for me, seeing that things were so sensitive. Not that I had a reason to be afraid; I just didn't want to take any chances.

The truth was, I hadn't meant to kill her, but the stupid girl kept squirming. I only wanted to talk to her to get more information, but she insisted on trying to escape. I'd gotten so angry that I didn't realize that my hands were tightening around her neck and I was choking her until she wasn't breathing anymore. Her last breath had been slow and deliberate. And as she fell limp in the chair, it hit me that I'd killed her.

I panicked when I realized what I'd done, and was in desperate need of a way out. I ran out of there so fast, Marion Jones couldn't have stopped me.

Thinking back to that day still made me shudder . . . .

I'd posted Twylah's bail, and afterward, she hadn't even said enough to me to form a paragraph the entire way home. I kept glancing over at her, waiting for her to make some sort of conversation, and she hadn't provided anything.

So, I'd decided to jump start it.

"T, aren't you going to say thank you or something for getting you out of jail?" I asked.

"Yeah, thanks," she said nonchalantly.

"Excuse me," I said, exaggerating my words. "I didn't know that you had the money to get yourself out, because had I known that, I wouldn't have posted your eighty-thousand dollar bail," I said as I rolled my eyes.

"Daphne, if you're going to make me kiss your butt for getting me out of jail, you're sadly mistaken." She turned to me. "You need me just as much as I need you," she said, looking back toward the window. "So please don't get it twisted."

I raised an eyebrow. That short jail time had made her a little feisty.

Nonetheless, she was the one mistaken if she thought that she was going to get away with talking to me like that. "I suggest you change your tone. Let's not forget all that I've done for you."

"No, let's not forget all I've done for you. I've betrayed a friend for months now for a few extra dollars." She crossed her arms over her chest.

"A few dollars? A few dollars? Huh! What a serious understatement! How about you call it for what it is . . . a couple of hundred thousand dollars! And in case you have forgotten, it was you who came to me because you so desperately wanted to have a lifestyle equivalent to that of a certain Michelle Johnson, so you could prove to an ex-boyfriend who didn't want you broke or with a few dollars in your bank account. So please don't you get it twisted," I said, clearly annoyed. "I came in during a time when you were desperate. And as they say, desperate times call for desperate measures."

Twylah turned back to me again. "How dare you! Don't try to throw your money up in my face! You were the one who was so infatuated with a certain Pastor Johnson that you were willing to sell your soul just to be close to him. If it hadn't been for me making sure you knew his whereabouts, as well as Michelle's, you wouldn't have gotten as close as you did. And if you hadn't been so greedy in trying to rush things, you might have had him by now."

She knew that was a low blow. She knew that more than anything in this lifetime, I wanted Darvin to myself. The only person that was standing in my way was Michelle. "Well, that might be true, but I have created for myself another opportunity, and like it or not, you are a part of that opportunity."

"Daphne, I'm done with your schemes. I can't take it anymore. I'm sick of your blackmails. Ever since you decided to come back here, I've been playing your dirty game. I don't like how this is hurting people."

Was she trying to back out of our deal? "Oh, no you don't. You are going to continue to do what I say. I have held up my end of the bargain, and you will hold up yours."

"I've done everything I said I would do. I told you in the beginning that I couldn't make any promises, and that still stands. I opened the doors for you, but we both agreed that it would be your responsibility to walk into them. Now, like I said, the games are over. I want out."

I laughed hysterically. She had really lost her mind. Didn't she know that you don't play with dirt unless you plan to get dirty?

"It's not that simple."

"And why not?" she asked. "You don't need me anymore."

"Oh, sweetheart, you are very much needed, and unless you cooperate, your sainthood will be for naught, because I will make sure that Pastor Johnson and Michelle know every dirty little secret that you have."

Twylah glowed with fury and frustration. She glared at me with frost covering her eyes. "You wouldn't dare! Because I might have to tell everyone your dirty little secrets, Daphne."

"You b—"

"You better not call me out of my name!" she interrupted. "Why are you doing this anyway? You have all of the information you need. You are several steps closer than you were two years ago, and now with you re-creating yourself, you're sure to succeed."

I could have knocked the taste buds out of her mouth for threatening me, but the truth was, I still needed her. I tried to take a softer approach.

"You don't get it. The plan is not complete until I'm Mrs. Darvin Johnson. And like it or not, you will see this through to the end."

She shook her head. "No. I won't do it. And that's all there is to it."

A thought suddenly came to me. "You want him for yourself, don't you?"

"What?"

"You heard me. You are secretly in love with Darvin and you don't want to admit it."

"That's ludicrous." She paused for a span. "Sure, I might have been a little attracted to him at one time, but to say that I'm in love with him is a huge overstatement."

"Yeah, sure." I didn't believe anything that she said.

"I'm serious. We all know that he's good-looking, sweet, charming, funny . . . but I've never desired him for myself."

"So, why do you want out?"

"After Michelle came to see me in prison, I thought about the backstabbing and the lies that I've told. I thought about all of the things that she said, and I realize that I've been wrong. I mean, I knew I was wrong in the beginning, but for some strange reason, I never stopped long enough to care.

Greed is a monster, Daphne," she said, staring out of the window.

"How selfish I've been. Breaking into their house was

way out of character for me. And to top it all off, I still didn't find any dirt on Michelle. Just like I told you before you demanded I do it—she's squeaky clean. So, it has to stop. She may have the life I wish I had, with a man to love like Pastor loves her, but what can I do about it? Besides that—she's pregnant."

I slammed on my brakes in the middle of the highway. Twylah knew that I hated for her to speak of Michelle in a positive way, and I especially hated for her or anyone else to mention that Michelle was pregnant with my man's baby. Michelle didn't deserve to be carrying his baby, and when I found out that she was, I was tempted to be mad at Darvin. But I couldn't blame him for wanting his sexual desires met. After all, my plan had taken far longer than I had anticipated, and he had to do something in the meantime.

Getting a man of Darvin's caliber took time. Dedicated and well thought out time.

Pastors were a different breed. They had to be more careful than the average person, because an affair that leads to divorce for them could cost them their ministry, which would mean losing their livelihood. And I definitely didn't need that to happen. I could hardly wait until he was sending me on endless shopping sprees and surprising me with exotic vacations—with his money.

The car horns jolted me back into the present, and I realized that the thought of my life with Darvin had placed a smile on my face. I resumed riding.

"Twylah, don't you ever again in your life mention Michelle and her baby to me. Especially not in a way that suggests that I should be happy for her or care one way or the other."

"Daphne—"

I interrupted. "You have got to stop calling me that. One day you might slip up and say it in front of the wrong person." She was really working my nerves. "It's Dawn. Daphne is in Florida recuperating from a nervous breakdown, so I would appreciate it if you never mentioned her again."

Twylah stared at me. "You are sick. A really sick individual. And you need some help."

I reached over and pretended to punch her in the arm. "Aren't we just the two sickos?" I laughed hysterically before I turned serious. "And you haven't seen crazy if you try to undermine me, Twylah. I'm serious. You don't want to cross me."

My tone must have made her nervous. She didn't utter another word.

Later that night, I drank an entire bottle of Riesling, and in spite of the guilt I felt, I knew I'd done the right thing.

I tried hard to shake away the happenings of that dreadful day. It was sad that things had to end on that note, but Twylah left me no choice. I'd planned to scare her and offer to give her enough money to leave town, but she kept making it worse. She kept insisting that she had to change her life and start living for Jesus again, as if she were born perfect. It turned out that it was for the best. I was too close to my dream for Twylah to sabotage it.

Bringing my thoughts back to the present, I took in the beautiful Sunday morning. The melody in my heart was that of an angelic choir. Today was the day that I put the rest of my plan into action. I'd done my homework, and I was ready for the final exam. I took one last look at my reflection in the car window and admired my own beauty. If I didn't look like the perfect first lady, then I didn't know who did. The simplicity of the apple red Ben Marc suit was downright breathtaking. Showing just enough cleavage to make your eyes wander, and a hem that stopped just above the knee of my shapely legs, I was ready to make my entrance. The suit was forming to every curve in my body and the matching hat, purse, and accessories were sure to get some of the deacons stirred up.

I smoothed my skirt, tucked my handheld purse under my arm, and walked toward the building. I was more focused now, and had to stay the course. So far, nothing had backfired in my face. No one had suspected my double identity, and the one person who did know was now dead.

Yep, everything seemed to be working perfectly. I approached the door, and a fine-as-the-morning-sun man dressed in a dark blue suit opened it for me. He was tall with a bald head, and had those bedroom eyes that would make you melt.

I put myself in check because just looking at him was making me hot and bothered, and I didn't need to be hot and bothered. Especially in the house of the Lord. I was too close to my destiny, and nothing was going to stop me now. Not even a man whose silent words suggested I meet him in the same spot after church. Nope. Didn't have time for that.

The ushers opened the huge wooden doors and let all of us who had been standing in the lobby, into the sanctuary. When the usher realized that he knew me, he immediately escorted me to a seat in the back.

Trying desperately to remain calm, I smiled, and through gritted teeth said, "I would much rather prefer something closer to the front."

The short, scrawny-looking man glared at me. "Look, I know you who you are, Ms. Carlton, and I suggest that you not buck me today. If you do, I won't be responsible for what I do. Now, you sit your demon-possessed behind in this chair right here," he said, pointing to the space he selected for me.

Suddenly, an older woman wearing a floral dress that looked more like drapery, and whose size would have petrified King Kong, took her purse and hit the usher in the same arm he used to point to the seat he was holding for me.

"Charlie, you need to stop your stuff. God loves sinners too. Now, I'm sure Ms. Carlton here knows she ain't no saint, but God loves her kind. And besides that, you know the protocol is that you seat from the front to back. Now, I might be old, but I can see that it ain't near full in the front yet, so you need to move Ms. Carlton closer. And just maybe some Jesus will rub off on her," she said as she stared at me through bifocals.

I had never felt so demeaned and humiliated in my life. True, I wasn't a saint, but did I have to be made to feel as if I were the scum of the Earth? I knew plenty of people who were worse sinners than me.

"Are you going to follow me, or are you going to stand here staring off into space?" He scowled.

"Charlie," I whispered, "you better be glad that we are in the church, because if we weren't, I would have to show you just what I do to men like you who try to throw their weight around."

He hissed and led me down to the third row. It must have been my lucky day because I got the end seat. When I got ready for my performance, I would have perfect access to the aisle.

Parishioners began to fill up the sanctuary within minutes of my sitting down. Before long the service was underway. I could hardly breathe while anticipating Darvin's entrance. I was sweating in my hands, on my back, under my arms . . . I was about to start a water ministry on the third row.

Finally, Darvin came out, and Michelle followed soon after him. One day that was going to be me, and I could not wait.

Darvin took his place and joined in the praise and worship service. I closely watched how engrossed he became, almost like being in a trance. I held up my own hands, trying to feel something, but I felt nothing but chills running down my spine. I knew I shouldn't have come back here, because I was no longer able to front. I used to have the whole church thing down to a science, but now it was like I couldn't even fake anymore.

Yeah, that was me as Daphne: speaking in tongues, shouting, participating in every ministry that was offered, and serving as an armor bear to Michelle—even though the last stint didn't last but a hot second before I'd totally lost my mind and failed my own plan. I got greedy and lost track of what I was supposed to be doing.

My plan had been to befriend her, but the more I got to know her, the more I realized that it was me who Darvin needed, not her. I was powerful, Category 1 beautiful, intelligent, had a way with people; while Michelle was the opposite. She was plain, Category 2 beautiful, and from the way she always complained, she totally hated her position.

After I lost it, I had to move back to Florida and get myself together. Shortly after I left, I knew I had to find a way to get back. I kept telling myself that the only reasonable thing to do was change my identity.

Standing there with my hands raised felt so foreign to me, but just in case Darvin noticed me in the congregation, I didn't want him to see me not worshipping. If he was going to worship, so was I.

The service progressed, and I kept my eyes on the prize. I watched every move he made. I even noticed how touchy he and Michelle were today, and how every once in a while, he would just look over and smile at her. The sight of it burned holes in my heart. That should have been me.

One day, I'd run into one of the ladies from the church at the grocery store, and the gossiping staff member told me that she suspected he and Michelle were having problems. That was obviously a lie, or they were putting up a good front. I heard pastors and their wives did that, but looking at them, it was too hard to tell.

Darvin moved to the podium, where he took his place to preach.

"Church, let's give God a praise," he said.

He must not have gotten the response he wanted, because he said it again. "I said, let's give God a praise. That was good enough for me, but not for the one who woke you up this morning. Not for the one who has you in your right mind, health, and strength. Not for the one who gave you those arms to lift toward heaven and that voice to sing praises. Surely, you can do better than that!" he exclaimed.

This time the crowd was on their feet. I smiled because Darvin never failed to get the crowd hyped. He always knew what to do and say.

That had been my only concern about myself. I was not as confident when it came to the church crowd, but could work any other social gathering effortlessly. But since I had not been attending church, I spent the last couple of months watching religious programs. I pretty much had the pulpit jargon down. I'd watched a couple of popular female pastors, and had imitated them long enough to feel comfortable to do it myself if I ever needed to. So, when the time came for me to be his wife, no one would doubt my capabilities. I was already one up over Michelle.

I spent the entire service daydreaming about my soon-to-be new role as first lady, and I almost missed my cue. Darvin was in the final stages of his message, the part where everyone came alive and was shouting "Yeah," "Thank you, Jesus," and "Pastor, you know you preaching," among other things. It was time for me to shine. Just as the organ got crunk, I fell out. In the spirit.

I lay there on the floor with my eyes partially open and tears running down my face. Ushers came from everywhere and were throwing sheets over me as if I were covered in leprosy, covering up what would be any chance of skin showing. I could see the prayer warriors were gathered around me, praying that God would speak or deliver; whichever I was standing in the need of.

I purposefully fell on my side with my face toward the pulpit so I could get Darvin's reaction to me sprawled out on the floor. He was too busy preaching to notice. I knew that when he stopped, he would see me and come down to lay his hands on me, as with everyone else who got "slained in the spirit." And I would cherish every second of it.

I kept the tears coming. I'm sure they thought they were tears of joy because of my gratitude for God. Nevertheless, they were tears of joy for what God was getting ready to do in my life. I couldn't understand how He would bless me so in spite of my sins, but He sure was doing it. Here I was plotting and scheming, trying to take someone else's husband, and yet He was allowing me to do it. It must have been in His will.

I closed my eyes for a brief second, and I felt a touch on my head. I tried to contain my excitement, as I knew it was Darvin coming to me. The hand moved from my head to my arm in such a gentle way I almost forgot why I was really lying on the floor.

"Get your floozy butt off of this floor. I'm on to your games, and I won't stand for it. You are one sorry excuse for a woman, but if you get up now, you might be able to contain what little dignity you have left," the voice whispered in my ear.

My heart started pounding and my hands balled into fist-fighting position. I opened my eyes to see Michelle bending over me with her very round belly in my face.

I had to quickly remind myself to respond as Dawn and not Daphne, because Daphne would have punched her right in the face. The Dawn in me had to keep my composure, because this was my last chance at Darvin.

I did the only thing I knew to do; I started speaking in tongues. Maybe not the real ones, but the one that you say so fast no one can tell the difference.

"E-ro-ha-shun-day," I babbled. "Un-tie-my-yellow-bow-tie," I babbled even more. "Como te llama," I said in Spanish. I kept saying those things over and over again, louder and louder, until Michelle was finally convinced that I was not putting on a show.

She slowly walked away, and the scrawny usher took her place. He was glaring down at me too, but I was certain that Darvin didn't miss my performance.

I wasn't sure if fear of Michelle had him scared to move, or if he was afraid that being in my presence would expose the true feelings he had for me.

After about five minutes, the ushers helped me up. They

were fanning me liberally with those Martin Luther King church fans, trying to fan away the spirit, so I would calm down. One usher straightened my skirt, and another one tried to smooth my hair back in place. While they were busy trying to put me back together, I kept searching until my eyes locked with Darvin's.

In that twinkling of an eye, I knew that I'd gotten in his head. I knew that my work for today had been done.

My intent was not to come in here and put on a shouting fit just for the sake of being seen in my cute outfit. My intent was to raise questions in Darvin's head: When was the last time anybody had been slain in the spirit as a result of one of his sermons? According to Twylah, not recently. When was the last time Michelle lost her first lady composure and shouted to one of his sermons? Again, according to Twylah, not ever.

Yes, those were the questions that I intended to raise this morning, and by the look on his face, I'd done my job.

I had learned that pastors loved the feeling of validation; and from now on, every Sunday, I would be Darvin's biggest fan.

Chapter Eighteen

Michelle

I cringed when I saw Dawn waltz into the church looking like a two-bit ho in that candy apple red suit—though I must admit it looked deliciously fantastic on her, but highly inappropriate for church. Interestingly enough, I wouldn't have expected that from her, but would if it had been Daphne. They were so much alike it was ridiculous.

Little did she know, but during the service, I caught her watching Darvin. It was that same kind of smitten look that Daphne used to have on her face. It was that sick, fatal attraction look. I shivered. Something was not right with that woman. I don't care if her temperament was slightly different than that of her sister, I wasn't taking any chances. It was time for a change to come, and I wasn't going to wait on it.

After tiring from watching Dawn pretend to be endowed with the Holy Ghost, I got out of my seat and headed straight for her. I went over to her and all but demanded that she get up off the floor. She had some nerve. And she had caught me on the wrong day. My pregnancy hormones at seven months were really kicking in and that "mean streak" my grandmother told me I would get, I had it.

Dawn finally got up, but it wasn't until after I'd walked away. One of the ushers assisted her back to her seat, and I almost shot daggers at her when I saw the smirk on her face. I could hardly wait until service was over because I planned to tell her a piece of my mind, woman to woman.

***

I kept watching Dawn out of the corner of my eye as she waited in the line to speak to Darvin. I made a mental note that beginning next Sunday, Darvin and I would stand together and greet parishioners. I didn't go out to greet often because my feet were normally swollen, but today and any other day that Dawn was there, I didn't care if my feet were as big as watermelons.

She was not about to do to me what her sister had done to me, my family, or my church.

Instead of waiting until next Sunday to put my new rule in place, I decided that it would start today. I sashayed over to where Darvin was standing, and just as she approached him with her little bony hand extended, I walked up to him and locked arms with him.

Darvin had been so sweet since we'd worked through our issues with his almost-affair, and true to form, he leaned down and kissed me on the lips.

I'm sure Dawn thought that we were trying to prove something to her, but he and I decided we would greet each other with a kiss any time we'd been out of each other's presence.

I savored the sweet kiss that he planted on my lips, and had we not been in the church, I would have added a little more spice to it. However, it didn't stop me from rubbing it in her face. Just in case she had any ulterior motives, she would know that we were not to be tampered with. I'd put up with drama for long enough. It was my turn to be happy again.

"Why, Pastor," Dawn said as she fanned herself, "I didn't know you had it in you. You better not let too many women see you lay a kiss on First Lady like that. Some women might feel a little left out."

"Well, First Lady is the type of woman that will make you do things like that," he said as he smiled down at me. He then walked away. I could have broken out into a cheer. It was as if he knew she was up to no good.

When he was out of listening distance, she said, "Mmm. If only we could all just be First Lady."

I knew in my heart of hearts that there was something behind what she'd just said, but I was no longer bound by fear.

"Sister Carlton?"

"No offense, First Lady, but I actually dislike when people refer to me as their sister when I'm not," she said. "However, I'll make an exception for you," she said.

"Please, by all means, don't let me offend you." I stepped closer to her to further drive in the point I was about to make. "Listen, Dawn Carlton. I have seen many like your kind: home wreckers. Women like you who lust after the pastor for all sorts of selfish reasons, but never stop to think about how your actions may affect their homes and loved ones. No, all you can see is the powerful man, the fame, the fortune, the expensive cars, and the lifestyle of the rich and famous.

"Well, let me tell you something, sweetie. This life ain't what it looks like sometimes. It's more than just being noticed and known when you walk into a local restaurant or store. It's more than just having people inflate your ego by calling you First Lady. This position requires hard work, spiritual dedication, a high level of tolerance and long-suffering, the ability to spiritually uphold your husband while dealing with women like you who just want his last name and not his virtues and vices, among many other things that you have no clue about. So, the next time you think you might want to be me . . . think again. Ask your sister, Daphne; she'll tell you."

By the time I'd gotten that entire statement out, I was nearly out of breath. I don't know if it was the amount of words or how fast I'd said them.

My temper was rising, and the blood was boiling in my veins. I was sick of women like Dawn Carlton always making those insensitive comments and thinking that being the first lady was a piece of cake. I was sick of people telling me what they would do if they were the first lady or the pastor's wife. You don't know what you'll do until you're in another person's shoes.

"My goodness, First Lady. Aren't we a little on the touchy side today?"

Dawn batted her eyelashes really fast. I could tell that she was really upset, and was also trying to see how many people had heard me diss her. But I didn't give a rat's butt who heard me or what she thought. It was time for my feelings to matter for a change.

"Dawn, you haven't seen me on the touchy side, and you better start praying now that you don't ever see it. My wrath is not one that you want to experience, because if I have to step out of my role and deal with you woman to woman, I will— with no hesitation." I'm sure my eyes were as red as fire, as they normally were when I got really upset. When I got upset, really upset, I couldn't mask it.

"For a Christian, you do know how to speak some very threatening words." She smirked. "Look, I don't want any trouble. You're right. Maybe I was a little out of line for my comment, but there is no need to get defensive. After all, he is going home with you, right?"

I don't know why I got the feeling that was a sarcastic question, and for whatever reason, I envisioned myself taking off my earrings, my Jack McConnell hat, and beating her tail like Sophia beat Harpo in *The Color Purple*. But I dismissed that thought. "You're right, Dawn. He's going home with me."

"So, if you know that, why do these types of women you're referring to bother you so? I'm sure you're going to be dealing with that for the rest of your life, and I guess I have to wonder if you're going to react that way to everyone you're seemingly intimidated by."

"You know? You and your sister are so much alike. I don't know why either of you think that you are someone to be

intimidated by. For the life of me, I just can't understand that."
I beckoned for Chanice to come over and bring my flats because my feet were hurting, but I refused to end the conversation like this. I also watched as, one by one, the other members who waited in line to talk to me and no doubt ask about the baby, walked away. I would have to speak with them next Sunday. The business at hand was more important.

I took the shoes from Chanice and replaced the heels with the flats. I said my thanks to Chanice in a way that let her know she could give me a few more minutes alone with Dawn.

"That's the thing that gets me about women like you. You're so sure that we are intimidated by you, and you dote on that fact so that you can try to use that against us. Believe it or not, Dawn, we pastors' wives have conversations about females like you, but we hardly waste our time being intimidated," I lied. "We concentrate more on how to teach you that it's in your best interest to find your own man and leave ours alone." I stopped talking long enough to wave at a little girl who had been dying to speak to me. "Do you better understand now the message that I'm trying to relay to you?"

Dawn rolled her eyes so hard that I could have sworn they would be rolling around on the floor at any second. Finally, she responded. "Madame First Lady, I appreciate your trying to *educate* me, if you will, on the do's and don'ts of 'women like me.' However, I feel that I must tell you that I've already been raised one time by a woman who is a lady. I've already been trained on how to get a man, and I've never had any problems at all getting any man that I want. Any man I want.

"And I also feel the need to tell you that you're right about my sister and I being a lot alike. Matter of fact, we are practically the same person, so there's no need for you to keep referencing her. Lastly, you don't need to place your concern with me. Because let's face it, we're both grown women with no need to hurl insults at the other. You just stick to your job as First Lady of Mount Zion Baptist Church, and I'll stick to mine."

She stepped closer. "Because I am going to become a very active member of this church the same way my sister was. And if you allow me to make your life a living hell, then that's your business. I'm going to enjoy mine."

With that, she walked off in the direction of a tall, handsome man who had noticeably been watching us for some time. Maybe she would set her eyes on him and get them off Darvin. I would surely hate to have to pluck them out.

I spoke to a couple of other members who were still lingering in the foyer before going to my office.

Dawn Carlton was mutilating my last nerve. I was growing weary by the day, rolling over, taking whatever she dished out, when she dished it out, as I did with her sister. It was high time for me not to allow another person to waltz into my life, create chaos, and walk away as if they'd done nothing. I was sick of her. She needed to see that this game she was playing was being played on my court. If she played by the rules, praise God. If she didn't, may God be with her.

Darvin and I drove home in bliss. I was acting as if nothing had happened today at church. I could tell he appreciated me not bringing up the situation. Most of our conversations now included ways to make our marriage better, not worse. That was another reason I refused to allow Dawn Carlton to disturb my peace. Not everything about my life was in order, but the areas in which it was, would stay that way.

We drove into the valet area of the Oceanaire on Peachtree Street, where we were having lunch. The Oceanaire was one of our favorite restaurants in Atlanta. It was the closest thing to being at a Florida eatery, getting fresh seafood. We left the car with the attendant and walked into the restaurant, where we were greeted by the manager, who knew us by name. He took us to our regular table in the back and took our drink orders. I got my usual Shirley Temple, and Darvin got his usual fresh squeezed lemonade. The Oceanaire was not only known for their food, but the restaurant itself was beautiful, and they had impeccable service.

Darvin and I made small talk about ministry, but then shifted the conversation to the baby.

"Sweetie, how are you feeling today?" he lovingly asked.

"I couldn't feel better. The baby is kicking more than usual, making me a little tired, but nonetheless, all is well."

Conversation about the baby always made me smile. Anyone who knew me knew I was anxiously anticipating the baby's arrival.

"So, you ready to talk about the nursery?" I asked. Darvin always avoided that topic, leaving me to try to figure out the theme on my own.

"Well, I was thinking a nursery with a basketball theme would be good."

He laughed after that statement.

I playfully hit him on the arm. "And what makes you so sure that the baby is going to be a boy?" I asked. He'd been crossing his fingers, his legs, and anything else he could cross in hopes for a boy. Each time we'd gone to the doctor to find out the sex, the baby had gone into a position where the doctor couldn't determine it. We'd done everything that we knew to do to get the baby to turn so we could see, but none of it had worked.

"I just feel it in my spirit," he said.

I smirked. "Yeah, whatever. You are going to be real disappointed when they say, 'Congratulations, Mr. and Mrs. Johnson, you're the new parents of a baby girl!'" I laughed at the thought of that.

"We will see, Mrs. Johnson." The smile on his face was priceless. I couldn't wait to make him a dad.

We continued to share moments of continuous laughter and bliss that lingered on longer than normal, and allowed ourselves to enjoy just being with each other. With everything that had gone on, it was good to just unwind and bask in the appreciation of our uninterrupted time together.

"You know, Michelle, I haven't said this in a while, but I'm so proud of you. You are an incredible woman, and I don't know what I would do if you were not in my life. You have been through so much," he said, taking a bite of his shrimp and grits appetizer. "I really would like to see you just enjoy the rest of this pregnancy. No stress. No worries. Just pleasure and relaxation. You deserve that and more."

I felt as if I was about to cry at his tender words. Over the course of the last few years, we'd lost our connection. Our romance. A part of our friendship.

"Thank you, baby. You will never know how much that means to me." I leaned over and gave him a kiss.

"I'm serious. I want you to enjoy the next couple of months, because once you become my baby's mama, it's going to be all about the little man from then on in," he said jokingly.

"There you go with that wishful thinking again." I took a sip of the Acqua Panna that I'd ordered. "It's all right, though. As long as I'm your baby's mama, I will give you as many babies as you want—until you get that boy."

Before he could respond, the maitre d' appeared with our entrees. I'd ordered the fish and chips with grouper and a buerre-blanc sauce, and Darvin had selected the crab cakes. After the food was placed on the table, we blessed it and immediately started eating. The way we dove into it, you would have thought that we hadn't eaten in days.

The food was delicious. The conversation was engaging. The atmosphere was perfect. Yep. Things in my life were taking a turn for the better. In the words of one of my favorite childhood poets, Henry Wadsworth Longfellow, all was well with the world.

Chapter Nineteen

Daphne

All my life I had to fight. I had to go above and beyond the ordinary to get the things that I wanted. I saw Darvin no differently.

It had been four weeks since my run-in with Michelle. But not one to be defeated, I got very active in the church as I said I would, and had been layering the icing on very thick ever since then. Each Sunday Darvin preached, I fell out in the spirit. I spoke in tongues. I shouted amen louder than anyone in the church. I sent emails to his personal email address almost every day, encouraging him to keep preaching, telling him that his sermons were changing my very life. Oh, yes, I was the perfect member—soon to be the first lady. And I was hoping that it was getting harder for him to see the monster I'm sure Michelle had made me out to be.

This past Sunday, I'd walked up to him and placed in his hands an envelope containing a love gift of twenty-five hundred dollars in cash. I knew there were some heavy hitters in the church, but none of them were dropping that kind of money in the love offering. I told him his sermon blessed me so much that God had spoken to me and instructed me to sow a seed into his life. After all, you reap what you sow, right?

His eyes had gotten large, and you couldn't have missed the smile on his face if all the lights were turned out. I knew from being on the inside as Michelle's armor bearer that pastors loved their love gifts. I couldn't have asked for a better plan than to have the opportunity to be as close to Michelle as

"Daphne" in order to find out what Darvin liked and didn't like. Therefore, I was able to trump all of the other women who had taken a liking to him. They had no clue as to who he really was. He was a man who liked his ego stroked as much as any other man; however, not in the usual way. He loved it when people spoke words of affirmation and expressed their love through gifts. Those were just his love languages, and I knew how to speak them. However, as "Daphne," my financial luxuries had failed to compare to what they were now.

It seemed that since my first investment had yielded my unbelievable dividends, I was on a streak of luck. In addition to my already lucrative portfolio, God had afforded me to be even more successful in my newest ventures—trading and selling stock market shares, as well as buying and flipping houses in the real estate business. I wasn't hurting for money in no sense of the term, and giving money and gifts to my future husband wasn't a loss; it was an investment.

Michelle had turned all kinds of shades of blue when I put the money into his hands. She was probably aware of the fact that it was another part of an ultimate plan, but I didn't care one single iota. Any time I had the chance to make her squirm, I would. And any time I had the opportunity to let my little light shine, then shine it would.

However, I must admit that Michelle's persistence was beginning to wear me out. The goal was to claim Darvin, but it would be a lot easier if I could just get her to snap and walk away on her own. The stress on her face that I was accustomed to seeing had been replaced with a look of peace. That could only mean one thing: It was time to shift the plan in another gear.

I knew that Darvin secretly desired a gray, two-door Bentley Continental GT. I happened to be at the church one night for women's meeting, and when I got up to go to the bathroom, I walked by the choir room and overheard him talking about it with the minister of music. Darvin told him that whenever he was ordained bishop, he would get one. I also heard him mention that some church in Baltimore had lost their pastor, and that it was a possibility that he might have to go there and fill in.

A smiled had crossed my face. I didn't know how to go about getting him ordained as bishop, nor did I know much about the church in Maryland, but his dream of owning a Bentley would soon be a reality. Church members did it all the time—bought their pastors and bishops expensive cars. To the man of God it was a gift; to the purchaser, it was nothing more than a tax write-off.

I'd done some investing for the owner of the Bentley dealership in Roswell that proved to be insanely lucrative, and even after getting my share, he still owed me a favor. He was involved in some dealings that I happened to find out, and let's just say that the price was high enough for me to keep my mouth shut. I would simply have to go down there, cash in my favor, give him about fifty-thousand dollars, and arrange to have it delivered on Sunday as a surprise for Darvin on his pastor's anniversary. I'd already planned to have the name plate read BISHOP.

I made the necessary call to have the owner meet me for lunch to discuss the particulars. This Sunday was going to separate the women from the little girls. While most of the single women—some married—were going to be bringing all sorts of gifts and alms, I was assured that nobody was having a Bentley delivered. Once I completed the purchase for the car, I would call the coordinator of the pastor's anniversary and make arrangements to have a place to speak on the program. I would have to be dressed to kill—only Michelle, of course—and my walk to the front of the church would have to be even more tantalizing. This would be one Sunday when I would not argue with the usher about being seated in the back.

I was becoming so excited about the upcoming Sunday that I picked up my Bible. I didn't know where the scripture was found, but I did know that somewhere in there was a scripture that said, "Oh, give thanks unto the Lord, for He is good." And good He was.

Chapter Twenty

Daphne

Getting dressed for the pastor's anniversary program was almost torture. I couldn't seem to get anything right. I didn't know why I was so nervous. Maybe it was because I knew that today would put me several steps closer to having my man. I couldn't believe that my plan was working this well, even with the minor distractions I'd experienced along the way.

The first thing that showed the condition of my mind was when I stepped into the shower and had forgotten to turn on the hot water. The cold water, along with the cool atmosphere, froze every particle of water into its place on my body.

After I recovered from shock and got dressed, I tried to figure out why my legs didn't fit into my pantyhose. After failing to succeed more than three times, I fell back on the bed in frustration. While it was my plan to make a late appearance, I didn't want to be too late.

I sat up, tucked my frustration back in, and tried once more to put on the pantyhose. This time I tried with more deliberate moves. I realized that I had been trying to put two legs into one hole. As petite as my body was, it wasn't petite enough to put two legs into a space that was only meant for one.

Laughing at myself, I put on my shoes and went to the body-length mirror to take one last look.

Dressed in a black-and-gold Donna Vinci suit that had rhinestones that ran along the edges of a deep-cut collar and along the hem of the skirt, I looked like a million bucks. I had barely eaten anything all week so that the suit would cling to my body in all the right places. The black-and-gold Michael Antonio shoes that I'd bought a few years back were the perfect ending to a perfect story. My hair stylist had blended some tracks into my short hair, and the soft curls that she'd made fell gracefully down my back. My makeup had been applied with the skill of a professional, and if there were such a thing as being flawless, I was the epitome of it.

The drive to church took longer than any other day I'd driven those same fifteen miles. Beads of sweat had totally consumed the palms of my hands, and even with it being the middle of the fall season, I had the air conditioning blowing generously in my face.

I pulled into the overflow parking lot because the main lot was already full. I concluded that it was too far to walk, and decided to drive to the main lot to find a parking attendant who would be kind enough to park for me.

When I'd first come into town as Dawn, the members of Mount Zion were hesitant to accept me. It had taken some time, but my recent involvement with them and the different ministries for which I volunteered had garnered me some respect among many of them. I worked tirelessly on my teams—always attempting to go the extra mile. After all, I had to do whatever was necessary so that when it was my time to become first lady, no one would have a problem with it.

The parking attendant took my keys and drove away in my car. I walked inside of the church and could hear the guest psalmist, who had been brought in for the special day, bellowing out harmonious notes. I pushed on the sanctuary's door a little so the usher would know that I was waiting to get in.

He opened the door. It was just my luck that I got the same rude usher every single time.

"Ms. Carlton, there are no more seats in the front. You will have to sit in the back," he said sternly.

I smiled and simply said, "No problem, Brother Charlie."

He led me to a seat in the next to the last row. I gracefully sat down and waited for the presentations to begin. I had not planned on listening to the sermon, but was focused on my well-prepared speech. It was sure to rock the house.

However, the guest pastor, Pastor Stanley Promise, was intriguing enough. He was so fine that if Darvin had not been the love of my life, I would have tried to see what I could find out about him. His wedding ring glistened under the stage lights, but that had never meant anything to me—at least not after my first encounter with one in college. I was low in money, and unlike my friends who had parents with money, I had nothing. I was a broke accounting major on the verge of being kicked out of my dorm when my friend, who was trying to help me get a job, introduced me to the manager of T.G.I. Friday's.

Dawson Phillips was one of the finest men I'd ever seen. He was nothing like those college boys I saw every day. He was a man. A real man with biceps and triceps that would cause any woman to fall weak. He was the man that held the answers to all of my problems.

After a brief conversation with him that day, he hired me on the spot. I knew he was attracted to me, as I was to him, so a couple of weeks later, I found myself in his bed, and was there every opportunity I got. That didn't give me a good reputation among the girls on campus (including my friend). Matter of fact, they labeled me a home wrecker. But I couldn't care less. He took care of me, made sure I didn't want for anything—until his job transferred him to another area.

From there, it was one married man after another. Married men were much more fun than single men. Married men always gave the very best of themselves, and took the worst of themselves back home to the wife to deal with. But I wanted my own man now. And while some people say you reap what you sow, it would be different for me, because I planned to be the best wife I could be—leaving no reason for my husband to seek out another woman.

I glanced toward the stage to the section where Darvin sat along with Michelle, the assistants, and other guests. There was a woman sitting next to Michelle who was no doubt this pastor's wife, and she was almost as sharp as me. I wanted to meet her . . . one first lady to another. I could learn a thing or two from her. I wondered if Michelle personally knew this woman. She seemed too exquisite to associate herself with a simple woman such as Michelle.

Pastor Promise's message was on point for me. His topic was, "Don't Let Nobody Turn You Around." He went on to preach about how you must be determined to go after what God has set aside for you, in spite of people who may try to get in your way. And he was more than right. That's why Twylah had to die. Michelle was the last person hindering me—and had been—since God had first told me that Darvin was supposed to be my husband.

The pastor said that sometimes you had to be persistent so you could let the devil know that you meant business.

"Amen," I hollered, because the devil sure was standing in my way. In a big, eight-month pregnant way.

When the sermon ended and the invitation had been given, I started feeling that nervousness again. It was almost time to make my presentation. I had purposely asked that the coordinator place me last on the program. I wanted everyone to give all of their little gifts, so just when everyone thought the gift-giving was over, I would stand and present Darvin with something that nobody had ever given him before.

I listened to all of the presentations. Monetary gifts. Cruises. All expense paid vacations. Gift cards. On and on and on. It wasn't until presentations started being made specifically for Michelle that I realized I had not even thought about her.

Oh, well. It was the pastor's anniversary, and she wasn't the pastor. Besides, I didn't care enough about her to spend one penny on her.

Finally, I heard the announcer call my name. I sat still for a moment, making my appearance even more dramatic, then stood and walked down the center aisle in complete runway fashion. I could feel the stares bouncing off every inch of my body. I smiled at the apparent attention I was getting. I couldn't have imagined this moment to be any better. I went to the stage, took my place behind the podium, and picked up the microphone.

"First giving honor to God, who's the head of my life. I give honor to my pastor, our first lady, the deacons, the deaconesses, all of the leaders of the church, and to everyone who makes us this beautiful sea of flowers in God's sight. Church, we serve an awesome God!" I said in typical church fashion, and waited for the applause of the audience to die down before I continued. "Today is a special day as we celebrate our pastor's anniversary. And though we should celebrate him each and every day, this is the day that we have set aside to honor him. And his wife," I said as I looked over at Michelle for good measure, because nothing else I said would have anything to do with her.

"So, I prayed and I asked God what He would have me do for my man of God. Amazingly, God did speak to me, and He gave me clear instructions. You see, God gave me special insight to be able to know what the desire of my pastor's heart was. He allowed me the ability to see those secret things that nobody knew about; those things that had not been spoken."

I looked over in Darvin's direction and could see that he was totally taken aback. The expression on his face showed a perfect mix of confusion and anticipation. On the other hand, Michelle's appearance was too complex to describe. It was a mixture of anger, disgust, and ugliness.

"So, today, I stand before all of you, humble, yet grateful for the ability to present to my pastor—a man who I've watched, who gives so much of himself, yet receives so little; a man who lives the life that he preaches, and walks the walk that he talks." I paused for a second. The crowd had begun to clap once again. I shifted my gaze to Darvin. "The man who forgave the sins of my sister and demonstrated the love of God by accepting me into his flock. The man who has made the biggest impact in my life with the sermons that he preaches—life-changing sermons, at that. Can I get a witness, church?" The church chimed in their agreements.

"So, as a symbol of my gratitude, and as a token of my love, I would ask that the church stand with me today and give honor to our chosen vessel, as I present to him the keys to a 2007 Bentley Continental GT coupe."

Before I could get anything else out of my mouth, the church was blanketed with oohs and ahhs, whistles, and cheers. I grinned like a schoolgirl, loving every second of it.

Darvin's shock was worth every dime I'd spent. The stare that Darvin gave me was one that I knew would tie our souls together. Forever. It was as if no one else was in the room but us.

Finally, the crowd settled down. "Just to give you an idea of the exquisiteness of this car, I would like to provide you a few details. The Bentley Continental GT coupe is unlike any sports car on the road. In case you're wondering what that means, it simply means that it's a real nice car."

That statement garnered light chuckles from the audience.

"The last thing I want to say to Pastor is, I don't know where God is going to take you in your life, but I'm sure I have some people here who would agree with me in saying that the office of bishop is somewhere in your future." The hand claps came again. Some even stood. Boy, did this feel good. "So, I took the liberty of prophetically having your nameplate ordered with the title BISHOP on it."

Every person, minus Michelle and the guest pastor's wife, was standing on their feet. I smiled as I looked around at the same congregation who'd turned me away as Daphne, but today was embracing me as Dawn. My eyes focused back on Darvin as I tried to will my shaking legs to move and take him the keys. Thankfully, Darvin was headed toward me and I didn't have to move.

He walked up to me, gave me a hug, and whispered in my ear, "Thank you so much. I will never in my life forget this day."

I smiled, all the while looking in the eyes of a very angry Michelle. She could have spit fire at me and drowned me in hell's flames. It's been proven that a certain percentage of all human language was non-verbal, so she and I underwent an eye argument briefly, with my last statement being, "Top that!"

Darvin took his place at the podium after the announcer said no more presentations were listed and that his new car was parked out in front of the church. I had to ask her to announce that because when Darvin put his arms around me, all rationale, all five of my senses, and my brain quit working.

"Church, I feel overwhelmed. I'm elated today that you all have shown so much love to me and my wife. I feel as if I'm not worthy to receive such honor, but I certainly am not turning any of it down," he said between a laugh. "I must say that I'm astonished by the last presentation. Now, I know that Mount Zion takes care of me very well, but, Ms. Carlton, if you only paid the down payment for this car, then Mount Zion is going to have to give me a raise so I can afford the payments." More laughter followed his comment.

I took this as an opportunity to turn around and respond before finishing my walk back to my seat. "No, Pastor." One of the ministers brought a microphone to where I was standing. "Silly me, I failed to mention that I have the title right here in my hand. It's yours . . . no money owed."

I was definitely going to get accustomed to the adoration by the church, because once again people were on their feet, clapping for me. I continued to walk to my seat as some people stopped me for a hug or to shake my hand.

Wow. If presenting the pastor with a Bentley awarded me this much attention, I wondered what they would say when I wrote out that big check to cover a large portion of the expenses to build the new Family Life Center.

"Ms. Carlton, I want you to know that I will cherish this gift for the rest of my life, and I do thank you for being so generous. Church, she was right. It has been a desire of my heart to own a Bentley, and I'm grateful that God has sent somebody to fulfill that desire. Touch your neighbor and tell your neighbor, 'Don't hate on Pastor.' " The church did as he asked. "Touch your other neighbor and tell them, 'Don't hate on Ms. Carlton.' " Once again the church responded accordingly.

My heart was about to explode from the joy I felt.

Instead of walking back to my seat, I walked right out of the door. My work was done. I wanted Darvin to enjoy his day free of any drama, other than what I had surely caused.

After making my way to the foyer, I turned around when I heard someone call my name.

"Daphne?" a male voice called.

Before I thought any better, I had already turned around.

"Yes?"

Standing a few feet away from me in the corner next to the church's bookstore was a tall, handsome man that I remembered seeing at church once before.

I put on my million-dollar smile, trying to mask the nervousness I felt.

He called me Daphne. Worse than that, I acknowledged it. I tried to dismiss the feeling; it was probably an honest mistake. After all, people thought we were twins. Besides, I was sure he must have wanted to talk to me about my high-dollar presentation.

I seductively walked over to his direction. Sure, Darvin was my goal, but I didn't have to stop flirting until I was officially Mrs. Darvin Johnson.

The man eased out into better view. The look on his face was anything but pleasant, and for some reason, my heart began racing along with the fluttering in my stomach. It was at that moment that I realized that this man could possibly know who I was. It was a chance that he knew the real me.

"So, you are Daphne Carlton? And Dawn Carlton . . ." He shook his head in disgust. "Well, well, well. You don't look so tough now. Matter of fact, you look downright scared." He moved closer to me. He was extremely intimidating, even for someone like me.

"Um, I answered to Daphne because I always do," I answered nervously.

"She's my sister, and she and I get that all of the time." I made a gesture with my hand that waved away the notion I was indeed one in the same.

He caught my hand in mid-air with a choking grip. "Don't play with me, Daphne," he said in a deep, husky voice. "If you cooperate with me, no one will get hurt. If you don't, then I'm not responsible if Mount Zion's new prized member comes up missing."

Terror had to be showing in my eyes, because it was occupying every space in my body. "I . . . I don't understand. What do you want? Money?" I stammered.

"No, I don't need your money. I wouldn't want your filthy money if I was a homeless man living under a bridge downtown."

I squirmed until my hand was out of his grip. I was getting upset. What did he want? "Well, what can I do for you, Mister—oh, I'm sorry, you didn't tell me your name," I said sarcastically.

He dropped his head in laughter. "You are a sad, sad woman, Daphne Carlton," he said as his eyes bore into mine. "Who I am is your worst nightmare. Who I am is the only person in this church who could expose you for who you really are."

I laughed nervously. "Whatever. I don't have time for games. I don't know who you are, what you're talking about, or what you want with me." I started moving away from him.

"I wouldn't walk out of that door if I were you. Unless you want me to do to you what you did to my sister."

I stopped dead in my tracks. It couldn't be.

"You heard me. My sister. You want to know who I am?" the man asked as I heard footsteps coming toward me. "I'm Solomon Andrews, the brother of Twylah Andrews. Does the name ring a bell?"

I whirled around and glared at him. "What do you want?" I shouted in the lowest voice I could muster.

"I want to know why you killed my sister," he said, standing so close to my face I could smell his morning's breakfast.

"Your sister committed suicide. Everyone knows that." My voice was practically quivering and my stomach was beginning to be upset. Could he know the truth?

"No, I believe you killed her, and I'm determined to prove it. Now, if you try to get in my way, you and I are going to have a much bigger problem."

"Look, Mr. Andrews, I don't know what you're talking about. I did not kill your sister! Am I making myself clear?"

I was as scared of him as a cat is of a dog, but so angry I could have killed him, too. What evidence did he have, and what gave him the gall to threaten me with it?

"Hmph. It's sad that you're forcing me to go to this level with you, but before it's over, you will wish that you'd never crawled out of your slimy hole. But I will tell you this: If you try to do anything stupid, there will be another hole with your name on it. And it's right out there in Mount Zion's graveyard."

I refused to let a single tear roll down my face for fear of showing a sign of weakness.

One of the church deacons walked up to me. "Is everything all right over here?" he said, looking back and forth between me and Solomon.

I wanted so badly to scream no, but I said, "Yes, everything is fine." I shifted nervously on my feet, hoping that the answer would satisfy the deacon.

Hesitantly, he walked away, and in the same fashion, I turned around to face the man who had managed to make me sick in all but ten minutes. How I wished this were a dream.

"Solomon—"

He interrupted. "This is not a game. This is not a dream. I'm really here to make your life a living hell, as you've so pointedly done for others. The same way you killed my sister and watched the life drain out of her body, I'm not going to rest until the same is done to you."

This time, the tear escaped against my doing. How had the day turned for the worse?

Chapter Twenty-one

Michelle

If the Lord didn't help me, I just knew I would surely fall. My grandmother used to say that all the time, but it wasn't until today that I realized just what she'd meant.

Today was our pastor's anniversary celebration, and I can honestly say that if I could have made myself melt, I would have poured myself down a drain. Even though I was no veteran at this, I was accustomed to the day being about Darvin, and people looking at me, trying to figure out how to acknowledge me so I wouldn't feel out of place. But I was not used to the stunt pulled by Dawn Carlton.

The tramp had come up into my domain and had taken over. She, in a matter of minutes, had everyone in Mount Zion dancing to the beat of her music—including Darvin.

Delisa, my girl from the group, had been there as a special guest with her husband, Stanley Promise, who'd preached the celebratory message. If she had not been there to stop me, I would have suffocated the life out of Dawn.

Delisa had tried to tell me not to be upset about Dawn presenting Darvin with a Bentley, but I couldn't help it. I was so torn about how I felt about it, I couldn't even be happy for him. I knew he wanted a Bentley—had for some time—but I just didn't think that my new archenemy would be the one to give it to him. Dawn had done a few vague things, but never anything this vivid for me to dislike her.

After everyone had cooed their congratulations to Darvin on his new Bentley and had tried to subsidize their lack of interest in me with equally as nice comments, we were finally ready to leave. I wanted to go home, change into a relaxing outfit, and kick my heels up with a glass of sweet tea. I wasn't in the mood for the annual fellowship brunch that was held at Ray's on the River. I needed my space to be alone to think.

Delisa and Stanley greeted members and guests alongside Darvin and me, and were also ready to go.

"Why don't we let the guys head on home, and you and I can stop by the store and grab something to cook, instead of going out," I suggested.

She exchanged looks with Stanley and Darvin before turning back to me. "Girl, we are exhausted. After that service today, I'm too tired to cook. Let's just go on to the brunch. I'm sure you'll enjoy it."

I tried to bore a hole into her. She knew good and well that I was trying to avoid the brunch so I could be alone and digest everything that had happened. I just didn't feel up to smiling and trying to be excited when I really wasn't.

Once again, this was not my day. This was the day for Darvin to be honored, and most of the time, people had nothing to say about me, unless they were just trying to appease me. Even though my heart told me to be excited for him, my head ached. My body screamed for rest.

I turned to Darvin. "I'll tell you what. Why don't you go without me this time? I'm tired, and I just don't feel up to going."

Not hiding the disappointment in his eyes, he said, "But, baby, this is our day. We can't just not show up to our own brunch."

"You know I will go to the end of the Earth for you, but this is not my day. This is your day. And before you go into the 'we're one' speech, I already know that. But let's be honest. This celebration is more for your honor than mine, so if I go home, people will notice, but will in the same minute get over it."

His displeasure showed on his face. I hated to disappoint him, but I didn't want to be the one to spoil the party. If I went, my sourness would be contagious.

"Baby, please don't do this. This is a happy time for us. Let's just enjoy brunch, and tomorrow we'll rest and relax all day. Our congregation really wants to see us both there," he pleaded.

I looked from Darvin to Delisa to Stanley, and back to Darvin, trying to make up my mind. I scratched my head in several places before I said, "No. You go."

Delisa, obviously irritated, pulled me by the arm and over to the side, out of listening distance of the men. "Listen, you know I love you and you are my friend, but you have got to grow up. What happened to the woman who just last week at our meeting was so strong and ready to take on any giant?

"Do you remember how determined you were to be happy? We were all so proud of you because you deserved it. You've been through a lot, and to hear you get your motivation back was like music to our ears. Now, you're standing here telling me that you're going to allow a woman who bought your husband his dream car take away all that you've worked so hard to get?" She pulled me closer as if she didn't think I could already hear her. "She may have the money, but you have that man's heart. And money cannot buy love, Michelle. How many times have you heard that?"

She looked over to make sure that the men were not listening. And they weren't. They were looking through the glass doors at Darvin's new Bentley.

She continued. "Now, I'm going to need you to get it together, Miss Thing. You are not going out like this. You are a month away from delivering your baby, and trust me, no Bentley or any amount of money will ever be able to replace the happiness that you'll give him bringing his child into the world. So let her buy all of those expensive gifts. Let her continue putting thousands of dollars in his hands. Aren't you the one enjoying the benefits?"

It was more of a statement than a question. "All right, now wipe that smug look off of your face. Take one for the team and go to this brunch. Besides, girl, I'm hungry," she joked.

I pondered what she said. Delisa was right. I needed to pack my feelings back on the inside and take this like a woman. I didn't need to get even with this woman. I already had Darvin, and I was secure enough in our marriage to know that a Bentley wasn't enough to get his full attention. Or was it? I shifted my focus back over to Darvin. The expression of joy and pride on his face was unmistakable.

"Baby," Darvin called, "are you going?"

I looked one final time at Delisa. "Yes, sweetie."

He flashed me his smile of approval. "Good. I want you to be the first one to drive my new Bentley."

I was floored. "Darvin! You can't do that. I know you want to drive it."

"I'll have plenty of time to drive it. But I want you to be the first," he said. Afterward, he walked over to me and said, "And my last."

Lord have mercy. That man always knew what to say and when to say it.

Once inside the car, I realized I had another problem.

There was no way I would be able to fit comfortably behind the wheel of a two-seater sports car, especially not with thunder thighs and a bubble belly.

Chapter Twenty-two

Michelle

My doctor's appointment was today, and I could hardly wait.

Darvin's schedule did not permit him to go with me, and I was less than happy about it. Once again, I was going to try to find out the sex of the baby.

I navigated my Navigator into a parking space at the prestigious Buckhead medical facility. Another woman in a Range Rover pulled up beside me, retouched her makeup, and got out. Her pregnant stomach was almost as big as mine.

I'd only gained seventeen pounds so far, but I looked like a hot air balloon. I was carrying our son or daughter all in my stomach, and a little in my hips. I never knew how much being pregnant would stretch your body in places you didn't even know would stretch.

I wasn't exactly in shape when I found out I was pregnant, but I had been holding on to a size twelve for years. Now, I was a size fourteen, bordering along the lines of sixteen, and I had this puffy face that made me look even bigger.

Darvin didn't seem to mind my weight gain at all. He often took pictures of me and my pregnant belly, and would save them on his phone's screensaver.

So many nights we stayed up talking about the baby and how our lives would change. On the nights the baby was kicking and wouldn't settle down, he would sing lullabies. After a couple of songs, the baby and I would both be asleep.

A smile turned the corners of my mouth as I thought about those precious moments. I turned off the ignition, grabbed my purse, and proceeded toward the doctor's office. I touched my stomach and willed the baby to be in a position that would reveal its sex.

I walked through the door and saw Nancy, the appointment scheduler, sitting in her usual spot, greeting all of us mothers-to-be as we walked in.

"Hey, Mrs. Johnson," Nancy sang. "Aren't you looking nice today? That brown skirt and rust turtleneck with that blazer . . . girl, you know you working it." She snapped her fingers. Nancy always made me laugh with her "sister girl" attitude. She was as white as snow, but you couldn't tell by the way she acted.

"Thank you, Nancy."

"Are you excited about your visit today? Girl, you're almost there. What? Four more weeks?"

"Yes, very excited. And yes, four more weeks, and I'm counting them down."

She laughed. "That baby is so lucky to have a mother like you and a father like Mr. Johnson. Speaking of Mr. Johnson, where is the handsome fellow today?"

"He's out of town on a speaking engagement. He will be back later tonight."

"Well, hopefully, you'll find out the sex of that baby and have some good news for him."

"Hopefully so. I'm planning something big in the event that I find out today."

"Honey, you go, girl! Don't forget how you got that baby. So, don't be planning too much, honey child."

"I can't get pregnant anymore until after I have this one, so whatever happens tonight, I don't think I have too much to worry about," I said, laughing at her humor.

"Girl, I'm almost sixty years old. You know I ain't got all of my scruples.

The elevator quit going all the way to the top some time ago."

And she wasn't lying about that. "You are crazy."

I shared a little more small talk with Nancy before going to sit down. I sat for about another ten minutes before they called my name. I followed my nurse, Carla, to the back, and went into the cold exam room to undress and wait for Dr. Stenzel to come in.

Dr. Stenzel was an amazing doctor. In the early stages of my pregnancy, I stressed about everything. When we were in the heat of all of our turmoil, I'd experienced some bleeding due to stress, and Dr. Stenzel on many occasions allowed me to call her after hours. She was German, with years of experience in obstetrics and gynecology, and had bedside manners that made her one of the most sought after doctors in Buckhead. Her waiting list was almost two years long.

I got moved up in the list after meeting her at a luncheon. We sat at the same table and hit it off instantly. At the time, I didn't know I was pregnant, and had gone to her because I'd been experiencing pain in my lower abdomen.

The pain turned out to be the stretching of my uterus because I was six weeks pregnant.

That day seemed like ages ago. Now, as I sat here four weeks away from welcoming my baby into the world, the feeling was overwhelming. As usual, the tears began to flow down my face, while the reality of being a mother was pressing its way closer to the forefront. I didn't know if I was ready to be a mom, but I was definitely excited about it.

Dr. Stenzel came in. "Hey, Miss Lady. How are we doing today?"

"We're fine," I said, rubbing my stomach for like the millionth time that day.

"Good. I like to hear that. We're too close to turn around now," she joked.

"I know. Hopefully, today we will know more about this little one, so we can get better prepared."

"Let's get started then. You know the routine. Lay back and let's get this party started."

I lay back as Dr. Stenzel performed a routine check-up. She then reached for the cold gel that always left me covered in chill bumps. She applied it to my stomach and turned the ultrasound machine so that it would face me. I crossed my fingers, hoping that the baby would behave.

After a few moments passed by, she said, "You're going to have a feisty little fellow.

"I know," I said. Then it hit me. "What did you just say?" I asked with my eyes as big as quarters.

"I said you're going to have a feisty little fellow," she said again.

Huge, mountain-sized tears streamed down my face. "So, I'm having a boy?" I breathed.

"Yep. That little thing right there better be on a little boy." She laughed.

She pointed to the screen and showed me the evidence that identified my baby as a male.

"Wow. Darvin is going to be so happy," I bawled out between tears. "Oh my goodness, it really is a boy." The baby had his legs wide open today, as if to reward me for my patience.

Dr. Stenzel turned off the machine after printing the pictures. She wiped the gel from my stomach, wrote brief comments on my chart, and it was over.

"How are you doing? Are you getting plenty of rest and taking care of yourself?" she asked.

"It has been a rocky road for a while, but I'm doing well. I still have my days, but I think about my baby and I tell myself I have a reason to live."

Dr. Stenzel rubbed my arm. "And that's a very good reason." She stood up. "Remember what I said. Where there's a healthy mommy, there's a healthy—"

"Baby," I said, finishing the statement for her.

Dr. Stenzel laughed. "Do I say it that much?"

I joined her laughter. "Yes, ma'am."

"All right, Miss Mommy-to-be, you are ready to go. I'll see you back here in a couple of weeks."

"One last thing. Darvin and I had planned a trip to Los Angeles for next week. It's our last chance to get away before the baby comes. Do you think it will be okay for me to fly?"

She looked skeptically at me above her black-rimmed glasses. "Hmm, I don't know, Michelle. How long are you planning to stay out there?"

"Just three days. We wanted to leave on Thursday morning and return on Saturday evening."

She continued to stare at me, trying to make up her mind as to what her recommendation would be. "You will need to check with your airline to make certain they will allow you to fly in your eighth month. In my professional opinion, I guess it will be okay. But you have to stay off your feet. And you have to make sure that you're not under any stress. I don't want you to have to worry about you going into premature labor."

"Yes, ma'am," I said in a military fashion. "I promise to be extra careful. This is going to be our last getaway for a while, so I plan to relax and prepare myself mentally to come back and take on my new role as a mother."

She still looked a little unconvinced. "I guess that will be fine. Like I said, be careful. I really shouldn't be agreeing to this, but since the trip is next week and according to your exam today, you're not close to a natural delivery, I'm going to make an exception."

I reached up and hugged her. "Thanks. I really appreciate it. You're the best. And because you're the best, I'm going to let you deliver all of my babies." I grinned.

"Yeah, whatever. You just take care of yourself."

With that, she walked out. I got off of the table and put

my clothes back on. I had to hurry and get to the store so I could pick up the items I needed for tonight. I had the perfect idea to surprise Darvin with the sex of our baby.

Later that night, I poured the honey glaze over the fresh salmon I was preparing, checked my French-style green beans, and cut into my red potatoes to make sure they were done. I put the freshly squeezed lemonade into the refrigerator, dusted my hands on the cloth, took off my apron, and went to my bedroom to get the decorations.

Darvin was due home in about an hour. I had to make sure that dinner was ready and the decorations were set by the time he got there. Little Junior was active tonight, slightly slowing down my pace. I don't know why I didn't guess he was a boy, if only by the kickboxing and movements that he made. He was an active little fellow.

I took out the pink bows, pink ribbons, pink balloons, the pink place settings and tablecloth, and started putting them in their appropriate places. I was going to trick Darvin and make him think we were having a girl, and even bring out some pink strawberry ice cream. I began to laugh at my own crazy idea. I would bring it around to the truth with a T-shirt that I had airbrushed for him, that said JUNIOR'S DADDY.

If I knew Darvin, he would not get the hint and think that I was trying to appease him with the shirt because I knew how badly he wanted a son. So, in the event that didn't work, I was going to just come right out and say it.

The hour went by faster than I realized, and it was about to be show time. I looked at myself in the mirror and admired how pregnant I looked. I was in full bloom, and for whatever reason, I had never felt sexier. The soft purple suede dress was form-fitting and exposed my swollen stomach. The short bob that I was sporting framed my round face, and the amethyst and diamond jewels that Darvin had given me a few years back were glistening against the light and the color of my skin, creating an almost angelic appearance, if I must say so myself.

When I heard the sound of the garage door, I quickly went into the kitchen and stood next to the counter so that Darvin could see me as soon as he walked in.

He entered the house, and just as he was about to call my name to let me know that he was home, he saw me. He slowly removed his suit jacket, and in the same manner, set his briefcase on the floor.

"Baby, you look beautiful," he said. He allowed his eyes to roam the length of my body, and I, in turn, absorbed the attention.

"Thank you, sweetie," I said, walking to him. I reached up and put my arms around his neck. He put his arms around me and allowed his hands to rest just below my waist. "How was your trip?"

We pulled back from each other, and I picked up his coat that he had let fall to the floor. "It was good. You know how it is. Revivals are revivals. I must say, though, God did an awesome work these last few days." He paused.

"I wish you would consider going with me sometimes."

I didn't want to have this conversation right now. This topic always ended in an argument, and I was too elated to let that happen.

"Honey, I'm glad that things went well. And maybe after the baby's born, I'll consider traveling with you."

That seemed to be satisfying, because the smile returned to his face. I was about to burst with the news if we didn't get the night underway. I leaned in and gave him a long kiss.

"Mmmmmm . . . that's why I rush home, baby."

He inhaled the sweet-smelling aroma of the spices that filled the air, and started walking toward the dining room. We weren't like the traditional family who only used the dining room for special occasions. Anytime we were eating dinner at home, we ate in the dining room. We were our own special guests.

He gasped at all of the pink decorations. He turned to me for confirmation, and all I gave him was a smile. He rushed over to me, picked me up, and swirled me around—all 170-pounds of me.

"A girl? Wow. Baby, this is great. We are having a girl." He loosened his tie as he sat down in his chair. "I'm going to have another woman in my life."

"Hey, wait a minute. I don't know about all that," I teased. "It's only room for one queen in this castle."

I took the glass covers off of the dishes that held the food and served Darvin his portions. I then poured his lemonade, repeated the same thing for myself, and sat down to enjoy the meal. He blessed the food and jabbed his fork into a healthy piece of the salmon.

He continued smiling. "I can't believe it. A girl. It's so surreal now that we know the sex. It's like before we were talking about a person that didn't really exist, but now we can put a name to her. This is so exciting, baby."

I smiled and allowed him to ramble on and on about how great it was going to be to have a little girl in the house. It was all I could do to keep quiet.

I got up from the table, went and got the ice cream and T-shirt, and came back to present them to Darvin.

"Strawberry ice cream. You're so cute." He laughed. "Really cute." He picked up the T-shirt and just as I thought, he thought I was trying to placate him. "Junior's daddy, huh? So you got jokes?" He ate a spoonful of the sweet dessert.

"Darvin, it's not a joke. At least the T-shirt isn't. The rest is a joke."

"I don't understand. What do you mean the rest is a joke?"

I walked around to where he was sitting and leaned over

him with my arms dangling across his neck. I kissed his neck and said, "It's a boy."

It took a second for it to sink in with him. He removed my arms and led me around to sit on his lap.

"Are you serious? It's a boy?" The look in his eyes was mesmerizing as small puddles filled them.

I began to cry. "Yes. It's a boy. I wanted to trick you with all of this pink stuff," I said as I motioned to all of the decorations. "It's the truth, baby; you're going to be Junior's daddy."

"Are you sure? I mean, what if it's a mistake?"

I went into the kitchen to get my purse. I retrieved the photos that Dr. Stenzel had printed and brought them back into the dining room. I returned to my seat in his lap and pointed to his son's "package."

"You see that right there?" I asked.

Realizing what he was looking at, he said, "That's definitely a boy!"

He stared at the pictures for a second longer with pride all over his face.

I looked down into his eyes. "You are going to make a wonderful father, and I can't wait to begin this new phase of my life. With you."

He kissed me tenderly. I relaxed my body and allowed myself to absorb the moment. It was times like this when I realized that the love Darvin and I shared was real, and could weather any storm.

Chapter Twenty-three

Daphne

I sat in my living room twiddling my thumbs, trying to determine what I was going to do about what I'd just seen. I was coming home from a late meeting with one of my clients, and just before I turned into my driveway, I saw Michelle sitting in Darvin's lap, kissing him. She was as big as their house, and poor Darvin probably had a blood clot in his leg from all of that weight stopping his flow. Lord knows I would not be that huge when I got pregnant with his baby.

Why did it look like they were celebrating? It wasn't a special occasion that I could remember, and I couldn't think of anything else that could give them reason to make merry. I was fuming, to say the least. Ever since my encounter with Solomon Andrews, I'd been in a terrible mood. I had not seen him since, and if I ever saw him again, it would be too soon.

My intention was to find out who he was and have him dealt with. I couldn't afford for anybody to mess up my plan. I was too close to the finish line. But the pressing matter was trying to find out what Darvin and Michelle were celebrating. It was driving me crazy.

Listening to the clock tick the seconds away, I decided that the only way to find out what I wanted to know was to go directly to the source. I had been living across the street from them since I'd been back from Florida, and no one had yet to find out. Back in the day, everybody knew their neighbors, but now, everyone was so busy with their own lives that no one stopped to pay attention to who was living next door.

As for me, it also helped that I had a garage in the back of my house. It was meant for a boat, but I never used the side garage doors, so I parked in there. And since the houses in our subdivision were behind black iron gates, unless you saw some-one coming home at an exact time, there was no way to ever really know who lived where. I had never really intended for Darvin not to know I lived across the street, but I had never planned to tell him either.

Tonight, it was time to make a friendly introduction. Darvin and Michelle had left their gates open, enabling me to sneak a peek at what was going on in their house. I'd gotten out of my car and pretended to get mail out of the mailbox, but took the opportunity to get a full view of what was going on in their dining room. What I saw made my stomach turn; Michelle put-ting her oversized lips on my man was the most disgusting thing I'd ever seen. When I was her assistant, I hardly ever saw them kiss.

That was partially because of me. I was causing so much havoc in their life that they only shared arguments, not kisses. That's why I couldn't understand why Michelle wouldn't just go away.

I got up out of my thoughts and went into my bedroom to put on something attention grabbing before I went over there. I didn't have much time, because I was sure that they were going to close their gate soon. It had to be an oversight; they never left their gates open. I selected a low-cut black sweater that exposed a dangerous amount of cleavage, a pair of jeans, and a belt to go around my waist. I grabbed a pair of four-inch Nine West pumps and went back into the living room. I stood there trying to think of what excuse I was going to make up for going over there. I realized that I didn't have one. I only had the truth. I was going to shock the living daylights out of Michelle, and remind Darvin of how fabulous I was.

I grabbed my house keys from the coffee table and walked out of the front door. At the bottom of the driveway, I pushed the button on my remote that opened my own gates, checked for cars, and walked into the driveway of Darvin and Michelle. It had been a long time since I'd been in their house. At one point, I was welcomed in the same manner as Chanice and Twylah had been. That had changed.

I bounced up the steps to the front door and rang the doorbell. Silence.

I rang it a second time and waited, but no one came to the door. What could they be doing? I knew they were in there.

I rang it again. Still nothing.

This time, I walked down the steps to see if I could see anything through the dining room window. The lights were now out. I went back to the door and tried the bell again. And again. What in the world were they doing?

I looked at the intercom system on the wall, but I really didn't want them to know it was me until they saw me. They would never answer the door if they knew I was out there.

Maybe that was it. Maybe they saw me walking up and had decided not to answer. The thought of that made me livid. My plan wasn't working, and it looked as if I was not going to be able to do anything to disturb the happy home tonight.

I started walking back toward my house, and as soon as I got through the gates, they were closing behind me. Fuming, I whirled around, only to see Michelle standing in her doorway waving at me. If I had the strength of Iron Man, I would bend those gates, go up there, and choke her the same way I choked Twylah.

I could see that Michelle was not going to be easily moved. Nothing I'd done so far had worked. She wasn't fazed for long at my return as my twin sister.

Now, looking at her smiling made me so mad that I started trembling. She had known it was me the entire time.

And I was sure that meant she'd seen me coming.

I walked back into my house and slammed the door. Who knew what they were doing in there now? Images of Darvin and Michelle laughing and talking about me flashed through my mind. Were they over there making fun of me? Were they talking about how stupid I looked as I walked away? Or were they over there kissing again, now that they knew they couldn't be interrupted?

So many scenarios played on the turntable of my mind, and were spinning out of control.

I went to the refrigerator and grabbed a bottle of Evian. I needed to refresh my body, because the residue of resentment had filled me. I went into the bedroom and kicked off my shoes and flopped down on the bed. What was I going to do?

The doorbell rang.

I looked in the direction of the living room and decided that whoever it was would have to leave, because I had not invited anyone over. As a matter of fact, I never invited anyone over. The only person that had ever stepped foot into my house was Twylah, and she was dead now.

The doorbell rang again.

Oh, well, they would have to walk away the same way I had minutes ago. I cursed myself for not closing the gates behind me. I was in such a rage that I'd forgotten.

The doorbell rang back to back to back more than six times, so I decided to answer. Without looking, I flung open the door. The anger that had set up residence in me had been evicted by sheer joy, as I looked into the eyes of my future husband, Darvin.

"Dawn, may I come in?" he asked.

Startled by his arrival and more so by his desire to come in, I said, "Sure, Pastor. Who would turn their pastor away at the door?"

I moved aside to let him enter. I strung together multiple curse words in my head when I saw how dirty the living room was. I had not cleaned up in more than a week, and the last thing I needed was for Darvin to see me not being able to keep house. But it was too late. He had denied all possible rationale that had to be screaming at him, telling him not to enter a single woman's house alone. It wasn't a good look for a pastor.

"Dawn, I didn't come to stay long. I just wanted to talk to you for a few minutes," he said with concern in his voice.

"Okay," I said hesitantly. "Why don't we go into the keeping room? The living room is a little messy. Getting ready for work some mornings is a pain, and I go from room to room, leaving something behind in each one."

"This is your home. It's not my place to judge you or what your house looks like."

"Well, I would still prefer we move into the other room. I have the fireplace going. It's a little cool out tonight."

I tried not to run to the keeping room. Enthusiasm was overtaking me. Darvin was actually in my house with me. Alone.

Once there, I motioned for him to sit in a chair that was close to the fireplace. "So, Pastor, to what do I owe this visit?" I asked, all while grinning from ear to ear.

He dropped his head, looking as if he was carefully choosing his words. And then it was like a thought appeared to him—one that had been on his mind. "How long have you lived here?"

I stared at him. He was expressionless. Maybe I should tell the truth.

"Since moving to Atlanta."

"I see. Any particular reason you chose this neighborhood—or this house—so close to mine?"

To be near you, stupid. "I think that was a huge coincidence, Pastor." I tried to sound honest. "Look, I know what you're probably thinking. The truth is, I didn't tell you I lived here because I didn't want you to think I was trying to harass you as my sister did."

He looked at me with tiredness in his eyes. "Dawn, I don't know how to say this, but you're causing problems. Major problems."

I was taken aback by his forwardness. "I'm sorry. How am I doing that?"

Maybe I was making progress after all.

"Let's face it. We both know that you and Michelle never got off to a good start, and with you purchasing me a car, giving me countless dollars every Sunday, and living across the street . . . it's not helping the situation. At all. I know that you might be innocent in all of this, but showing up at my house tonight wasn't the best thing to do. I can't fight in your defense and ask Michelle to overlook the other, when you're coming to the one place she should be able to have privacy." He paused and leaned forward in his chair.

"I really value you as a member of the church, the same way in which I did your sister, but, Dawn, sometimes I guess I do have to question your motives, if any."

I raised my eyebrows, as if that were going to help me soak in everything that he'd just said. I cleared my throat before speaking. "I'm a little shocked, Pastor, that first of all you would think I have motives in giving you anything. Several members bless you on a weekly basis, and just because I have the finances to go above and beyond the average, I should be blamed for that? Secondly, I'm a little appalled at the notion that I'm to blame for the problems that you're having in your home. I don't mean to toot my own horn here, but, as much as I know that I have it going on, I don't know if I'm capable of interfering with your marriage."

Sweat was forming on my brow, and even though Darvin wasn't here for the reasons that I wished he was, I still didn't want him to see me looking like a melting pot. I reached for the remote that operated the fireplace and turned the flame down a little.

"I didn't say that you were the cause of my problems at home. I'm simply saying that if there were any, you're not helping it."

I laughed. So, there were some problems. Maybe my plan was working after all. I needed to make him more comfortable, to see what else I could find out.

"Pastor, I'm sorry for being rude. Can I offer you something to drink?"

"No, I really must be going. I just wanted to come over and ask if you would refrain from coming to my house. Michelle is beside herself now that she knows you live across the street."

Who cared if Michelle was anything? Certainly not me.

"Once again, I didn't tell you or First Lady because I knew how you felt about my sister. I didn't want you to think that I was spying on you or anything." I should have won an Oscar for this performance.

He was silent as he studied my face for any traces of lying. I sure hoped that he wasn't operating in the prophetic right about then, because he was sure to see that everything I'd just said was indeed a lie. A big one.

I continued. "I'm sorry for not saying anything before now. In hindsight, maybe I should have told you. That's why I came over there earlier. I saw your gates open when I went to the mailbox, and decided that it was long overdue that I introduced myself as your new neighbor, so to speak," I said, trying to make light of the situation.

Darvin's silence was making the atmosphere difficult to slice through, and it was making me nervous.

"I had no idea that we were neighbors. I don't know what I'm going to do about this," he said as he put his face in his hands.

I moved closer to the end of the couch that was directly facing his chair.

"Why do you have to do anything about it?" I asked in a soft voice.

He looked at me. Then he laughed. "Come on, now. How many times do I have to say it? Michelle isn't fond of you. You are a nemesis to her, and could you blame her? You are the sister to the woman who tried to destroy our lives," he said, sounding frustrated.

I honestly, for a very brief second, felt bad about all of the drama that I'd caused him. I never stopped to think about the stress that it might have been causing him. However, my thoughts of pity were just as quickly erased with a flashback of Michelle standing in her door, waving at me earlier.

"What do you suggest I do? Move out of my house so that your wife can be comfortable? Or would she like it better if I just moved out of the state altogether? Tell me, what do you want me to do?" I was heated now.

"I don't know what to tell you to do." He looked as if he was contemplating his options. "I'm not suggesting that there is any easy solution to this. I mean, Michelle is probably over there climbing the walls because I'm over here. I just didn't know what else to do."

"About what?" I said, hoping she really was climbing the walls.

He looked at me again with those piercing eyes. "This is really hard for me. I'm torn because you are a member of my church who has technically done nothing wrong. You've been nothing but nice to me, but at the same time, that's my wife over there. She has her own opinions about your motives. I don't know what to do to fix this." He stood up and moved directly in front of the fireplace. "I mean, I can't ask you to leave your home. I can't even ask you to leave the church, because then what type of pastor would I be?"

Exactly.

"Would you even consider asking me to do either of those things?" Time for a home run. "Do you not care about my soul, or me, in the least little bit?"

I forced tears to form in my eyes. Judging from the look on his face, not only had I scored a home run, I had knocked the ball way out of the field. I held my breath, waiting for him to answer.

"Of course I do. I'm your pastor. I care about all of my members."

Wrong answer.

"What about just as a person? Would you care about me as a person even if I wasn't a member of your church?"

"Yes, of course," he said as he walked back to the chair and sat down.

"However, I think the best thing to do here is to ask you to just stay back. Don't try to prove anything to me. Don't buy me any more gifts or give me any more money. If you want, I'll return the Bentley to you. And if you have an accounting of the monetary gifts, I'll give that back to."

With every word, my heart was breaking in half. I had to do something and quick. "I don't know what to say," I said and dropped my head. This time I allowed tears to flow; something I never did. I was sure it was going to get his attention. It worked.

"Please, don't cry," he said desperately. "You've got to understand the position that I'm in. I have no other choice. It's you or my marriage."

I cried harder. "Why is your marriage so fragile that you even have to make this decision?" I lashed back. "Pastor, you need a woman who can handle things like this and women like me. You can't have this conversation with every woman who poses a threat to your wife. If she was so sure of what the two of you have together, then why would she put you in this position? Why would it even matter?"

I could see the struggle in his eyes.

"I guess it's different when you're in her shoes. I don't really know what it feels like for her to have to deal with something like this."

"I don't know either," I said, "but I do know this: I know that if I were her, I would cherish what you and I had," I said with emphasis. "I know that I would never let anyone come between us, no matter what. I know that I would spend more time figuring out how to better our relationship than worrying about who's trying to tear it down. That's wasted energy that she could be spending on you." I moved closer to him.

"Pastor, I have never tried to disrespect you, First Lady, or anyone else. All I've ever wanted to do was show you that I love you. I knew it would be difficult, because I knew how hard it would be to live past what my sister did to you. But I kept trying. I never gave up on you." At that point, I allowed myself to completely break down. I cried uncontrollably. "I just don't know if I will ever be able to live here without being blamed for my sister's sin."

Even with my head down, I knew that Darvin was staring at me. I could feel his eyes wandering my body, trying to figure out his next words; something he'd been doing all night.

"I'm sorry," he said remorsefully.

I lifted my head. "Really? Hmph. Not as sorry as I am. I have tried my best to fit in. You know what, Pastor? I meant what I said at your anniversary. You have changed my life, even if it has been a short time. Your messages move me to my core, and I always leave better than when I came. I can't imagine what I was doing before I started attending Mount Zion. You have been such a wonderful influence to me, and to think that I might have to give that up really hurts."

I cried so hard, Darvin reached for tissues that I kept on the coffee table. He passed me a couple of them.

"Listen, you don't have to leave the church. I'll figure out a way to work this out," he said, stroking my arm.

Currents of electricity shot through my body faster than the speed of light. Every hormone related to desire was standing at full attention. I had waited so long for him to touch me in a loving, caring way, and had almost forgotten what I'd imagined it would feel like. It felt better than any daydream. I allowed myself to dissolve into his touch, and the burning sensation it caused traveled directly to my womanhood.

"Pastor,"—I touched his hand as it slid up my arm—"that's music to my ears. I could never leave your teachings. I don't think I would make it. I know God sent me to your ministry for a reason, and since I've been blessing you, He's been blessing me. Not only have I been blessing you, but I've been paying my tithes too. I've honestly seen God do some powerful things in my life since I started living by your messages."

He didn't even realize that my hand was still on his, so I felt compelled to continue the ego stroking. "Pastor, you are an awesome, awesome man, and don't you let anybody tell you anything different. I wouldn't care where you went; I would follow you. Literally. I would travel across the country if I had to, just to be under your leadership."

Tongue tied, he said, "That's very sweet of you. Thank you. Those words mean a lot to me."

"You sound surprised to hear them."

"Well, I don't hear it all that much. People walk up to me and tell me I preached a great sermon, but it's not often that people just lay it out the way you just did." He paused. "Or shout the way you do on Sundays." He smiled at me.

So he had noticed!

I saw him drifting into another place. He left a door open that I had to walk in. "Well, I'm sure First Lady tells you all the time."

He stared into space. "She used to. Lately, we've been through so much, I wonder if my sermons are really ministering to her anymore. She's been through so much being married to me. Even still, she has always been my biggest fan. I almost expect it out of her," he said, looking into my eyes. "It's just good to know that you're touching someone else's life. It helps me to know that my labor is not in vain."

I wanted to kiss him—the force of love was almost willing me to—but I shifted slightly, and the movement highlighted Darvin's hand on my arm, and he removed it.

"Your labor is not in vain. And anytime you need to hear or know that, you can always call on me. As a matter of fact, I hope that First Lady won't mind sharing the cheerleading section with me, because when she gets tired, I'll be right there to cheer you on," I said with more meaning than he knew.

"Thanks. While that is very flattering to me, I think it would be best if you lay a little low until I figure out how to handle this. I'm going to have a talk with Michelle again. I don't think this is anything that the three of us can't clear up. Maybe we can get together one night at the house and talk this out. I'm sure that Michelle just has apprehension because of what Daphne put us through. But I'll talk to her. We'll work this out," he said, getting up to leave.

I smiled at him. "That's a great idea," I said as I stood as well. We walked back through the kitchen to the living room. I slapped myself playfully in the forehead as if I'd forgotten something important. "Pastor, I know that you have to leave, but would you care for something to go? I have grape juice, water, sweet tea, and some apple juice, I think." He looked as if he thought I was trying to come up with something to get him to stay a little longer, so I had to divert my plan.

"On second thought, why don't I give you something to take to First Lady? I have an unopened box of brownie sundae cheesecake from the Cheesecake Factory," I said, smiling and eliminating any shred of doubt that he might have had concerning my intentions.

He looked toward the door, possibly knowing that if he didn't leave Michelle might think something was going on, but maybe out of some sort of obligation, he surmised that the least he could do was accept my offer.

"Oooh . . . that's her favorite. I'm sure she would love that," he said, walking back toward the kitchen behind me.

I smiled. "And what about you? What can I get for you?" If only he knew what I meant by that question.

"Nothing. I'm fine. I really do need to get going. We were sort of in the middle of something. We found out the sex of the baby tonight—it's a boy," he said proudly.

I almost tripped over my own two feet. I'm sure he could see the blood boiling in my veins. Why did he have to bring that up?

"That's fantastic." I tried to sound happy for him. It didn't work. "Okay. I'll grab the cheesecake and get you a grape juice to go. I heard it was your favorite."

I moved to get the items from the refrigerator.

"I think I'm going to run to my room and get a gift bag for First Lady," I said. As I turned around, I purposefully bumped into Darvin, sending grape juice flying all over the place and staining the white cotton T-shirt he was wearing. "Oh my goodness! I'm so sorry. I didn't mean to—"

"No apologies. It was just a mistake," he interrupted.

I hurried back to the kitchen with a smirk on my face, grabbed a dish cloth, ran some cold water on it, and tried to dab the juice from Darvin's shirt. The feel of his chest underneath the cloth was sending hot flashes to the most sensitive areas of my body. I could only imagine what it would feel like to run my hands across his chest. And if I had my way, my little impromptu plan to spill the juice and get him to stay a little longer would yield exactly that.

Darvin must have felt a little uncomfortable. "It's really okay. If you'll just get that bag, I'll be on my way." He took the cloth from my hand and dabbed at the stains.

"Do you want me to bring you another white T-shirt? I would hate for you to go home with grape juice all over yourself. If Michelle already has a problem with me, what will she think if you went home like this?" I asked as I pointed to his shirt. "How would you explain that?"

He looked at me, and I knew he had not thought about that. It wasn't like it was a big deal, but he knew it would be to Michelle. He looked down at his shirt and back to me. "Is the shirt exactly like this one?"

"Just like it. My brother left one the last time he was here," I lied. The truth was, I had been buying small items and keeping them at my house, because I already anticipated the day that he would spend the night with me. I had underwear in his size, socks, T-shirts, pants, shirts, and a couple of hats, some shaving cream, a razor, and other toiletries that an overnight male guest might need.

"Okay, well, I guess that would be a good idea."

I grinned. "All right, give me one second and I'll grab that and the bag."

I rushed to my room to grab the items. While in there, I refreshed my makeup and spritzed some perfume on my neck and behind my ears. I pushed my bra up to make my breasts perk up a little out of my sweater, took a book from the nightstand, and hit the side of the wall.

"Are you okay?" I heard Darvin ask from the living room.

"Not exactly," I said, sounding as if I were really hurt.

"What happened?" he yelled.

"I ran into my dresser trying to hurry back. I think I sprained my ankle," I said as loud as I could. The living room was close to the bedroom, but far enough so that you had to speak at a decent volume to be heard.

"Do you need any help?"

"Would you mind? I can't seem to move," I said.

Silence. Finally, I heard footsteps coming toward my bedroom. Darvin peeked around the corner as if the flames of hell would consume him if he walked any further. Seeing me on the floor, he said again, "Are you okay?"

I laughed. "Yes, Pastor, I'm fine. I might need you to help me get up."

Just as I said that, his cell phone buzzed.

"Excuse me one second. This is First Lady calling me."

I tried to smile, but Michelle really had bad timing. I was finally getting my way, and she was interfering.

"Hello?" he said. "Hey, baby. Yes, I know. I'm on the way back over to the house." Pause. "Yes. Well, in just a few minutes. Dawn fell, and I think she sprained her ankle. I'm going to help her off the floor and I'll be right home."

He paused. "Michelle, please. What do you want me to do, walk out and leave her on the floor?" he asked, patience sounding thin. "She fell trying to get something for you." He turned his back to me. "We will talk about this when I get home. What could I possibly be doing, especially across the street from my house?" He paused again. "Okay, like I said, we will talk about this when I get home," he whispered loudly.

He hung up the phone and turned back toward me with a half-crooked smile on his face. "Sorry about that. Let me just help you up so that I can be on my way."

He reached down and practically lifted me from the floor. I allowed myself to fall limp into his arms and enjoyed being carried by him to my bed, even if it was only three steps. He sat me down, kneeled to the floor, and examined my ankle.

"I think you'll be fine. I don't think you sprained it either. I've had many sprained ankles in my college football days, and yours doesn't look like one. Just wrap it up and you should be good to go."

The examination had ended too soon. That darn Michelle. "Thanks, Pastor. I really appreciate all of your help." I saw the T-shirt that I'd gotten for him lying on the corner of the bed. "Oh. Here's the shirt," I said as I leaned over to get it. "Do you still want to change?" Seeing a little hesitation cross his face, I said, "I couldn't help but overhear your conversation with First Lady, and I don't think I need to reiterate that you need to get out of that shirt before you head home."

He took the shirt from my hand. "You're right. I'll just

go in here and change and I'll be on my way." He walked out of the door, but came back almost immediately. "Do I need to lock up for you on my way out?"

I slowly stood on my ankle, not wanting to give away the fact that I had not the slightest pain anywhere in my body, including my ankle.

"I think I can get it," I said as I hopped to the door.

I pretended to stumble a little bit, and Darvin was at my side almost immediately.

"I really think you should get back into bed. If you follow me all the way back to the front door, I'm not so sure that you'll be able to get back in here without hurting yourself."

"That's sweet, Pastor, but I have to go back in there anyway. I have to clean up that grape juice that I knocked out of your hand, and besides that, I haven't eaten anything tonight. I am going to make a sandwich and then go to bed."

"If you say so. But let me help you at least get to the kitchen."

I locked arms with Darvin and hopped into the kitchen. The walk there put an image in my head of our future wedding day. One day we would lock arms and never have to part. And Lord, what a day it would be.

"I really hate to leave you like this, but I have to get home. I'm just going to change this shirt. Can I step back into your bedroom?"

You can get into my bed if you want, I wanted to say.

"Sure. And don't think anything of having to leave me. When you're single, you get accustomed to fending for yourself. And I've been single for quite some time now," I said as I smirked. I wasn't single by choice. I was waiting on him.

"You'll meet someone. Just give it time. Your knight in shining armor will appear and you'll forget about all of your lonely days and nights," he said and disappeared.

I grabbed the cloth just as the doorbell rang. I glanced toward the door.

For the second time tonight, I had a visitor. And since Darvin was here, this other person was not welcome. I wanted to savor what few minutes I had left with him without being disturbed.

I set down the cloth. The doorbell rang again. I was getting pissed. No one ever came to see me. No one knew where I lived. I hurried past the entranceway to my bedroom. I didn't want Darvin to see that I was practically running, but I wanted to get rid of whoever it was so that I could get back to spending time with my man.

I flung the door open without looking again, and for the second time that night, I was speechless.

"Where is my husband?" Michelle demanded to know as she pushed her way past me and into the house. She had fury in her eyes that suggested that everything in her path would be destroyed if put in her way.

However, she had yet again underestimated me. No real scandalous diva, would allow such a prized moment to escape. "He's in my bedroom . . . changing," I said, as I walked toward my kitchen.

"Changing what?" Michelle asked.

"His clothes," I said with no emotion.

"Since when does my husband have clothes at your house?" She paused for a second as if a light bulb came on. "What is going on between you and my husband?"

I gently laughed at Michelle's incredulous accusation. She was really sad.

"Why don't you ask him what's going on? I'm not married to you; therefore, I owe you no explanation."

Michelle pursed her lips together into a thin line. "You're right. Where is he?"

"Again, he's in my bedroom," I said, smiling. The night was turning out better than I could have ever planned.

Michelle's mouth flew open. Her worst nightmare was

coming true. She thought her husband was cheating on her with her sworn enemy.

At that moment, Darvin came out of the back, tucking in his shirt and saying, "Thanks for the shirt. I don't know how I would have gone home with the other shirt on. Michelle would have killed me."

It was then that he saw her.

"I'm not going to kill you. It would do you a favor. I'm going to leave you, Darvin," she said just above a whisper. "I've had enough."

"Michelle . . ."

She threw her hands up. "Please, don't try to explain, because I don't care to hear another explanation. I'm tired of your explanations. I'm tired of having to always understand your explanations. I'm tired all the way around. It's over, Darvin," she said as she turned to walk out of the door.

He ran after her, took her by the arm, and swung her back around. "You don't mean that. I was just—"

Darvin was once again interrupted.

"I do mean it. I'm so, so tired," she said through tears. "I'm tired in my spirit." She made her point by pointing to a place on her chest as if it held the treasure of her soul. "I can't take it another day." She took her hand and ran it down his face. "I've tried, and I've concluded that I'm not cut out for this. My expectations, my needs—everything—are so different from what's needed to be your wife, or the wife of any pastor. So, I bow out. I bow out gracefully." She gazed at me, and then, in the same manner in which she spoke, she walked out of the door. Darvin stood watching her walk away.

I released a breath that I'd been holding in as I witnessed the moment that I'd been waiting for take place in my living room. My job had been done.

Michelle had released Darvin, and now he was free to be mine. The feeling I felt was nothing short of amazing. She had handed him over to me right in my own house. I couldn't believe it. She must have really been fed up to give me that satisfaction.

"Um, Pastor, I'm so sorry about what just happened. I don't know what to say."

He continued to stare at the door. "It's not your fault. It's mine. I should have never come over here. I shouldn't have done a lot of things."

He slowly turned the knob and walked out of the door, this time leaving me standing and staring.

It was a bittersweet victory. Darvin appeared to be genuinely hurt. His marriage was ending; I guess I would have reacted the same way. It would take some time to get over, but he would. And I would help him. I would be there with him every step of the way.

I walked back to my bedroom and whispered a prayer of thanks to God; for once again, He had come through for me. My mother used to always tell me that God made His sun to shine on the evil and on the good, and sent rain on the just as well as the unjust. Her words had proven to be true.

With that thought, my mind wandered to my mother. It had been a while since I'd spoken to her. I grabbed my cell phone from the nightstand and punched in her number.

The phone rang three times before she picked up.

"Hello?"

"Mom? Is that you?" I asked.

"Daphne? Baby, are you all right?" Pause. "It's pretty late."

I smiled. My mother called it late a minute after the sun went down.

"I know, Mom. I just called to check on you. I wanted to hear your voice," I said, holding back tears. I missed her, and I could imagine her smile.

"How you faring up there, baby?

You taking care of yourself? You ain't in no trouble, are you?"

Why did she have to go there?

"Ma, contrary to your belief, I'm not a troublemaker," I said, clearly irritated.

"I know you ain't, Daphne. It's just that you left here so suddenly and against my wishes. I didn't think you were ready to go back around those people."

"Well, turns out you were wrong. Turns out that I'm about to get married," I said, exhilaration returning.

"Married? Daphne Carlton, are you telling me the truth? You fixin' to be married?"

"Yes, ma'am!"

Maybe Darvin hadn't proposed yet, but now that Michelle was out of the picture, it would be any day now.

"Oh my goodness!" she said enthusiastically. "To who?"

"Pastor Darvin Johnson," I stated proudly.

Silence.

"Mom, you there?"

"I'm here. Daphne, what have you done?"

What! Did she not just hear me? Why couldn't she just be happy for me, instead of always criticizing?

"I don't have time for this. I was expecting a different reaction from my mother, but you never have been able to understand me. You never did want to see me happy," I accused.

"Now, you know that ain't true. I've wanted nothing but the best for you, child. But I ain't never wanted to see you destroy somebody else's life trying to get it. You were told to stay away from that man and his wife, and you promised me that you would. I don't want to see you end up in jail this time."

"Well, I lied. I had to follow my heart," I said bitterly.

"Don't let your heart lead you to hell, Daphne. You will reap what you sow."

With that, I hung up the phone.

I didn't want to hear another word.

Tonight, God had answered my prayers, so if my heart was leading me to hell, then to hell I was going.

Chapter Twenty-four

Michelle

The tears stung my eyes as I struggled to pack as much of my belongings into my suitcase as I could. The pain and anguish that I felt tore at my heart, and stabs of hurt pierced my body. As I placed each piece of clothing into my bag, I felt as if I were putting my marriage in there one day at a time. Memories of the good times that Darvin and I had made the tears fall harder.

I didn't understand how he could throw it all away for someone like Dawn. Was it because she was attractive? Financially successful? Was it because she was able to offer him so many more things than I could? Somehow, I had honestly believed that what I gave him was enough.

I laughed because it was almost funny how Dawn had come in and finished what Daphne had started. Daphne had not been successful in destroying us, and after she left, Darvin and I had become closer than we had ever been in our marriage. Dawn, on the other hand, had appeared, and had almost perfectly devised a better plan to obliterate my life. She had done it. I was done. It was over.

Trying to grasp that thought was difficult. So much of my life was intertwined with Darvin's, and trying to erase him out of it as if he were never there would be difficult. My head started hurting, and I tried ignoring the sharp pains that I was feeling in my stomach. The baby. What were we going to do about the baby? How would we raise our son?

I swirled my head in circles, in hopes of ridding myself of the headache and the reality of what was happening. And what about the church? What would we tell them? I thought about the members of Mount Zion and how I would miss them. They had become so close to me, and I to them. Life without them would be hard, even if they sometimes got on my nerves.

I thought about the many tender moments that Darvin and I had shared over the years. I thought about all of the things that we had survived together, endured together, and fought through together. I would never forget those things. I would never forget his touch, his scent, his smile, those mesmerizing eyes, the way he managed to make me laugh at just the right moments, the way he stared at me, admiring my beauty until I was uncomfortable; his protectiveness, the way we finished each other's sentences, the way he gently made love to me until he rocked me to sleep—I would miss him terribly.

I sat down on the side of the bed and allowed the screams that I'd been holding in escape. I cried until my body shook, and until I heard the sound of the bedroom door open.

"Michelle, are you okay?"

He had some kind of nerve. "What did you just ask me?"

"I know that's insensitive of me to ask and a tad bit re-dundant, but I don't know what else to say. You wouldn't let me explain."

I had no energy to argue. "There is nothing more to say. It's over. It's that simple." I stood up and continued to pack.

He walked toward me. "You don't have to leave. If this is what you want, then I'll leave. You're pregnant, and I don't want you trying to find anywhere to go."

I was sure going to miss that thoughtfulness too. Lord, how did we get here? "I'll be fine. I was making it just fine before I married you," I said sarcastically.

Defeated, he took the clothes that I was about to place in my bag from my hands. He then took the items that were in the suitcase and placed them back in their respective places.

"I won't let you go. Baby, I need you. I just can't allow you to give up on us," he cried. "You can't leave me. You won't leave me."

Anger rushed from my body like water from a faucet.

"You can't tell me what to do anymore! I am not your wife. And for the record, I didn't give up on us. You threw us away. So why don't you go across the street and tell Dawn what to do? Both of you deserve each other! You make me sick to even look at you. How could you throw away our life like this? How could you do this to us? Our family?" I broke down, and the sobbing started again.

He was at my side before I could blink. I allowed him to hold me for what might be the last time. I put my head in the crease of his arm and wept until I had no more power to weep. No one could have told me that we would end this way.

He allowed me to cry without saying anything. When I felt I had released everything that I needed to get out, I was tired and ready to go to sleep. Fatigue outran my rush to leave, and I decided to wait until the morning. No sense in not getting a good night's sleep on account of this drama.

Darvin tucked me into the bed and just as he did every night, kissed me goodnight, as well as the baby. I watched him walk out of the door.

When sleep overtook me, I had the same dream over and over again.

I dreamt that I was shooting Dawn.

Chapter Twenty-five

Michelle

    The morning came sooner than I wanted it to. I turned over on my side only to see a letter resting on Darvin's pillow. I rubbed the remnants of sleep from my eyes, grabbed the letter, and turned onto my back to read it.

> Dear Michelle,
>   I hope that you slept well last night, and I pray that you find it in your heart to read this letter in its entirety. I know you said that you didn't want an explanation of what happened last night, but I didn't want us to separate without you knowing that nothing ever happened between Dawn and me. I was in the back changing my shirt when you walked in because I'd wasted grape juice on the one I was wearing. Dawn convinced me that I needed to change so that I wouldn't further upset you. I know now that was a stupid mistake, and if I could take it back, I would.
>   I love you, Michelle, more than I love myself, and the last thing I want, is to be without you. So, I'm begging you, pleading with you—before you make a decision to leave me—just think about it. Think about us. Think about our son. Think about our life together. And if you decide to believe me, forgive me, and give me another chance, I promise to spend the rest of my life making you happy and putting your feelings first. No matter what.
>   I love you, and breakfast is waiting for you downstairs. I'm going to the office if you need me.
>
> Love,
> Your Husband

I held the letter to my chest and cried. As much as my head was telling me not to believe him, my heart confirmed that what was written was the truth.

However, the point was no longer about what had happened at Dawn's, but was about whether I could handle this life anymore; whether I was strong enough to handle being the first lady anymore.

My thoughts were interrupted by the trickle of water sliding down my leg. It took a moment for me to realize what was happening. When it finally set in, my body went into a myriad of emotions. Fear, joy, and excitement were all overtaking me. I was afraid to move for fear of doing something to the baby.

Wait a minute.

I wasn't due for another four weeks. I couldn't be going into labor. It wasn't time.

Panic zipped through my body. I reached for the cordless phone that was on the nightstand and dialed Dr. Stenzel on her private number.

"Hello?" Dr. Stenzel answered.

"Dr. Stenzel, this is Michelle Johnson," I said nervously. "I think I'm in labor."

"Okay, Michelle, I don't want you to panic. Just continue to breathe. Everything is going to be just fine. What happened that makes you think you're in labor?"

"My water broke."

"Okay, I want you to meet me at the hospital. How long ago did your water break?"

I didn't answer for a second because a labor pain was starting to form.

"It happened just before I called you," I finally managed to say.

"Hmmm . . . Is Darvin with you?"

"No. He's at the church."

"Well, you need to call him and have him rush home

immediately. I need you to get to the hospital as soon as possible, to see what's going on."

"Okay," I said, trying to control my fear.

Dr. Stenzel knew me all too well. She said, "I know you're scared, but I have no doubt that you are going to deliver a very healthy baby boy, who's going to be just fine. Now hang up and call Darvin so you can get to the hospital."

I hung up and immediately called Darvin.

"First Lady Johnson's office," Sabrina, my executive assistant, said.

"Goodness. Hi, Sabrina, this is First Lady. I'm sorry. I meant to call Ann. I'm trying to get in touch with Pastor. I didn't even try his cell because I remembered Ann telling me that he had a meeting this morning."

"Hey, First Lady! Yes, he's in a board meeting. Do you need me to get him?"

"Yes. Please tell him that it's an emergency," I said, trying to conceal my labor pains.

"Are you all right? Should I call Chanice?" Sabrina asked, almost out of breath.

"Sabrina, just get Pastor for me."

"Yes, ma'am. I'm going right now. Hold on one second," she said as she put me on hold.

I was holding for about two or three minutes before Darvin got to the phone.

"Hey, baby, are you okay? Sabrina said it was urgent. What's wrong? Did something happen?"

He was throwing so many questions at me I almost forgot why

I was calling. "I'm in labor. I need you to get home right away." The pains were now coming more frequently.

The phone went to a dial tone before I had a chance to say good-bye, and I whispered a little prayer for Darvin that he would make it home safe.

I got up and went to get dressed. Once in the closet, I chose a skirt set to wear, grabbed my flats, and walked to the kitchen to wait for Darvin. I looked in the coat closet next to the front door and grabbed my hospital bag that I'd packed when I first found out that I was pregnant. I had changed some things in it over the course of the pregnancy, but whatever was in there now would have to stay in there.

I heard the garage door opening and looked at my watch. Darvin had made it home in ten minutes flat. I grabbed the overnight bag and went to meet him at the door.

He rushed to me. "Baby, are you okay? How do you feel? Are you in any pain? Do I need to get anything for you?" he asked, out of breath.

I motioned for him to take the overnight bag from me as I went toward the passenger's side to get into the car.

After getting me settled in, he got into the driver's side. He squeezed my hand. "It's going to be all right, baby. And the baby is going to be just fine," he said.

He always had an uncanny way of reading my mind and deciphering my worries. Since my water had broken, I'd been petrified that the baby wouldn't make it. All of the horror stories about babies being born early—especially male babies before the 37th week—were wearing on me. I knew I needed to activate my faith, but it was so hard to do right now.

We made it to the hospital in twenty minutes flat, and by the time we arrived, tears had soaked my face. The pain was unbearable. I don't know who told me not to get an epidural, but it must have been a man, because no woman who'd ever experienced child birth could possibly tell me to go natural. The pain was so bad, my eyes were crossing.

Darvin jumped out, grabbed a wheelchair, and rolled me into the ER.

"Excuse me, ma'am, my wife is in labor and we need to see our doctor immediately," he said to the hospital worker.

"Okay, sir. Just fill out these forms and we'll get her back in just a few minutes," she said as she took a sip of whatever was in her cup.

"No. You'll see her now. Her doctor said that she would be waiting on her, and I want her to be taken back now. Those papers can wait," he said in a stern voice.

"Sir, there is protocol that must be followed. You have to sign her in, in order for us to treat her. So, if you would just do that, we can get her into the system quicker. I know that you're anxious to get her back and meet your new baby, but we have to follow the proper steps," she said, this time a little nicer.

Darvin snatched the clipboard from her hands and scribbled his John Doe on a few forms.

"There. Is this good enough? Can my wife now see her doctor?" he said impatiently.

"Who's her doctor, sir?" she asked as she rolled her eyes.

"Dr. Stenzel. Jacqueline Stenzel."

The attendant paged Dr. Stenzel and proceeded to take down all of my insurance information. Within minutes, Dr. Stenzel was coming through the big metal doors with a carefree look on her face. I was glad everybody else was calm, because my nerves were a mess.

"Darvin, Michelle, we have everything set up for you. I'm going to do an exam, and if the need be, perform an emergency C-section. By the expression on your face, you are already in labor. If you've dilated too much, you may have to have a normal delivery," she said in her medical tone.

I shook my head in agreement to whatever she wanted to do. I was not in any position to argue. I looked up at Darvin, who was trying desperately not to look worried.

Dr. Stenzel wheeled me through the doors and into a room that was as clean as the board of health. Everything was either white or chrome. Medical equipment flanked the large room, and the bright lights were almost blinding.

A team of people stood in place, ready to get started at the word of Dr. Stenzel. They helped me up onto the table, and Dr. Stenzel checked to see if I'd dilated too far for a C-section.

"You've only dilated two centimeters. I have a mind to stop the labor, but I don't think it would do much good. I think you would be back in here in the next couple of days." She looked at her team, and with a nod of her head, people started moving into place.

"The anesthesiologist will be here in just a few moments to administer meds to you. We're going to do a Caesarean. Do you have any questions?"

Not able to get my words out for fear of going into another crying spell similar to the one from last night, I shook my head no.

Once all of the prepping was completed, the actual C-section lasted a total of about ten minutes. They whisked the baby to a table that had a warming light above it, and began the suctioning and cleaning process. I watched and listened, waiting to hear him cry, or make any type of noise that said he was alive and well. But the deafening silence was the only thing that flooded the room.

Panic rose through my body. Was he alive? Oh God. My baby had to live, and he had to be all right. I tried to stop the tears from flowing, but the dam had broken. My little boy was over there fighting for his life, and there was nothing I could do about it.

I looked at Darvin only to see a look of uncertainty in his eyes. The giant that I had come to know had been reduced to a man who was standing powerless as he waited for his son to breathe his first breath.

My thoughts were interrupted by the nurse, who announced that they were rushing the baby to the special unit for infants.

"Dr. Stenzel, what's going on? Why are they taking our baby?" Darvin said in a panic.

"Calm down. Everything will be fine," she said.

I heard the words that came out of her mouth, but the story she told with her eyes was different. She, too, looked afraid.

"Will he be okay?" Darvin asked with a shaky voice.

"I'll be honest. I believe that everything will be just fine, but it's going to be touch and go. We have to hold on to our faith, pray, and believe the Word of God."

Dr. Stenzel finished working on me, and left to check on the baby. Darvin moved closer to me and grabbed my hand.

"Sweetie, don't worry. The baby is going to pull through this. We've fought through too much and prayed too hard for this baby not to make it. Let's touch and agree right now."

As Darvin prayed, I journeyed into a place deep within my soul to find that peace that surpassed all of our understanding. I needed God to hear my plea and pity my every groan. We needed a miracle. All I had to hold onto was the faith that had been instilled into me as a child. I could hear my grandmother's words: "Baby, when you can't count on nobody else, you can always count on the Lord. Even when the way seems dark and dreary, He'll be the light that brightens your path."

The thought of her words gave me small comfort. I knew that this was out of my control. I knew that the only option I had was to put everything—my fear, my doubt, and my troubles—in God's hands. He saw this day before it ever came, and if I was the woman of God I said I was, I had to learn how to lean not to my own understanding.

We were in the recovery room for what seemed like days before Dr. Stenzel or anyone came to update us on the status of our baby. Every time I started drifting off to sleep, my eyes would pop back open for fear of missing something.

I was in a little pain, and the anesthesia was threatening to overtake me. On the other hand, I would not rest until I knew my baby was okay.

Finally, Dr. Stenzel came in. "How are we doing?"

Darvin and I simultaneously said, "We're fine."

"Well, I have some good news and some bad news," Dr. Stenzel said. My heart sank. How can you have both good and bad news at the same time in a situation like this? "The good news is that your son is going to be just fine."

Darvin let out a sigh of relief, but I kept my eyes fixed on Dr. Stenzel because I wanted to hear the bad news before I let go of my breath. She continued. "The bad news is that he's going to have to remain in the hospital for at least a week or two for monitoring, unless he shows crucial improvements before then. His lungs are a little undeveloped, and he needs to gain some more weight."

"Is that it?" I asked, wondering if that was all the bad news.

"That's it," she said, turning to look at me.

Tears of joy fell. So what if I had to wait a week to take my baby home?

As long as he was going home at some point, I could deal with the wait.

I wailed in thanksgiving to God, for He had heard the prayers of my heart. I secretly promised God that for the rest of my son's life, I would raise him according to His will. However, I knew that no promise I made to God would be enough to express my gratitude to him for sparing my baby's life.

"I'll take it that those tears are tears of joy," Dr. Stenzel said.

Darvin grabbed my hand and kissed it. "Yes, they are. And, Doctor, we appreciate everything that you've done for us, as well as your entire team. We couldn't have asked for a better physician."

"And I couldn't have asked for better patients." She patted Darvin on the shoulder. She then turned to me. "Honey, you get some rest. You're going to need it. You actually get another week or so to be duty-free before the rest of your life changes. I'll be back in to check on you a little later." Dr. Stenzel smiled at us both, and walked out of the door.

Little did she know, my life had already changed, and would never be the same. From the moment that I saw my baby come into the world, my priorities changed. My view of life altered. My reason for living became clear. My desire to impart something into his little life became more evident. I was a new woman.

Chapter Twenty-six

Michelle

A little more than a week later, Darvin and I were taking one final look at the nursery. We had both decided that we would nickname the baby DJ, and today was the day that DJ was coming home.

We surveyed our work in hopes that everything was perfect. His nursery was decorated in multiple shades of blue and yellow, with a mural of water and ducks on his walls. Every imaginable thing that a baby—and his mother—might need was in his room.

The nursery had a flat panel T.V. on the wall, a DVD player, a microwave, a mini-refrigerator, a portable pantry, and an oversized rocking chair, all of which was for me. I'd always dreamed of what my baby's nursery would look like; the dream and the reality matched perfectly.

I'd had several baby showers, and Darvin and I had hardly spent any money buying him anything. My first lady friends had thrown me a shower about a month ago at Houston's, during one of our weekly Thursday night meetings. Their gift cards equaled $2,500, with them each giving me $500. I couldn't have asked for better friends.

Almost each department and ministry at the church had also thrown me showers, not to mention the two elaborate showers that my family and Darvin's family had given me. Our baby was the first grandbaby on both sides, so no expense was spared.

Both sides of our family had gathered at our home just prior to us leaving to pick up DJ. We were having a big "Welcome Home" party, and family members were busy scurrying around, as well as guests, who were still arriving.

We made our way downstairs and were greeted by applause. Warmth filled my heart as I looked at all of the people that I loved and cared about. Our mothers were crying just as hard as they were on the day that DJ was born. They said their babies had had a baby, and it went on and on from there.

Once at the bottom of the last step, Darvin addressed the crowd. "We would like to thank all of you for being here today, to share with us on this special day, the day that we bring our son home for the first time. As many of you know, Michelle and I have endured a lot in the past few years and we are eternally grateful for all of your prayers, words of encouragement, and anything that you've done to show your love. We plan to have a great time today, so enjoy yourself, eat plenty of food, and let's just thank God for our miracle."

Everyone applauded again. I waved my hand to silence the crowd, because I too had something to say.

"As Darvin has said, we've endured so much. We've had moments in which I thought I would be overtaken with grief and sorrow. But God is a good God and He's worthy to be praised." People started clapping again. "I thank God for each of you, but I wanted to openly and publicly thank my husband," I said as I turned to face him.

"Baby, we've seen our share of ups and downs, but God has kept us. He never promised that this life would be easy; He only promised to never leave or forsake us. There have been times when I didn't think I deserved you, and there have been times when I felt I would abandon the call on my life to be your wife. Nevertheless, I stand here today whole and complete. I stand here today loving you more than I did the day I married you. I stand here as your wife, your one and only, your forever and always."

Darvin allowed the tears to openly fall. He leaned in and kissed me passionately, and I honestly felt in my heart that the worst was over and that the best was yet to come.

We drove up to the entrance of the hospital and Darvin pulled around to let me out at the front door. I was moving around better than everyone had predicted I would be after undergoing my C-section. The first few days afterward were like torture. It hurt to breathe, and getting up to use the bathroom was worse than that.

Today, I was at least walking normally. The operator who sat at the front desk had grown accustomed to seeing me come in early in the mornings or leaving late at night. She waved at me as I walked through the doors.

"Mrs. Johnson, is this the big day? Are you taking the little man home?" she asked happily.

I put on my proud mother grin. "Yep. It's the big day."

She clapped her hands in excitement. "I'm so happy for you. Li'l DJ couldn't ask for a better mother."

I laughed. "I'll have to bring him by in a few years, and we'll see if he feels the same way."

Darvin walked into the foyer and kissed me in the sensitive spot on my neck. I giggled like a school girl. "You know that tickles when you do that."

He looked at me seductively. "Really now? And what happens when I do—"

I slapped him on the hand to interrupt his next statement. "What is wrong with you? People can hear you," I said, half serious and half jokingly.

"And who cares? Girl, do you know how long—"

I interrupted him again. "Darvin! Get a hold of yourself. We don't want everybody in our business."

"I can't help if I miss you," he whined.

"Well, we are on a mission right now," I said as we walked to the elevators. "We'll have to come back to this discussion later." I pressed the button that led to the labor and delivery floor. "Besides, I'm not going to be one of those women pregnant at her six weeks check-up."

"Hmph," was all he said.

We exited the elevator and went directly to the nurse's station to sign DJ's discharge papers. After taking care of the necessary paperwork, a nurse wheeled DJ around to us. He was dressed in the Superman outfit that I'd left for him the night before. Darvin and I both had mile-long grins on our faces.

"Mr. DJ is all ready to go," Rachel, his day nurse, said.

"And we're ready for him to go," I said.

In the car, I watched DJ the entire time as we drove home. He was sound asleep. We pulled into the driveway as everybody who had been watching for us came outside. Darvin came around and got DJ and his car seat out of the car as my dad helped me out.

Inside, the eating and entertainment began. People were in almost every room downstairs. The ladies were oohing and ahhing over the baby, and the men were in the living room trying to convince Darvin to smoke a cigar. I smiled as I took in all of my surroundings. Right, wrong, or indifferent, there was nothing like family.

I found my purse so that I could get my cell phone and call the girls. Our weekly meeting was in a couple of days, and I wanted to try to get them to all come over to my house for the meeting, instead of going to Houston's.

When I realized that I had left my cell phone in the car, I snuck out the side door, because I didn't want a million people stopping me and giving me 101 reasons why I shouldn't be moving around too much.

I grabbed my cell phone and noticed that I had received

a text message: **Congratulations on bringing your baby home. Well wishes, Dawn**

For good reason, I'd spent the last two weeks trying to forget that she even existed, and had done a good job of it, until now. Dawn was a force to be reckoned with, and I didn't have the energy to deal with her anymore. I'd spent a great deal of time with God in prayer and devotion, and one thing I had learned was that this battle was not mine, it was the Lord's.

I had said this before, and I reneged. But now, I was no longer going to worry about Dawn and her motives. I was going to live my life like it was golden, and not worry about her childish tantrums. Darvin and I were together, and we were going to stay that way. Not even a woman with all of Dawn's attributes could tear us apart. What we had had been bound in heaven, and no man or woman was going to set us asunder. If she wanted to get to me, she would have to come through Jesus Himself.

I made the calls to the ladies, and after chatting with them for a few moments, I sauntered back inside.

Darvin met me at the door. "Hey, you," he said tenderly.

"Hey, baby."

"Where have you been?"

"I went outside to make a call."

"Oh." He pulled me into him for a hug. "Have I told you lately that I love you?"

"Hmm . . . let me see." I pretended to think. "I believe you told me yesterday." I grinned.

"Well, let me tell you today. I love you."

"I love you, too."

He kissed me affectionately. I temporarily forgot that we were standing in the middle of a room filled with people. I didn't care a single bit; for this joy I had, the world didn't give it, and the world couldn't take it away.

Chapter Twenty-seven

Daphne

It had been a month since Michelle had been to church, and I loved every minute of it. I had become so visible in the ministry and meetings around Mount Zion that people had started to call on me when they needed something. Money might not buy you love, but it sure buys you a whole lot of power. Ever since I had started funding the youth trips, parts of the remodeling phase, and other financially deprived areas of the church, I was getting much respect around the place.

Darvin had made it practically easy for me too. Since the birth of his son, the last thing that seemed to be on his mind was the church. His answers to everything I suggested were "yeah" and "un-hunh." Lord knows if you give me an inch, I will take a mile. So, I was marching around Mount Zion as if I were already the first lady.

That thought made me smile. Not only had I been busy around Mount Zion setting things up, I'd been setting things up away from Mount Zion.

After that night at my house, when I became sure that Darvin and I would be together, I went ahead and assumed the role of his wife. I even had all of my bills switched over to my new name, Dawn Johnson. I started a blog, Ladies First, for other first ladies to come and gain support from other ladies who just wanted to be normal ladies first, and first ladies later. I formed a charity in Darvin's name in small, remote towns outside of Atlanta, and became the spokeswoman. Much to my shock, people loved me. Because he was so widely known, the few people that I interacted with as his wife were surprised they hadn't heard about his divorce via the news outlets.

Truth was the media would have had a field day with that story. But leave it to me to have an answer for everything. I simply told those who inquired that it had been kept under the rug in an effort to do as little damage as possible to his reputation. They all bought that answer.

Actually, being his wife was easy. I couldn't understand why Michelle had ever complained. The only problem I ran into was in the person of Sabrina, Michelle's assistant. She had a tendency to pounce on my last nerve. We had a brief argument one day when she accused me of trying to take her first lady's place. She treated me as if I had already fired her, which was going to be the first thing on my agenda as the official, new first lady.

I hadn't interfered with Darvin too much because I knew that he was going through a stressful time with his son being born premature. Quite frankly, I didn't care about the baby; however, I was concerned about him, being it was his first child.

I wasn't particularly overjoyed when everyone at church was shouting about how the baby had pulled through the crisis, because I didn't want Darvin tied to Michelle for the rest of his life. I didn't feel like having to deal with baby mama drama. She was sure to make our lives a living hell.

Other than that, all else was well. Darvin was planning to come to the church tonight for a meeting that I had set up. I'd told his assistant to block two hours of his time so I could speak with him concerning some ministry ideas that I had, and to give him updates about what I'd done since Michelle had been gone.

He had come to the office one day, and I stopped him on his way out and told him that I had heard about what happened and would step up and take over Michelle's duties while she was away. Interestingly enough, he didn't object, and I had not gotten a call from her signaling her displeasure. So, I did what I said: I took over.

That showed me that he indeed trusted me and didn't see me as a threat, but an asset. I planned to be just that, so he would see that I was capable of handling the role.

In the times when I happened to think about them going and coming with the baby, I would get a little troubled, but I would quickly dismiss those thoughts, for it was only normal for him to want to be close to his son. I was sure that Michelle was only tolerating him at this point. I had won. The game was over.

I went into the restroom of the guest office where I had been working at the church, and reapplied my lipstick. Darvin was set to be in the conference room in five minutes. I planned to be early with my reports, ready to present to him. I smoothed my hair, checked my teeth for smudges of misplaced lipstick, dabbed a little perfume on my pressure points, and headed out to meet my man. I had ordered take-out from The Pecan, one of his all-time favorite restaurants in East Point, and had it waiting for him.

I entered the conference room and set my folder on the wooden executive table. I checked the food order for accuracy, pulled his chair out so that all he had to do was sit down, and went to wait on him by the floor-length windows that flanked the oversized conference room.

I stood there for so long, daydreaming about the journey I was about to begin, that I didn't realize that Darvin was more than fifteen minutes late. He was a very prompt person, and if he was ever late for anything, it was because something was wrong.

My heart sped up, and I stepped outside to ask Sabrina if she had heard from him. Of course, the little wench wouldn't have told me if she had, so I stepped back inside. Darvin's assistant, Ann, had taken the week off, so I couldn't ask her. I contemplated calling his cell phone, something that I had not done since moving back. As Daphne, I used to call it at least once a day for one reason or another.

I paced the floor until finally I decided to walk over to the place where I set my things down to get my cell phone from its case. I scrolled down my new BlackBerry's contact list until I got to his number. I dialed, and it went directly to his voicemail. I looked over at the steak dinner that was rapidly getting cold. My one mind told me to call his house to see if he was okay, but I knew Michelle would have a darn fit if I did that.

I tapped my fingers on my arms that were now crossed over my chest. I didn't know whether to be mad or worried.

The knock on the door stopped my thoughts.

"Sorry for disturbing whatever meaningless things you're doing," Sabrina said. "You have a call holding on line three." She then walked out of the door.

I raced to the phone, sure that it was Darvin. "Hello?" I said.

"Dawn, hey, this is Pastor. How are you today?" he asked, chipper as ever.

I glanced down at my watch. He was now twenty minutes late. "I'm good, Pastor. How are you?"

"I'm well, thank you. Listen, Sabrina told me you were waiting on me. I apologize, but I'm not going to be able to make our meeting today."

"But, Pastor, I already have your lunch waiting. I ordered a steak dinner from one of your favorite little spots," I said, trying to convince him to come anyway. "And also, I have a ton of things to go over with you."

"I see. Well, I'm not going to be able to make it. Something more important has come up."

I raised an eyebrow. What could be more important than discussing matters of the church? I'd spent all of my time preparing to accept this role as his wife knowing that with it came hectic hours. That was why I decided to get involved, so that our hours would intertwine.

"Wow, that's interesting, Pastor. I haven't ever known

you to miss a meeting unless it was a matter of life and death." I paused. "Is it a matter of life and death?" I asked, agitated.

"No. Everything is fine. I just decided to take a day off and spend it with the family."

"In the middle of the week?" I snapped.

He chuckled. "Yes. In the middle of the week. If I had any sense at all prior to now, I would have spent more time with my wife instead of at that church. Whatever is pressing can—no—will have to wait until later. Life is just too short, Dawn."

I heard the sounds of his son cooing in the background. I was livid at the thought of him having family time with anyone other than me. Michelle was supposed to be on a fast track to being history, yet he was spending the day with her? I didn't understand. I was sure that things were over between them. Then I thought, men get sensitive about their kids, especially boys. Maybe it was the baby. Maybe the baby was the thing keeping them together. I began to wonder what would happen if the baby didn't exist.

"Okay, um, I'll just have to reschedule," I said with disappointment lacing my voice. "Do you think we can get together before the end of the week?" I asked, holding on for any sign of hope.

"I don't know. I'm considering taking off the entire week."

What had Michelle done to him? He sounded as if he had been brainwashed. Spending time with the family? What kind of hogwash was that?

"Well, all right. You enjoy your day, and I will push this aside to a later time."

"Okay, you have a blessed one," he said before he hung up.

I was standing in complete shock with the receiver in my hand. Had I been so secure in my plan that I'd forgotten to account for setbacks? For this was certainly a setback, and one that I had not expected.

I slammed the phone back onto its cradle, wheeled around on my heels, went and stuffed the lunch I'd bought back into the bag, and held it up over my head for a dramatic slam dunk into the trashcan. I grabbed my purse and stomped out of the door. I practically sprinted past Sabrina, because I knew she was waiting to gloat in my face.

Darvin had greatly disappointed me, and on top of that, my heart was hurting. I'd done everything that I could to prove my love to him, and it was almost as if he didn't care. I was trying to ignore the anger that was becoming apparent, but it was overriding the normal feelings that I felt for him.

As I walked to my car, I became more and more upset. I thought about all of the changes that I had gone through to be with him. The changing of identities. The endurance of people judging me. The ridiculous amount of money that I'd spent . . . all for him. And he had the nerve to dismiss me as if I were nothing.

By the time I got to my car, I was in tears. How could he do this to me? This was not the man that I'd fallen in love with. He had eagerly taken my gifts. He had, although with slight hesitation, allowed me into his life. Had I loved him in vain?

I beat my steering wheel until my hands hurt. I cried and cried until my heart was sick. I cried because once again, it looked as if my desires were slipping through my hands. Once again, it seemed as if what I wanted didn't matter. Why was it that every time I got almost to my finish line, it moved? Why was it when I got heaven in my view, hell's flames blazed on top of it?

How do you heal a broken heart?

I concluded that there was only one way to do it.

With revenge.

Chapter Twenty-eight

Daphne

A week had fizzled by since Darvin had cancelled our meeting. While he had taken the time to spend with his little family, I had taken that time to get my strategy back together.

I had decided that I was no longer going to allow myself to be defeated. Michelle had obviously done something to him. He was acting too strange. That could only mean one thing: It was time to get rid of Michelle. If she thought her life was hell now, my new plan would have her living there—permanently.

If she thought she was going to flounce around me, brag about her perfect marriage, her perfect son, her perfect church, and go on about how good God had been to her, then she had fallen and bumped any good sense she possessed out of her head.

Tonight, she was making an appearance at the church for the first time since having her baby. My plan was rock solid. It was sure to work. Soon, I would smell the sweet fragrance of victory.

People were scurrying around, getting ready for the one-night revival we were having. The guest choir had already moved into place, and I took my seat on the second row, as I had for the last month or so. I didn't even worry about making an entrance.

The sanctuary was filling up quickly as the guest choir began to sing a praise song. The people who were already there rose to their feet and rocked or swayed to the beat of the music. Some sang along.

I clapped my hands off beat, my attitude evident. I went along with the service. I did the normal things. My body was there, but my heart wasn't. Once my mission was over, Darvin and I would be going on a vacation; I had made the final arrangements a day ago. I booked us a seven day retreat at a resort in the U.S. Virgin Islands. I had arranged every detail, and it all related to relaxation, because by the time it was all said and done, we would both be exhausted, and would need the rest.

Not to mention, Solomon Andrews had been popping up in unexpected places, attempting to terrorize me. He would make his presence known, but wouldn't utter a word. The bookstore. The grocery store. The church. It didn't matter; he was there. Each time, he bore holes into me, and each time put more fear into me. I had to figure out a way to get rid of him, too, but first things first.

Michelle had to go.

Darvin, Michelle, Chanice, and the baby made their appearance on stage, as everyone stood to clap.

"Boy, do we miss seeing her around here," a woman next to me said.

"I know that's right. Things haven't been the same since she's been gone. Pastor hasn't even preached the same," another woman said.

"I know. It just looks right to see the two of them together," the first woman replied back.

They both nodded their heads in approval when Darvin kissed Michelle on the cheek and went to take his position at the podium.

I wanted to go up there and wipe the residue of happiness off her face. I was sick of her to the utmost.

"Praise the Lord, church!" Darvin shouted. The church responded in typical fashion. "God is good tonight. Can I get just one witness to testify that God is good?" he asked. Several people stood, agreeing that God had been good to them. "Tonight is a special night. I stand before you this evening a different man. For so long, too long, I've put this church and the needs of this church before my own wife and family. But this recent ordeal that I've been through has taught me that life is too short to take for granted." A thunderous applause followed that statement. He continued. "So tonight, I ask for your forgiveness because I've gotten the biblical order out of order. God established the family before he established the church, and going forward, we are going to honor the institution of family more here at Mount Zion." Once again the claps came.

"A lot of the reason the body of Christ is paralyzed is because we have leaders standing up in the pulpit, and home ain't right. The Bible clearly states in I Timothy 3:5 that if a man know not how to rule his own house, how shall he take care of the house of God? Pastors are falling day by day, because we refuse to stop and deal with the necessities. We refuse to stop majoring in the minors, and instead focus on what's important, in prospective order.

"But I'm changed, church! I've had a Damascus Road experience like Saul did in the book of Acts, and I, like Saul, have been brought down to my knees. I stand before you tonight a whole man. A better husband. A better pastor."

People were standing to their feet, shouting their amens. Once it had settled down, he continued. "So please help me welcome my wife and my new son to the podium."

Michelle held their baby as she walked to the podium, and once again Darvin kissed her on the cheek. He acted as if he couldn't get enough of her.

I rolled my eyes in disgust and looked at my watch. I couldn't wait for this service to be over.

"Church, I want to thank all of you for your prayers, gifts—anything that you've done to show your love and support to me and my family. I ask that each of you will continue to keep us lifted up, and also that you join me in raising our son. We all know that it takes a village to raise a child." People began to clap. "May God bless all of you, is my prayer."

With that, Michelle went back to her seat.

The crowd was still clapping when Darvin grabbed the microphone to speak again. Somehow, he lost his composure, sending the crowd in an even bigger uproar. I rolled my eyes in frustration. I was surer than ever that Michelle had him under a spell. In all of the time I'd known him, he'd never behaved the way I'd seen him behave recently.

Someone from behind me passed me a note and interrupted my thoughts. I turned around to see Solomon Andrews.

Fear jerked through my body, and the chills that ran the length of my spine felt as if someone had poured cold water on my back.

I unfolded the tiny piece of paper, and read: MEET ME OUTSIDE—NOW.

I nervously placed the message into my purse and looked to see if anyone recognized the panic on my face. I could make a scene and draw attention to myself, or go out and face Goliath. If I made a scene, he was sure to expose me.

I decided to do as ordered. I slipped out of my seat, and while drawing curious stares, I took the seemingly mile-long walk to the foyer.

Solomon was on my heels.

Outside, I whirled around with fury in my eyes. I pointed my finger in his face. "What is your problem? Why are you following me everywhere I go?" I asked.

He stared at me for a moment. "Get your finger out of my face," he said sternly.

I relaxed my trembling hand to my side.

He continued. "I thought you might want to know that my sister has been found."

For some reason, I could hear more behind what he was saying. Had they discovered my fingerprints on her body? No, that couldn't be it. She'd been tossed in a lake. Surely, any evidence or trace of my DNA was long gone by now. Or was it?

"And why would I want to know that?"

He looked amused by my question. "Daphne, Daphne, Daphne. I wish I could pay to see the look on your face forever. You resemble nothing comparable to the force you pretend to have behind you."

What was he talking about?

"Solomon, if you don't mind, can you go ahead and make whatever point you called me out here to make? I would like to hear at least some of Pastor's message."

He laughed. "Do you think that you are in a position to make any demands of me?" He lessened the gap between us. That move caused my heart rate to speed up. "But you're right; the sooner you know how close you are to being exposed, maybe you'll do the right thing and leave town—while you can."

This time, despite the traces of fear, I laughed. "You are amusing. Leave town? Please. I am not—"

He interrupted me. "Because, you see, not only was my sister found, she was found alive."

The absence of saliva was causing my mouth to rapidly become dry. I felt the strength in my legs crumble at his earth-shattering words. It was difficult to speak above the lump lodged in my throat, so I stood there, hoping he would say it was all a joke. But I knew it wasn't. This was too serious to joke about.

In the midst of emotions that failed to behave, I cleared my throat.

"I'm . . . I'm . . . happy for you. For us. I can't believe it," I managed to say.

"Believe it. It's true."

He walked closer to the main entrance. Something willed me to follow.

"How—"

He interrupted me again. "She was found in another

town. I guess the trauma she experienced in some way caused her to forget who she was, or where she lived. She's been living in this town ever since that dreadful day," he said, his voice cracking with emotion.

I felt as if I was going to faint. Twylah was alive? And to think, all this time, I thought I'd killed her. I'd been happy, even, when I learned those burglars had stumbled upon my dirt and had disposed of it for me. And after all of that, she was still alive? How could she have survived?

"Solomon,"—I walked closer to him—"I don't know what to say." I paused. "At least now you know she didn't commit suicide." I paused again. "Nor was she murdered."

A new set of tremors traveled my spine. If I didn't kill her, that meant . . .

"No. She was not murdered." He turned to face me. "One of the reasons I came here was somewhat to apologize to you. I'm sorry for accusing you of murdering my sister." He cast his eyes to the floor. "Twylah called me the day before you were to bail her out of jail. She told me everything about you: who you were, what she'd done for you. The lies. The schemes. Everything. She even went so far as to say that she didn't know how you would respond to her telling you that she wanted out. So, when they told me it was presumed she'd committed suicide and the whole story about the intruders, I felt it was all a lie, and that you killed her and had those guys cover up your dirty work. I'm still not convinced that's not the case. But for now, I apologize."

Why hadn't I made sure she was dead? Why did I run out of her house that day like a bolt of lightning? Listening to Solomon tell the story, it would have made all the sense in the world to pay somebody to do it for me. Why hadn't I thought of that?

He continued. "So, I came to tell you that I'm going to get my sister, and

I'm bringing her back.

"Up until right after her memorial, I'd been on a tour in Iraq. Prior to that, I lived in South Carolina. But I've decided to make Atlanta my home, and now that this has happened, I want both my mother and my sister to be with me."

And what did any of that have to do with me?

"And before you ask what any of this has to do with you, let me remind you that I do know the real you." His expression turned cold again—one I'd grown accustomed to seeing. "So, here's what I'm proposing: In exchange for your freedom, you leave town and never step foot in this city again. I don't want you anywhere close to me, my sister, or anyone else I care about. You have bribed her for the very last time." He grabbed my arm. "So, do you think we can make a deal?"

I heard the sounds of the musicians playing and the choir preparing to sing what would be their last song before everyone filed out of the sanctuary. I had obviously missed Darvin's entire message. The longer I stood there not answering his question, the tighter his grip became.

"I . . . I can't just pack up and leave," I stuttered. I have a job. A home.

A church that I'm heavily involved in. How do you expect me to just move so hastily?"

He released my arm as people began coming out. "You have two weeks to do whatever you need to do. After then, if you are still here, I promise you I will be having a meeting with the pastor and his wife. I'm sure they would love to alert the police of your violation of their restraining order," he said as a smirk came across his face.

Doubt crept into the crevices of my mind. How could everything I'd worked for be vanishing before my eyes? I'd done everything to not get caught, but had yet gotten caught. If he or Twylah exposed me, then I was sure to end up in jail. No judge would ever understand that I'd done everything I'd done in the name of love. No one would understand the depths or the heights one was willing to journey to be with the one they cared about.

"Do we have a deal, Ms. Carlton?" he asked again.

"Yes," I replied.

He smiled. "Good."

I turned to walk away.

"Oh, and Daphne?" he called, louder than I wanted him to.

"Yes?"

"Nice seeing you again."

With that, he went the other way. I watched him saunter away, proud of what he'd done. Little did he know, this was not enough to stop me. I had two weeks to figure out what I was going to do, and when you'd been waiting as long as I had to finally get what you wanted, nothing would stop you.

And two weeks was plenty of time.

Chapter Twenty-nine

Daphne

Three days had passed since my encounter with Solomon. I'd tried unsuccessfully to find out the whereabouts of Twylah. She was the biggest threat to me; not her brother. Hopefully, that amnesia was still in effect, because the last thing I needed was her returning and stirring up trouble for me before I could accomplish my goal.

Today, my newfound plan was going into full swing. I realized that my hopes of staying in Atlanta after Darvin and I were married had been dashed.

If Twylah was going to be living here with her brother, then surely they would cause trouble for me. So, the question then became, how would I ever convince Darvin to leave the sacred Mount Zion Baptist Church?

I smiled at my own brilliant plan. I could not believe that after all of this time, I never even considered the possibility of what was to come.

As I maneuvered my way through security at the Hartsfield-Jackson International Airport in Atlanta, I looked down at my plane ticket. I was headed to Baltimore to meet with the fine folks of the Bethelite International Baptist Church. They had been trying to contact Darvin in hopes of getting him to replace the pastor that had recently died. I remembered hearing

Darvin mention it a time or two, but I didn't put much thought into it.

Until now.

The members at Bethelite had been brushed off time after time by those intercepting the calls at the church. All staff and leaders had been instructed by Michelle to forward all calls from them to the voicemail—ultimately to the trash pile.

I happened to be in a meeting one night when a call from Mrs. Ruby Jiles, chairwoman of Bethelite's pulpit search committee, had come through. Tony, our church's graphic designer, picked up the call, and later explained to the three of us in the meeting that the woman had been desperately trying to get a phone conversation with Darvin. At that time, I couldn't fathom Darvin speaking with anyone from another church, especially if they were trying to recruit him. I didn't want him to even consider moving away from Atlanta. Away from me.

Three days ago, I changed my mind. It was the perfect solution to my problem. Bethelite was a much-respected church in Maryland, and according to the gossip floating around in the various ministry circles, every hopeful pastor and current pastor alike was trying to court Bethelite's search team in hopes of becoming their next pastor. They were a five-thousand member congregation in one of the richest counties in Baltimore. From my own research and findings, I discovered that the coveted position meant a substantial, high six-figure salary, a comprehensive benefits package, four weeks paid vacation, a sprawling 10,000 square-foot mini-mansion (in the name of a parsonage), two vehicles—one for the pastor and one for his spouse—and other perks that made me hop on Priceline.com to book my plane ticket.

I had a friend from back home in Florida design a new website for Mount Zion, which boasted a picture of Darvin as the pastor and me as his new wife. When I'd contacted the church office, I gave them the link to the "new" site that posted additional contact information for Darvin. Mrs. Jiles returned my call within the same hour, and was immediately thrilled that she had finally made headway, in hopes of trying to secure Darvin as their next pastor.

We had a great conversation. I informed her that Darvin would not be able to make the initial visit that they were requesting with their board of directors, but that I would come in his stead, to make the initial introduction and express any concerns or questions he might have in considering their offer.

Much to my surprise, it worked. She was more than happy to have me come up and speak to them. She expressed that they had been trying to reach his wife, when unsuccessful at reaching him, but to no avail. So, speaking to me was just as good.

I smiled as I took my first class seat on the plane. In a few hours, I would be taking on my first major role as Darvin's wife, at the new church we were going to be leading. I had no doubt in my mind that they would offer the position to Darvin; they had sought him too aggressively. And by the time I finished my introduction, they would be calling before I could land back in Atlanta, practically begging him to take the job.

I squiggled in my seat until I found the most comfortable position to lay back and get some rest. There was a long day ahead of me, and I needed to make sure I was alert and ready for any questions they might throw at me. I was sure they were going to ask what happened to his first wife, but I already had an answer. A good one, too.

The limo driver picked me up, and talked the entire ride about how excited everyone was about meeting me.

"Lady Johnson, we have been planning for the last couple of days to make your stay in Baltimore a very comfortable and enjoyable one," he said.

"We are elated that you are here."

Lady Johnson. I loved the way that sounded.

"And I sure do appreciate all that you've done. The hotel accommodations that you all made, I must say, were truly above par."

"Well, we try to display a spirit of excellence in all that we do, and we stop at nothing to make sure our leaders and our guests are taken care of," he said, placing emphasis on *leaders*.

I was at a loss for words. So, is this what it felt like to be a first lady? I could definitely get used to this. I looked out at the scenic attractions we were whizzing by, and silently thanked God for once again coming through for me.

When I walked into the massive edifice of Bethelite International Baptist Church, I was awestruck. It reminded me of the first time I'd gone to Mount Zion, only this church was twice its size. Every imaginable amenity a church could have was found in this building. There were flat screens built into almost every wall, with videos of ministers welcoming anyone who might walk through the doors. There was a coffee shop located off of the main lobby, and a bookstore attached to it.

Now, as I was standing in the foyer, tears were forming in my eyes. Here I was, preparing to meet with a team who would one day consider me their first lady. It was such a relief to know that no one at this church could ever hold anything over my head about my past, or anything I'd done. No one here would ever find out who I truly was. Yes, I was safe here. Peace and serenity enveloped me like a mother to her newborn baby. The fight was almost over.

"Lady Johnson," a small, petite woman said as she made her way to me.

She extended her hand to shake mine. "My name is Sister Charlene McHammond. I am the church's executive director of administration, and will be escorting you to the area where the meeting will take place. On behalf of our great staff and board, we are so glad that you made it to our city safely, and we anticipate a wonderful evening of fellowship with you."

"Thank you. I'm honored to be here."

Wow. What a professional introduction. She could teach Mount Zion's staff a thing or two.

We both said our good-byes to the limo driver, and I thanked him for his hospitality.

The woman and I went down a hall and through some double doors that led to another part of the huge building that was labeled THE ADMINISTRATIVE WING II

We breezed by one office after another. I wondered how many people were on their staff. From the looks of it, it took an enormous amount of people to run such a large organization.

As we walked, I took in the photographs of former pastors, their wives, and children, if they had them. I couldn't wait for Darvin's and my face to grace the church's hall of fame.

There were also pictures of children playing at past events, and pictures of celebrities who were either members or had visited the church at one time. However, the last picture struck a nerve with me. It was a picture of Jesus, with a scripture underneath it that read:

BE NOT DECEIVED, GOD IS NOT MOCKED: FOR WHATSOEVER A MAN SOW, THAT SHALL HE ALSO REAP. —GALATIANS 6:7

I almost went into a coughing fit. Those words inscribed on that gold plate underneath that picture were the same my mother had last spoken to me. I hated I'd ever seen that darn picture, because now I would be haunted by its words.

"Is everything okay, Lady Johnson?" the woman asked, noticing my slower pace.

Once again, hearing someone refer to me as Lady Johnson sparked my fire. "Oh, yes. I'm sorry. I was just taking the time to admire the pictures on the wall," I lied.

"Okay, well, we are here."

Butterflies, birds, and any other flying creature were flying around in my stomach. Nervousness was overtaking me. Excitement had the best of me. I was becoming an emotional mess.

We walked in. "Fellow church members and board of directors, please welcome Lady Dawn Johnson," Charlene said.

Applause erupted in the room. Were they clapping for me, at my arrival? Say it wasn't so.

"Thank you—all of you. It is such a delight to be among you this evening."

An older, bald gentleman wearing a three-piece suit with an antique timepiece hanging out of its front pocket, said, "No, we are delighted that you've come. My name is Elijah Skoch." I could tell he was very distinguished.

"Lady Johnson, I'm Ruby Jiles. We've been speaking on the phone the last couple of days."

"Aw, yes! How are you?" I moved to hug her. I felt as if I'd known her forever.

She smiled. "Let me introduce you to the rest of the team."

One by one, she introduced me to two additional females and three additional men. Alice Manning was the first female. She looked to be in her late forties. Bertha Parker was the other woman, and reminded me of my high school librarian. I wondered what part she played in the decision making. Deacons Larry Parkison and Scott Wilborn were the last two men to be introduced. They seemed to be the no-nonsense type, and had very formally shaken my hand.

"Now that we've all had our introductions, why don't we get started with this meeting?" Mrs. Jiles said.

They pointed to the seat they had reserved for me at the head of the twelve-person conference table. At my place, someone had positioned a notepad, a pen, a bottle of Evian, mints, and a tray of assorted fruits.

"Lady Johnson, I guess we'll get straight to the question we're all dying to know. When did the wedding take place between you and Pastor Johnson?" Mrs. Jiles asked. She looked around at the others. "We thought it was a little odd that he was married again so soon. We remember when he got married to his first wife a few years ago. Never really met her, but because Pastor came up to preach often, we knew of his nuptials."

Okay, so they were going for the big one off the top. I

was already prepared. "Well, we are newlyweds, Mrs. Jiles. We've tried to keep it under the radar a little, because we didn't know how people would accept our decision to be married so soon after his divorce became final. But, nonetheless, Darvin needed a helpmate to assist him in this ministerial journey, and that happened to be me. We were in love, and I'm sure you know that you can't help who you fall in love with, or when you fall in love with them." I took a sip of water. "So, here I am."

"What happened to his first wife? Why did they divorce, if you don't mind me asking? Was another woman involved?"

Bertha's questions came at me so fast, I didn't know which to answer first. "Ms. Parker, I honestly don't know how to begin to explain what happened between him and his first wife. Simply put, I think she was tired of the entire church arena and the life that came along with it. I believe the pressure of being the first lady ultimately caused her to choose a different path." I paused. "I can't say that I'm altogether upset about that, because after all, a beautiful relationship between us emerged as a result."

I waited to see how they would respond to that last comment.

"Lady Johnson, you don't have to apologize in any fashion for falling in love. As long as the two of you are happy, we are happy," Bertha said.

Everyone else chimed in their agreement.

I released my breath. I was on a smooth journey downhill. It would be easy from here on out.

"So, is Pastor Johnson interested in being our next pastor?" Deacon Wilborn asked.

I placed a grape in my mouth. I wanted them to see a more relaxed side of me. "Yes, he is very much interested. As I stated to Mrs. Jiles prior to my coming here, he wanted very much to attend this meeting with me, but was already obligated to another preaching engagement."

"We certainly understand that," Deacon Parkinson said.

"We watch him on the Word Network, and the way he preaches, it's a wonder he has time for anything but that."

"Yes, I can surely see why he's in such demand. His sermons are so uplifting, but are applicable at the same time. Those type of sermons are the key to reaching people in this generation," Alice said. She had been quiet the entire time. At one point, I'd caught her staring at me, and it had made me nervous.

"Well, I can tell you, Sister Manning, that people in Atlanta, Georgia love him to the ends of the Earth, and will travel that distance to hear him preach. If he and I weren't riding together to church on Sunday mornings and Wednesday nights, I don't think I would get a parking space. Folks are there almost an hour early sometimes, trying to make sure they get a good seat."

"I know. The last time the broadcast came on, we saw that the place was packed from door to door," Deacon Wilborn replied.

The broadcast. I had not thought about that. I hoped they hadn't taken notice that Michelle was still being shown on the broadcasts. I made a mental note to do something about that.

"Those broadcasts don't show you the overflow area. People are literally everywhere. There were talks about going to a third service," I added.

"Lady Johnson, you don't have to say any more. We know the quality of pastor he is. When our former pastor was alive, he would invite Pastor Johnson up every year to preach our Empowerment Revival. And every time he came, people were lining up to get in. And Lord knows the man can sing himself crazy," Ruby laughed.

Everyone appreciated that point being brought out.

"Girl, you better be glad you married him before I found out he was single, because I would let him sing me to sleep any night," Alice said sheepishly.

Ruby hit her on the arm. "Alice, get some dignity about

yourself, woman. You do not say things like that in front of our future first lady."

That statement brought a grin to my face. Her comment let me know they had pretty much decided Darvin was going to be their next pastor. I just had to get Darvin to come to that same conclusion.

I brushed off her comment with a wave of my hand. "Oh, it's not a problem. I understand how you feel. I admired him from a distance myself. It was almost unbearable to see him go through what he went through with his first marriage, while standing in the background secretly being in love with him."

"I'm sure it was," Bertha said. "I couldn't have done it. I probably would have just up and left town or something. I don't see how you did it."

If you only knew, I thought.

Deacon Parkinson, bringing the meeting back around to the business at hand, said, "Lady Johnson, I'm sure you have already been made aware by Sister Jiles of the salary package we are prepared to offer Pastor upon his acceptance of our offer. Is that feasible for the both of you?"

Hmm. Let me see. Do I play hardball? Or do I show humility? Gosh, being a first lady might be hard after all.

"Deacon, you and I both know the asset that Darvin is going to be, not only to this great church, but to this area as well. The last thing I would want to happen is to not take that into deliberation while considering your offer." I paused. "With that said, if you feel that is the very best that you can do, we are in a position to accept it—as long as you allot the opportunity for revisions in the future."

The two deacons looked at each other.

"That sounds reasonable to me. I can't speak for the entire board, but I'm sure that we will all agree to revisit the package in a year, and possibly add to it. I'm sure that finances will substantially increase at his taking over, so we have no problem at all making concessions to give him honor for that."

I smiled a smile of satisfaction. This was probably the easiest thing I'd ever done in my life. I couldn't wait to get back home and put the rest of my plan into action. Darvin would be delighted at this news. No pastor in America would turn down this opportunity. And I was going to see to it that he didn't either.

I ate more grapes and pineapples while we made small talk. They asked about our plans for children. They asked about our families. They asked about everything they could, until I informed them that I was tired and would like to rest before my early morning flight back to Atlanta.

We concluded the meeting, and before I knew it, I was back in my hotel room, lying on my back, looking up into the ceiling as if my future were painted on it. And what I saw were the days that lay ahead, when I became the First Lady of Bethe-lite International Baptist Church.

I couldn't have planned a better ending to my life's story. I had coveted Michelle's position as First Lady of Mount Zion, and God had something better for me the entire time.

At that moment, I wished I had a girlfriend to call and tell all of what the Lord was doing for me. But I had no one. However, it was okay. Just like the old hymn said . . . . What a friend we have in Jesus.

Chapter Thirty

Michelle

With taking DJ to doctor appointments and running my weekly errands, time had not been on my side as of late.

I parked my truck into its space at the office, grabbed DJ from the backseat, went inside, and whizzed by the receptionist. I had drunk two bottles of water on the way, and desperately needed to use the restroom. I waved at Sabrina on my way through to my office.

I didn't even notice the troubled look she had on her face until I came back out to properly greet her.

"Sabrina, is everything all right?" I asked.

"No. Pastor is quite upset with all of us right now."

"All of whom?"

"The entire staff is on probation. He found out we have all been interceding his calls from the people at Bethelite in Baltimore."

My heart started racing against its own beat. How could they have found that out? I thought only a few people knew, and all of those I'd trusted to never breathe a word.

"He's probably just huffing and puffing as he does sometimes. You know how he gets. He'll get over it, Sabrina. Don't worry about it."

"I don't think so, First Lady. He's pretty upset. He made Ann give him the number, and said he was going to call and apologize for his staff's incompetence." She looked at the main phone system. "His light is on right now. He must be talking to them."

I glanced at the phones, and sure enough, he was talking to somebody. I didn't know who it was, but I intended to find out.

"I'll be back. I'm going to talk to him."

"First Lady, he knows that you were the one who told us not to alert him of their calls," she said, dropping her head.

"And just how does he know?" I asked, perturbed.

"I think Dawn told him. She said something about running into an old friend who was here visiting, who also mentioned to her that Bethelite's search team had been trying to get in touch with Pastor."

Dawn had told him? Why was this woman always sticking her nose in places it didn't belong? Why couldn't she just leave well enough alone?

I left Sabrina and walked down the hall. When I got to Darvin's office, I heard the muffled sounds of him talking to someone, so I knocked on the door. After he said nothing, I decided to enter.

What I saw had me seeing all kinds of shades of green. Dawn was perched on her broom, as any witch would be; only the broom was my husband's nice leather chair. She and Darvin appeared to be engaged in a deep conversation.

I cleared my throat.

"Excuse me, am I interrupting something?"

Darvin cast angry eyes at me.

"No."

"I knocked, but you didn't answer, so I decided to come in." I looked over at Dawn, who was looking at me as if I were the one out of place.

"Should I come back?"

Hesitantly, he said, "No."

He was killing me with those one-word answers. He knew

that infuriated me. So, he was mad. I knew that, but that was no excuse for giving me the cold shoulder—and especially not in front of Dawn Carlton.

I turned to Dawn. "I'm sorry, but can you give Pastor and me a few minutes alone? I need to speak with him in private."

"Sure." She looked around me to look at Darvin. "Pastor, I'll be waiting outside when you're done. I wanted to finish talking to you about what we were discussing."

For the first time, I saw Darvin smile. "Sure thing. I'll only be a minute," he said pointedly.

What! Had he lost his mind? Was he openly disrespecting me in front of a member of our congregation? No sooner than Dawn could walk out the door, I whirled around to face Darvin.

"What is your attitude about?" I asked, putting my hands on my hips.

He got up and took a book from the bookshelf. He flipped through a couple of pages, as if trying to make me even more upset.

"I don't have an attitude, Michelle," he finally said.

Liar.

"Yes, you do. I already heard about the Bethelite situation."

His gaze met mine. "What Bethelite situation? Because as far as I know, there is no Bethelite situation."

The intensity of his stare made me shift on my feet. I lessened my resolve, and sat down in the chair opposite where Dawn had just sat.

"Baby, I know you're upset, but you have to understand that I did what I thought best for you. For us."

"How can you determine what's best for me? Huh? Am I not the man of my house? Am I not the priest of my home? If I can't pastor my own household, how can I pastor Mount Zion,

Bethelite, or any other church, for that matter?" He slammed the book shut.

"Did you ever stop to think that just maybe I deserved to make my own decisions? Do you believe that after all of this time of hearing from God, He would either suddenly stop speaking, or I would stop listening to Him?"

He walked to his mini-refrigerator and took out a Red Bull. For every second he was drinking it, angst rushed through my veins. I knew I had been wrong in intercepting those calls, but I also knew that Bethelite was serious about acquiring him as their pastor, and I couldn't let that happen. We couldn't leave all of these people at Mount Zion. They were like our family. Besides that, our relatives were here, and Lord knows I needed them, especially after having DJ. No, they were just going to have to find another pastor. God bless Bishop Cloud's soul, but it was not my fault that he died and they were now without a pastor.

"Sweetie, I didn't think you wanted to be bothered with the affairs of Bethelite when so much is going on here at Mount Zion."

"Would you just stop it? We both know that's not true. You blocked those calls from getting to me because you were too selfish to think about anybody but yourself. You thought that I might consider going up there, and you didn't want it to happen, so you told my staff to make sure I never knew about any of their attempts to reach me." He tossed the Red Bull can into the metal trash bin.

"And to think Dawn Carlton had to be the one to tell me. Out of all of the people, Michelle, Dawn was the one who told me. I pay nine people to work for me, and not one single one of them, including you, could do the simplest thing: pass on a message."

In one step, he was back sitting behind his desk, pretending to be engrossed in some paperwork.

"That's not fair," I said softly. "I try to never make selfish decisions. Even with all I've been through, I've still thought of others before myself. And since you mentioned Dawn, you can't possibly be telling me that you're now on her side. That you guys have teamed up and she has your best interests at heart. Because I would really question your judgment."

"Well, question it," he blurted out. "I'm not saying we're a team or anything of the sort, but I am saying that my own wife was plotting behind my back to keep a brotha down." He shook his head. "I never thought I would see the day that you would go to this level." He leaned back into his chair. "I knew you weren't particularly head over heels with this lifestyle, but I just never fathomed that you hated it so much, you would come between potential advancement opportunities for me."

"Advancement opportunities? Is that what you call those people in Baltimore? If so, then what are these people in Atlanta called? You sound as if you've forgotten the real mission here. The true purpose for your calling."

He slammed his hand on the desk. "Now, you wait a minute. I don't need you sitting in here telling me what I've forgotten, or insinuating that I've abandoned my calling. How dare you? The last time I checked, my ratings were higher than ever. More people tune into my broadcast than any other broadcast coming out of Atlanta. Last time I checked, every Sunday people are flooding the altar, giving their life to Jesus and desiring to become members of this church." His eyes were red as fire.

"When was the last time you did something for the Lord, Michelle? When was the last time a person came to Christ because you led them to Him? When was the last time a person joined this church because of the way you impacted their life?" He paused. "I don't hear you. When?" he yelled. When I didn't say anything, he said, "That's what I thought."

I sat there defeated. He was right. Who was I to interfere with any of his ministry dealings? Was I so wrong to want to build my life here, in Atlanta, around the people that I'd grown to love?

Tears escaped from behind their water gates. I put my hands to my face to cover up the shame I felt. I found myself asking a familiar question: Was I really called to this? To be his wife? Was I ready to continue to make sacrifices that I would never benefit from? I knew that everyone had their crosses to bear, but the cross of being a first lady was again becoming too heavy for me.

Chapter Thirty-one

Michelle

Instead of the usual sermon preparation I was accustomed to Darvin doing on Saturday evening, he was packing his bags to go to Baltimore.

We had argued until our voices were lost in the atmosphere. No matter what I said, he was still bent on going to Bethelite. I was angry, to say the least.

Tomorrow, he would not be in Mount Zion's pulpit; he would be in Bethelite's. He was giving the morning message, as well as the Sunday night message there. And to top it all off, he seemed to be excited.

I walked into the bathroom, where he was packing his toiletries.

"Do you need any help?" I asked, attempting to call a truce.

"No, I think I almost have everything."

"Okay, well, I hate to see you leave, but I know this is something you feel you have to do."

He stopped packing to look at me. "Please, let's not go through this again. Let's just leave things as they are, until cooler heads can prevail. I don't want to argue anymore." He resumed packing.

"Me either. I just want you to be happy, and if going to Maryland will make you happy, then I'm happy." I forced a tiny smile to appear.

"Do you mean that?"

I hesitated. "Yes. I mean it."

"Good." He walked to the doorway where I was standing, and placed his arms around my waist. "Listen, I'm not going to ever do anything without first considering how you feel, and how it may impact our family. And we both know how you feel," he said playfully. "I just need you to trust me on this one. I'm not saying that I'm going to take the position; I'm just going to check things out."

I smiled genuinely this time. "I hear you, baby. And I do trust you," I said, planting a kiss on his lips. "I'm sorry."

"Good. Why don't you pack up and go with me? One of our mothers would love to keep the baby."

"You're asking a bit much, don't you think? I'm just getting warmed up to the idea of you even considering this new church. I certainly am not ready to meet them."

He threw up his hands in surrender. "Okay, okay. I just thought I'd ask. You never want to go with me on any of my preaching engagements, but I thought maybe you'd want to check them out with me. But, hey, it's cool. I won't pressure you," he said, moving closer to me. "Now, do you think we can get in a few minutes of alone time while DJ is asleep?" He looked down at his watch. "I still have about two hours left before I have to be at the airport," he said seductively.

I responded with a deeper, passionate kiss. He picked me up and carried me into the bedroom, where he gently placed me in the middle of our king-sized bed. He reverenced my body, thanking God for it with every stroke of his finger and tongue. He skillfully began to touch my soul with the power of love and romance that only he and I knew existed. Somehow, our troubles moved to a distant place.

After our intense lovemaking session, I felt better about him going to Baltimore. Inwardly, I knew he would make the right decision—whether I liked it or not.

***

Two hours later, I dropped him off at the airport. I kissed him good-bye and watched him disappear through the revolving doors. I didn't know if he would come back as Mount Zion's Pastor or Bethelite's.

I sighed as I drove away. No one could have ever prepared me for the role of a first lady. There were simply no books to read that would adequately depict this life I lived. Not one single one.

The buzzing of my cell phone suspended my thoughts for the moment. I looked at the caller ID, and didn't recognize the number. I decided to answer anyway.

"Hello?"

"Is this First Lady Michelle Johnson?" the voice asked.

"Yes, it is."

"Sorry to bother you, ma'am. Do you have a few minutes to talk?"

"Um, maybe. May I ask whom I'm speaking to?"

"I'm sorry. Please forgive me. My name is Solomon Andrews. Twylah's brother."

I was at a loss for words. I had not heard from anyone in Twylah's family since the day of her memorial service. I'd wanted to call her mother on several occasions, but didn't know if the time was right. Getting a call from her brother was unexpected, to say the least.

"How can I help you, Mr. Andrews?"

"Just call me Solomon. And actually, I need to tell you something very important. But it sounds like you're driving, and trust me, you wouldn't want to be driving when I say what I have to say."

My heart was doing somersaults. For some reason, his tone suggested bad news was on the way. Again.

"I'm fine, Solomon. Just tell me what you have to say."

"Can we meet somewhere? Maybe the church?"

I had not intended to go to the church tonight. They were having quite a few meetings, and I knew if I went, I would end up working.

"I wasn't planning on going to the church this evening," I said. "But I'm willing to talk about whatever you wish to discuss over the phone."

Silence.

Finally, he said, "Okay, that will have to do, I guess. Before I get into what I really want you to know, I must deliver some rather shocking news."

From somewhere deep in my belly, laughter erupted. If only I had a hundred dollars for every time someone gave me shocking news.

"I'm accustomed to such news. Nothing you will say can shock me any more than I—"

"My sister is alive," he stated simply.

Okay. I was wrong. There was something that could be said to shock me, and he'd just said it. But how could it be true? Maybe it would be easier to accept had I not gone to Twylah's memorial myself.

"Excuse me? Who are you? Is this some type of joke?"

"I would never joke about something as serious as this. Hold one moment."

Silence.

"Hello?" a female voice said.

Time ceased to go on at the sound of Twylah's voice. I didn't even realize car horns were blaring at me for not moving through the traffic light. I'd come to a halt, and couldn't find the sense to continue to drive. Somehow, I managed to pull over to the shoulder, to collect not only my thoughts, but the brain cells that escaped a mile or two back.

"Twylah, is that you?" I asked nervously.

"Yes. It's me. Michelle, before you say anything, I just want you to know that I'm sorry. I'm so sorry for everything," she said as she burst into tears.

Tears produced in my own eyes. And before I could respond, Solomon was back on the phone.

"Mrs. Johnson, I'm sorry. All she does is cry. And talk about you, of course. She can't get over what she's done to you and your husband. She starts talking, and then the next thing I know, she's crying hysterically. I figured the only way for her to get on a progressive journey was to make one step by apologizing to you."

Again, I was at a loss for words. I couldn't believe my ears. I couldn't believe that Twylah was actually alive. How did she survive? Had she really tried to kill herself? Had three men really thrown her into a lake? If so, wouldn't she have drowned, even if she hadn't killed herself when they tossed her in?

Too many questions were running through my mind.

"Where are you?" I blurted out.

"I'm in North Atlanta right now."

"Maybe we can meet downtown," I suggested.

"I'll meet you at the Starbucks in Midtown in about an hour," he said before hanging up.

I sat at a small table at the Starbucks, sipping a latte with a dash of cinnamon, when a tall man entered the establishment. He was almost the identical image of Twylah. I knew instantly that the man was Solomon Andrews.

I stood from the table and went to the door.

"Are you Solomon?" I asked.

"Yes, I am. You must be Mrs. Johnson," he said, extending his hand toward mine.

"I am. My table is over there in the back," I said, pointing toward the area I'd been sitting in.

He followed me to the table, and we sat down in an awkward silence.

He was the first to break it. "I'm sorry to have to disturb

you on a Saturday evening. I'm sure your husband is not too enthusiastic about you meeting me—a total stranger."

I didn't want to address his last statement. While I was probably out of my mind for meeting a stranger in light of all that had happened recently, I would have really lost my senses if I told him Darvin was out of town. I didn't need Twylah or her brother breaking in on me.

"It's okay." I sipped my latte. "So, can you please tell me more about this situation with Twylah? I'm sure you know I have several questions."

He smiled and sort of dropped his head. "First, I'm grateful to God that my sister is alive. I didn't get a chance to make it to her memorial service because of my tour in Iraq. I harbored so much guilt about it; I thought I'd never get over it. So, when I found out she was alive, I was more than relieved. It was a week ago tomorrow that I got the call.

"An older couple in Alpharetta found Twylah standing dangerously close to a lake in their neighborhood. They got out of their car, approached her, and asked was she okay. Twylah, I guess, began to cry and tell them that she couldn't remember who she was, or how she'd gotten there. They said that she appeared to have been wandering around for many days. They took her to their house out of the kindness of their hearts, allowed her a hot bath, a hot meal, and a place to stay.

"After a few weeks of nurturing her, Twylah began to remember certain things. My name was one of them. From there, they researched, found me online, and contacted me. I went up there to verify that it was her, and it was."

He took out his cell phone and showed me a picture of a woman who'd lost a tremendous amount of weight, but nonetheless was Twylah.

I hadn't even realized that I was crying.

"Don't cry. She's all right. And she feels terrible about all of the things that she's done to you in the past. She is sorely regretful, especially for the break-in. That was the last thing she can remember the two of you discussing before she was presumed dead."

"It was," I said as my thoughts wandered back to that day. "So, are you saying that Twylah never attempted to kill herself?"

"From what I can gather, she had been contemplating thoughts of suicide. She mentioned something about a suicide letter she wrote the night she broke into your house. She never got rid of it, and I'm assuming that is the reason the police ruled it a suicide. However, someone did try to kill her, and after that person left, coincidentally, those three men came in and discovered her—nearly dead.

"Since then, we've learned that they panicked, and for fear of being charged with murder, removed her body, drove her to that lake, and tossed her in. And I'm assuming that when they dumped her, the cold water brought her back to consciousness, and she was able to float back to the bank.

"We are still a little unclear about that part, but it explained why that couple found her there. She had been venturing out to the town area, but kept going back to the lake, attempting to trigger her memory or something. The police discovered that those three men were residents in the vicinity of where they left her, and had traveled down to South Atlanta and broken into several homes. Long story short, God saved her life," he finished by saying.

"Wow. I can't believe it. I'm overjoyed. I mean, your mother must be very excited. I'm sure you all are."

"We are thankful, simply put."

"I'm very happy. This is good news."

"There's more."

"Really?"

"Yes. I wanted you to know about Twylah being alive, but I also wanted to talk to you about the person who tried to kill her that day."

My interest was piqued again.

"What does that have to do with me?"

"Everything," he said seriously. "And I've tried to figure out several ways to approach you, but there's only one way to do it, and that is to do it."

"Wait a minute," I said, throwing up my hands. "You're saying that the person who was trying to kill her is somehow connected to me? Because I'm going to tell you right now, I had nothing to do with it, and I certainly don't know who was responsible for it."

"Calm down. I know that you're not responsible, and I know you had nothing to do with it."

"So, what are you getting at?"

"Twylah and this person got into a very heated argument that day, and they got into a tussle. From what Twylah can remember, this person began choking her, and from there she can't remember anything else until she woke up in the water."

"Who is this person?"

I could see the signs of anger developing in the creases of his forehead, and in the flames of his eyes. His jaw hardened, and he wrung his hands together tightly.

I gently touched his hand. "I hope I'm not overstepping my boundaries, but are you okay?" I asked cautiously. "Who is this person you're referring to?"

"Daphne Carlton."

In that moment, my heart threatened to stop beating. My nerves packed up and ran out of the door screaming, *We can't take any more!*

Chapter Thirty-two

Daphne

Darvin and I had the most fabulous time tonight. We'd laughed like school kids. His subtle, flirtatious gestures had all but driven me insane with desire for him.

He was tremendously surprised to see me when I bumped into him in the lobby of the Marriott hotel where we were staying.

"Dawn, what are you doing here?" he asked, taken aback.

"Pastor," I said shamefacedly. "I knew from Ann that you were flying up here today, and I wanted you to have some support. I figured that with all of the people not wanting you to come here, it would do you good to see someone standing by your side." I saw him get uncomfortable. "You know, as a follower of your ministry," I said, hurrying to dismiss any adverse thoughts he might have.

"I'm at a loss for words, Dawn. I'm impressed that you would go to such lengths to show your support."

I would go through anything for you, Darvin.

"Well, here I am," I said, displaying my perfect white teeth. "Are you waiting for someone?" I asked, looking around the lobby.

"No, I was going to grab a bite to eat in the hotel's restaurant after I called my wife."

But I am your wife.

"Oh, I see. That's funny, because I was headed out to dinner too. I didn't know if the food here was good."

"It usually is. I typically eat here at least once whenever I preach up here."

"So, you would recommend it?"

"It's pretty good."

I didn't need to seem too desperate. "Well, I'm sure you want to get in a quiet moment. I'm going to just go down a block or two and see what I find."

He looked down at his Rolex. "It's a little late, Dawn. Maybe you should consider eating here. I would hate for you to be out at this hour by yourself."

His concern for my well-being made me want to do backward flips. "Are you sure? I really don't want to intrude."

"No intrusion here."

We walked up to the host at the restaurant, and Darvin ordered a table for two. Once seated, we ordered appetizers and talked all about the folks at Bethelite. I reiterated to him the fact that I was extremely proud that a church of that caliber was recruiting him and he was my pastor.

A few times he pulled out his cell phone, no doubt calling Michelle, but the gods in heaven were in my favor, because she had not answered.

I spent the remainder of the evening allowing Darvin to confide in me personal goals and aspirations. He shared that he really wanted to accept the offer to pastor Bethelite, but was sure Michelle would be in dire straits before she allowed that to happen.

"Pastor, you have to do what the Lord is leading you to do," I said. "If First Lady is truly meant to be your wife, she will follow your leadership. I mean, what could be so bad about moving to Baltimore? Sure, it will be an adjustment—major adjustment—but in time, she'll get over it." I paused.

"Follow the voice of God. It will never lead you wrong. It has never led me wrong."

I could see the appreciation of my words reflecting in

his eyes. I had scored major, major points. It was time for truth or dare.

"I have something to tell you," I said, lowering my lashes.

I could see the muscles in his face harden.

"What is it?"

"You don't have to be nervous," I said, letting him know I could sense his tenseness. "I just need to let you in on a little information . . . about what to expect tomorrow."

He took a sip of his water. "Expect? What do you mean?"

"Well, the day that I revealed to you that Bethelite had been desperately trying to reach you, I failed to mention one little small detail."

"And what was that?" he asked, taking a bite of the filet mignon he'd ordered.

"The reason I was able to get so much information from the search team was because I called them, pretending to be your wife."

He started choking. For a minute, I thought he was playing, but he really had gotten strangled.

"Are you okay?" I asked.

"Did you just say you pretended to be my wife? You mean to tell me that you couldn't think of any other way to get information? Like approach me with the fact that the church had been trying to reach me?"

I had not seen this going this way in my mind. I thought he would consider it a joke.

"No, I didn't consider that option. I only knew that I had to find out what was going on. I wanted to help you. I knew they would have never given any details about the call to the staff, because they wouldn't have wanted anyone to know the reason for their call. So, when I found out that Michelle had obviously talked to them about their offer, I figured the only way I could get details was to pretend to be her," I said, throwing the heat back on Michelle. "So, I did. I flew up here and—"

"You flew up here?" he interrupted, practically screaming.

"Yes. I met with the search team—as your wife. I gathered all of the information, brought it back to you, and here we
are."

I knew I'd taken a big risk telling him all of this, but it
was either now or tomorrow. When I walked into the church,
no doubt they would be treating me as First Lady Johnson, and
Darvin would want to know why.

We sat in silence for what seemed like an eternity. It
was pushing me closer to the brim of madness every second he
remained quiet. If only he would scream, shout, yell—something.
Anything.

"Dawn, I'm disappointed in you. I understand your motives, but your methods were all wrong. You should have never
done anything like that, because what am I supposed to tell
those people tomorrow when we arrive to church?" He paused
and signaled the waiter for the check. He sighed.

"Thank God Michelle isn't here or coming. I would
have the biggest mess on my hands."

"Pastor, I'm—"

"You know . . ." he interrupted, "this is something that
your sister would have done. I would have never expected this
from you, Dawn. I thought you had much more class than that.
I must say, you're definitely your sister's sister."

Those words were murder to my self-esteem. He had
compared me to Daphne. Even though I was Daphne, I hadn't
wanted him to remember her.

As far as I was concerned, she was dead. And the only
three people who knew the truth were my mother, Twylah, and
Solomon. This is why I had to convince him by tomorrow that it
was me who should be his wife.

I had already planned to send for my belongings, so
I would never have to set foot back in Atlanta. Everything that

I'd arranged in Atlanta in the name of Dawn Johnson had been cancelled. I would stay here and build a life with Darvin, and no one who knew me would ever hear from me again. I had already prepared myself to have to deal with Michelle occasionally, because of their baby together, but even that wouldn't be often.

"I really hoped you would be able to see the goodness in what I'd done. Had it not been for me, you wouldn't be here right now. You would have never known, because the one person you were supposed to trust to assist you in your destiny schemed, and withheld what could prove to the biggest opportunity of your ministerial career. And you have the nerve to sit here and harp on the fact that I pretended to be your wife, for the sake of only obtaining information? In my mind, I could hear you saying, 'Thanks, Dawn.'

"True, my sister has her ways, but that woman was in love with you. Truth is, I feel that I may be falling in love with you, but you know what? I pushed my feelings aside, and I did this for you.

"Imagine if you take this position. I don't benefit from it. I set this up for another woman who was too selfish to make the trip to support you. And you're appalled by me?" I pulled a hundred dollar bill out of my Versace wallet and laid it on the table.

"Dinner was on me. Consider it a love gift," I said as I began to walk away from the table.

I walked out of the restaurant and to the elevators. I pushed the button, and saw Darvin approaching me.

"Dawn, I'm sorry."

Bingo.

"Don't mention it. It's not a big deal."

"Yes, it is. That was very rude of me to behave that way back there. I guess when you said that you had pretended to be my wife, it struck a chord. We dealt with so much with your sister; I had a flashback. Please forgive me."

The elevator doors popped open. I stepped inside, and Darvin followed. I pushed the button for the nineteenth floor. He didn't know it, but my room was across the hall from his.

"What floor?" I asked, trying to sound annoyed.

"I guess we're going to the same one. I'm on nineteen."

We rode in silence.

"I'm sorry," I spat out. "The last thing I planned to do was make you upset. I love you, and I would never intentionally hurt you," I said, a lone tear skiing down my face.

I was surprised by my own words. I hadn't meant to tell him I loved him, but my heart got in the way.

The elevator doors opened again, and we walked out. I paused in front of my door.

"Did you know you were staying across the hall from me?"

I knew that was coming.

"How could I know that if you've been gone all day?"

I saw him deliberate the validity of my answer, as I turned and slid my key into the electronic lock system.

"So, are we going to figure out how to deal with this tomorrow? Exactly how many people think you're my wife?"

"The entire search team, as well as the limo driver coming to pick you up in the morning."

He rolled his eyes and released a breath of frustration.

"There's no way we can continue this façade. They are sure to find out the truth at some point—like, for example, when I accept the pastorate."

So, he was going to accept it? At least one thing was accomplished. The rest I could work on.

"I'll tell you what; you don't have to tell them tomorrow. You know how big the church is. I'll sit in the back, or in the overflow section, and nobody will ever know I'm there. I don't have to be on the front row, or be the first lady to show my support. All that matters is that you know I'm here."

Approval graced his face.

"Dawn, you're—actually, I don't know what else to say," he said, gazing into my eyes.

I did what came natural. I kissed him on the cheek, turned around, and went into my suite. Inside, I looked through the peephole and realized that he was still standing in the same place.

I leaned against the door and moaned. I wanted so badly to fling that door open and drag him into my room and make sweet love to him. I was tired of going to sleep alone. I needed my man. My female needs needed to be met, and only he was able to meet them.

Tomorrow would be different. I had a wonderful evening planned for us after he was done with both services. It would be a night that he would remember for years to come. I knew it would work, because I was in his head now. And when you have a man's head, you have access to his heart too. There was no separating the two, as far as I was concerned.

I got into bed, closed my eyes, and dreamt terrifying dreams of Michelle trying to kill me.

Chapter Thirty-three

Michelle

Last night was the most restless night I'd had in all of my life. After my meeting with Solomon, I drove home in a daze. The events of the night quickly took their toll on me. I knew I had to be tired because when I got home, Chanice was putting DJ to bed—something I always did—and I thought nothing of it.

In a zombie-like state, I went to my bedroom and submerged into my sea of comfort, hoping to gain some sense out of everything I'd learned.

Darvin had tried to reach me several times on my cell while I was talking to Solomon, but I'd missed his calls. He finally resorted to leaving a message—expressing his displeasure at not being able to reach me—and to let me know he'd left his battery charger in the car when I dropped him off at the airport. I tried to reach him back via the hotel's number, but I'd only gotten his suite's voicemail system. It frustrated me to my wit's end, but I didn't want to share with him the information about Daphne by way of a message; I wanted to tell him myself.

This morning, I'd gotten up, made a phone call to Florida, dressed DJ, and was now sitting in church, listening to Mount Zion's senior assistant pastor, Scott Randall, begin his sermon.

However, my thoughts were far away from this morning's message. My mind was solely focused on confronting Daphne Carlton when she waltzed her behind up in the sanctuary. I was going to take the microphone, expose her for who she really was, and then have the police to haul her lying, trifling butt away.

I had already spoken to the chief elders, Chanice, and a few other key people in leadership, to let them know what was going on. Security had been contacted, and they were on standby. Although I couldn't have her arrested on the charges of impersonating someone who didn't exist, I could at least have her locked up for violating our restraining order.

I was furious, to say the least. I was blowing hell's inferno from my nostrils. I shivered at the thought of Dawn Carlton actually being Daphne Carlton. She was brilliant, and had played us all for fools. She somehow convinced us that she was a twin, when according to the phone call I made to her mother this morning, she had no sisters.

"Hello?"

"Hello. May I speak with Ms. Carlton, please?"

"This is she. How can I help you?"

"This is Michelle Johnson. You don't know me—"

She interrupted. "I know who you are."

Taken aback, I stammered for my next words. "Well, I was calling about your daughter, Dawn."

"You mean Daphne."

"No, your other daughter, Dawn."

"Listen, I don't mean to be rude, but I don't have a daughter named Dawn. I have one daughter, and her name is Daphne."

After the reality of what was going on set in, Daphne's mother told me all about how she'd tried to convince her silly daughter to leave us alone, and how she knew one day this would all backfire on her. And she couldn't have been more right.

It was almost the end of Pastor Randall's sermon, and Daphne still had not made an appearance. It was unusual for her not to have been here by now. Maybe she'd gotten word that she was about to be out in the open, and had tucked her tails and ran. Or maybe . . .

"First Lady, are you going to go out and greet visitors today?" Chanice asked, cutting into my thoughts.

"No," I said firmly. "Did you notice whether or not Daphne walked in?"

"No, ma'am, I didn't. I will ask Elder Spencer."

Chanice beckoned for the elder, and after conversing with him for a moment, we discovered that Daphne had not shown up for service—not this service, or the one before it. Something seemed very strange about that.

After service had ended, I went to my office and retreated to my couch.

Why hadn't Daphne shown up? Did she leave town? Did she discover I was about to bring her down? It was all driving me insane.

"First Lady, I wouldn't worry about it too much if I were you."

"That's the thing, Chanice. You are not me. You don't know what this woman had done to me, my family, and our church. So, please, do not give me unsolicited advice right now. I need to think."

Chanice resigned and walked out of the office to give me some time alone. That was one of the things I loved about her. She was able to know what to do without me having to tell her.

I had to think. I glanced at the desk clock; it was almost time for Darvin to be getting up to preach at Bethelite's second service. I thought about calling the church, but I didn't want to alter his train of thought before his message. However, I needed to talk to him before the night service. I had been in the game long enough to know that he would probably be busy all the way up to the evening service with brunches, meetings, and other things the church had planned for him to do. I was afraid that I wouldn't get the opportunity to tell him what was going on.

Knowing Daphne, she was planning something. And I knew enough about her twisted mind to know that if I didn't move swiftly, she would destroy us all.

A thought occurred to me. I walked to the door and opened it.

"Chanice, get my mother on the phone. Tell her to meet me at her house in an hour. Let her know that I need her to keep DJ overnight. Afterward, find Sabrina and tell her that I want her to book me on the next flight to Baltimore."

Chapter Thirty-four

Michelle

The plane ride to Baltimore had been smooth, unlike my nerves.

I retrieved my bags from baggage claim, and proceeded to the rental car zone. Sabrina had taken care of my arrangements for me, and in no time, I was making my way to the Marriott hotel. Ann had given me Darvin's hotel room number, and I planned to go there first.

MapQuest led me straight to the hotel without getting lost. I got out, left my car with the valet, and went inside. At the desk, I requested an extra key to Darvin's room.

"I'm Mrs. Johnson, and I need an extra key to my suite, nineteen thirty-four."

"Sure, Mrs. Johnson," the clerk said. She looked into computer, and then frowned. "Wait a minute. I have you listed in suite nineteen thirty-one. Are you sure that your suite number is nineteen thirty-four?" she asked, confused.

"Yes. The room is listed in the name of Darvin Johnson, and I'm his wife."

With that, she looked at me as if I'd spoken a different language. She input something else into the computer.

"Can I see your ID please?" she asked.

I was getting agitated, but I pulled my driver's license out of my wallet and presented it.

"Hmm. Mrs. Johnson," she said, handing my license back

to me, "there's a slight little issue here. You are right. You are in nineteen thirty-four, but for some reason, there are two suites listed under Darvin Johnson. I guess you're also in nineteen thirty-one," she joked. "I'm sorry for the confusion.

Let me get you that key."

She walked away as my head began to throb. I kept telling myself not to panic or get prematurely upset, but why were there two suites in Darvin's name? I knew for a fact that his armor bearer did not travel with him, because I had been the one to drive him to the airport. Besides that, I'd seen his armor bearer, Shadar, at church earlier this morning. Darvin had insisted he go alone, because he didn't want Shadar all up in the air about his reason for being in Baltimore.

She came back and gave me the key.

"Is there anything else I can do for you, Mrs. Johnson? I'm about to end my shift, but would be glad to assist you with anything further."

I forced a smile. "No. That will be all."

I managed to pick up my feet and walk toward the elevator. Inside, I pressed the button for the nineteenth floor.

Once to the suite's door, I held my breath, not knowing what to expect when I walked in.

I dropped the key card in the lock, and at the prompt of the green light, opened the door. The scent of Darvin's HIMistry cologne was still lingering in the room. I inhaled. I'd missed him in the short period of time we'd been away from each other.

My sacred moment was interrupted when I caught a glimpse of a receipt lying on the desk. I picked it up as if it had leprosy.

My fear suddenly became my reality. Darvin had dined with someone last night in the hotel's restaurant, and I was sure that someone was occupying suite nineteen thirty-one.

I was so shaken; I backed into the bed and helplessly sat down. I stared at the receipt, trying to will away the notion that

Darvin had been with another woman. A part of me wanted to convince myself that it was harmless—maybe someone from the church. But I knew better. Only a woman would order a grilled chicken Caesar salad for an entrée. Only a woman would care to eat so light. A woman who was watching her weight.

The light in the room grew dim. My head was spinning and my heart was pounding faster than the speed of light. I could have sworn that the room was closing in on me, as rage was being injected into me by the syringe of hatred. I had come all this way only to find out that my husband was cheating on me. Was it that woman from months ago, who he'd admitted to almost sleeping with? I remembered him saying how supportive she was. Maybe since I had refused to accompany him, he'd relied on her for encouragement.

This just couldn't be. My emotions were playing on a see-saw in my heart, and my soul ached at its core.

The sound of something being slid under the door made me snap out of my pain for a moment. I went to the door and picked up the white envelope. I flipped it over and saw the red-lipstick imprint of a woman's lips plastered on it.

I opened the envelope and read its contents:

> Dear Pastor,
> By the time you read this, you will have already accepted Bethelite's invitation to become their next pastor. Service was phenomenal this morning—I've never been so proud in my life. I heard that you were meeting with the search team to discuss the transition (a little birdie told me), and so I know you won't have time to talk before you preach the evening service.
> However, I wanted to be the first to congratulate you on your success. If you are willing, take the key inside and meet me at midnight in the hotel's penthouse for a small celebration dinner. Last night's dinner started out wonderfully, but things seemed to take a turn for the worse. Let me make it up to you. No strings attached. No funny business. Just dinner. You deserve it.
> By the way, after you make the big announcement tonight to accept the church, I will have a big one for you as well. Oh, what the heck—I'll tell you

now. I'm planning to relocate here to assist you however I can.

Remember, I told you last night that I'm a lifelong supporter of your ministry, and that means wherever you go, I'll be there. And I'll be there to serve in whatever capacity you may need me.

Okay, enough for now. I'll tell you the rest later. See you at tonight's service. Well, I'll see you, but you won't see me. (smile)

Dawn

P.S. Although simple, I hope the kiss meant as much to you as it did to me. Your reaction was priceless.

It took heaven and the entire host of angels, to keep me from running out of that room and kicking down Daphne's door. How could Darvin fall for her, out of all women?

I paced the floor angrily, trying to figure out what I was going to do. My strategy had been to come here, surprise Darvin by showing up at the evening service, and spend a quiet evening informing him about the latest of Daphne Carlton. The nerve of him to be having dinner with the enemy!

I was unsure of how I wanted to deal with this.

No, I knew exactly how I wanted to deal with it, but I knew I couldn't behave improperly as a first lady.

I picked up the phone and placed a call to the bellman to come and get my bags. I needed to get another suite in order for me to carefully devise my plan. I couldn't take any chances; one mistake would push everything awry.

Two hours later, I drove up to Bethelite International Baptist Church. In all of the times Darvin had preached here, I'd never come. I wasn't into being the traveling Pastor's wife, preferring more to tend to the things at home.

The church was beyond striking, and thousands of people filed into the building for tonight's service. My heart warmed at the thought of these people coming to hear what my husband had to say. Darvin had definitely achieved an elite status among Pastors, and it showed tonight as parishioners hurried inside to get good seats. I was only planning to stay long enough to get a message to Daphne. I prayed that God would hear my prayer, and I would easily be able to slip the note to her.

I took a seat in the back of the church as others breezed by not knowing who I was. Service was soon underway. it felt abnormal being a part of the audience and not being on stage.

After the usual praise and worship, and all other elements of the program, Darvin entered the massive pulpit. The church erupted in applause. I went from being angry with him to feeling a sense of joy. I was so caught up in the moment, I almost missed Daphne bouncing in like a spring chicken. I must admit, she was dressed to kill. With every step she took, my fists balled tighter. I could just see myself knocking her teeth out. But I had to stick to my plan. For now.

Once she was seated, I motioned for the usher. He walked over to where I was sitting.

"You see that young lady over there in the powder blue suit? The one who was just seated over there on the end?" I pointed.

"Yes, ma'am."

"She's a friend of mine, and I'm going to have to run. I didn't want to walk down the aisle, so if you could just give her this note, I would appreciate it."

"I sure will. I'll do it right now."

I watched the usher walk over to Daphne and give her the note that I'd expertly written in Darvin's handwriting. As his wife, I'd done it a million times for one reason or another. By the time she unfolded it, I'd disappeared.

As I walked back to my car, I smiled. I would get rid of Daphne once and for all.

Forget being a first lady.

Forget the expectation that I had to take whatever was given.

Not anymore. Never again.

Yes, I still had to deal with Darvin, but I would concentrate on him later. Right now, my target was the woman who'd tried to wreck my life.

And this time, I aimed to bring her down.

Chapter Thirty-five

Daphne

Just as Darvin was entering the pulpit, an usher handed me a note.

Chills raced the length of my spine. The last time I received a note in church, it was from Solomon. Surely he wouldn't have followed me here. Or would he?

I opened the note written in Darvin's handwriting, and a huge smile spread across my face. It read: **Just wanted you to know that I'm thinking of you—only you. Thanks for all that you do. —Pastor**

I wanted to stand up and shout, "Hallelujah!" I'd finally won him over. He was finally able to see just how much he meant to me. The way I felt right now was enough to make me forget all of the hills I had to climb to get to the top of the mountain. It didn't matter anymore, because my new life had just begun. Tonight, Darvin would accept Bethelite's proposal, and tomorrow morning, I would wake up in his arms.

I watched Darvin in his element as he maneuvered the crowd with the exquisite manner in which he spoke. Thousands of people watched him with an eye of respect, grateful that God had sent him. Some were even throwing money at his feet, further pushing him up the sermonic cliff.

"Church, no matter what the enemy tries to do, God is still in control," he encouraged.

Amens rang throughout the building.

"I have found myself in the lion's den, just as Daniel. I have found myself facing a Red Sea, just as Moses. On many occasions, I've found myself in the valley of dry bones, just as Ezekiel. And Lord knows I've found myself in the valley of the shadow of death, just as David." People were nodding their agreements. "But, saints, I'm here to leave you with a word of hope. I'm here to let you know that we serve an awesome God. I'm here to tell you that Jesus can bring you peace in the midst of a storm. There is a way out of no way. Reach over and tell your neighbor, 'you can make it.'" Everyone did as told, and he continued. "I want to inform some woman who's at the end of her rope that God can and He will deliver. Some man, tonight, might be on drugs—my brother, you don't have to get high on crack. You can get high on Jesus!" he shouted.

By this time, not a single person was sitting, including me. For the first time in a long time, I actually felt the spirit fill me. I could testify to everything that he preached. I was a living witness that just when you feel all hope is lost, God will throw you a lifeline.

The church service had been awesome—that was, up until Darvin made the shocking announcement that he would not take on the pastorate at Bethelite. Everyone was stunned—including me.

Hours later, I was waiting in the penthouse, hoping he would show up. My hopes and dreams of becoming the First Lady of Bethelite had been crushed. I was so sure that he was going to accept, I hadn't intended on a defeat. I concluded that something must have happened between the morning services and the evening service. There was no way any pastor in his right mind would turn down such an opportunity as he was given.

Needless to say, I was a little perturbed. Tonight was my last chance to get Darvin to fall in love with me before we were back in Atlanta.

Atlanta.

I couldn't go back. There was nothing there for me if I

didn't have Darvin. I'd arranged to move everything here. If I went back, Solomon or Twylah were sure to expose me. Even if they didn't have any proof of my true identity, it was still too risky. I was beginning to get depressed. Darvin had destroyed everything.

Dressed in a black negligee with a satin robe serving as my covering, and standing amidst the dimly lit room, I walked over to the window and gazed down at the buzz going on outside in the busy street. I then cast my focus to the city's skyline. I was growing more disappointed by the second. Baltimore was supposed to be my new home.

Drowning in my despair, I nearly missed the faint sound of the key unlocking the door. My heart quickened, and the dejection I felt seconds earlier was all replaced with hope—hope that Darvin wouldn't leave this penthouse without expressing his love for me. If he did that, I could work on getting him to change his mind about Bethelite.

I inhaled and exhaled a deep breath all in an instant. The moment I'd been waiting for was finally here. A part of me had believed he wouldn't show up.

Without moving away from my position, I decided to break the ice. The moonlight was only casting its glow on me; the rest of the penthouse was in total darkness. I couldn't see him, but I could smell his scent—almost feel his touch.

"Pastor, I'm glad that you came. I was unsure about inviting you here, but after last night, I felt that the attraction between us was too strong to resist." I paused for a moment, and when he didn't say anything, I continued. "I hope that you don't feel I'm being too forward, as I was last night when I kissed you, but I couldn't go another day without telling you how I feel. You see, I'm in love with you, and I have been for a long time.

"Now, before you say anything, I'm sure this is a surprise to you. I've been trying to determine the proper time to tell you, but there never seemed to be one. You're so vague about your feelings, and I was afraid that they weren't mutual. For so long, I've wanted to just hold you in my arms and give you the treatment that you deserved. Oh, Pastor, you're such a good man."

He cleared his throat. "Dawn, I never saw this going beyond platonic reasons."

"I know. I wanted to tell you so badly," I said, walking closer to the sound of where his voice was coming from. "Pastor, if you only knew how much I loved you. What I've done to be with you. The depths I've traveled to prove my love for you."

"I think I know."

"Really?" I was relieved that he had noticed my advances.

"Yes, Daphne, I know."

My heart stopped beating. The Earth stopped rotating. I believe hell even froze at the sound of my real name coming from his mouth.

"Pastor, you just called me Daphne," I said nervously.

"Stop the games," he said. "I know who you are."

I remained as still as the morning dew. I kept swallowing, hoping to wash away the lump in my throat. I didn't know what to say.

He continued. "Why didn't you just tell me who you were? How do you know that I wasn't in love with you as Daphne? How do you know that I wouldn't have been thrilled to know that you were back?"

Huh? What did he just say?

"Excuse me?"

"You should have just been honest with me," he said.

I felt his presence drawing near.

"Would you have really accepted the fact that I was Daphne, after you and your wife made it clear that you didn't want me anywhere near you? After all, you treated me like scum, and even invoked a restraining order to keep me away. What was I supposed to do? Run up to you and say, 'Hey, Pastor, I'm back'?"

"The truth would have helped. How am I supposed to be with you knowing that you've lied to me? What if I had taken that church tonight, and began a new life with you as Dawn, when in actuality you've been Daphne the entire time?"

So, I was the reason he didn't take the church?

"How did you find out that I was really Daphne?"

"Is that really important? The point is, I found out. And I'm hurt, because I trusted you."

His words sliced into my heart deeply. I couldn't believe that I'd had his love all the time, and had nailed myself to the cross with my lies.

"Darvin, I'm so sorry," I said as I moved toward him. "Please, please forgive me. I only did this because I love you. I want to be with you. I want to be your wife," I said through tears.

"Is that why you've been posing as my wife?"

"Yes," I said hesitantly.

The room grew quiet.

All of a sudden, the lights came on. The force of the light in a room that had been dark was blinding, but it was not too blinding to notice that Darvin and I were not in the room alone.

Michelle was standing next to him.

Chapter Thirty-six

Michelle

The expression on Daphne's face as she stood helpless was as exhilarating as the day I got my first kiss. The way her eyes bulged out of her confused head almost made me laugh at her pathetic self.

"It's funny how things change when the tables are turned, huh, Daphne?"

"Michelle . . ."

"Don't you dare speak my name out of your mouth," I said through gritted teeth. She didn't know how close I was to exploding. "I'm doing the talking in here. I want you to shut your mouth. As a matter of fact, I want you to sit down in that chair next to the lamp and shut your mouth—until you're spoken to."

She did as I ordered. Boy, did this feel good.

"Michelle, we have what we need for the police; her admitting that she's Daphne," he said, referring to the tape recorder he was holding that had captured her entire confession. "Let's just stop and wait for the police to get here."

"If you don't shut up talking to me, you will regret anything else you might say tonight." I glared at him, daring him with my eyes to test me. "Neither of you will tell me how to feel. I've been through enough of this hell, and you will not tell me what I need to do. Is that understood?"

Defeated, Darvin just looked intently at me.

"Good. I'm glad both of you understand that this is my show—my game—and we play by my rules."

"Michelle . . ."

Slap!

"Heifer, didn't I tell you not to speak my name out of your mouth? Huh? Are you hard of hearing?" I yelled at Daphne.

They were both appalled at the fact I'd slapped her. And if she didn't do as I told her, I would do more than that.

"Now, Daphne, can you please tell me why you have done everything in your power to destroy my life? I mean, if this was all about Darvin, why not just seduce him like most other women would have done? That way, at least, it would have been fair game."

She didn't say anything.

Slap! Slap! This time I slapped her twice; one time for each side of her face.

"Don't you hear me talking to you, you sorry excuse for a woman?"

I saw tears stream down her face. Sadly for her, I wasn't fazed one single bit. For all I was concerned, it was an act. And she definitely deserved an Oscar for her recent role.

"Answer me when I'm talking to you! I thought you were so bad. What happened to the bully that's been going around bribing everybody? Why aren't you trying to choke the life out of me like you tried to with Twylah?"

"What!" Darvin exclaimed.

I forgot that he didn't know any of the information I'd discovered. I hadn't had time to tell him when he had finally arrived at the hotel. I was waiting for him in his room, and had only shared the basics of what was going on.

I continued. "You left her for dead in that house. It wasn't good enough that she turned on me thinking she had a friend in you. No, no. You had to take it further and try to get rid of her when she realized her mistake. What kind of animal are you? What kind of tramp would do all of that just to get a man? And now you're sitting here looking at me like a sick puppy. You make me sick to my stomach."

"I never meant to hurt anyone. I only wanted to be with Darvin. By any means necessary," she said, looking into my eyes.

Then out of nowhere, she gained momentum.

"Why do you care? You don't want this lifestyle anyway. You're never there to support Darvin, and what little he asks of you, you reject. Who he needed was a woman like me to come into his life. A woman who knew the type of man she had at home, and knew how to take care of him. And if I get my way, that woman will be me," she finished, satisfied with herself.

I stared holes into her for more minutes than I could count. There was no doubt that she was totally insane. I recalled everything that she'd done to me, and the more I thought about it, the angrier I became.

Rage swelled in my chest.

Wrath plagued my eyes.

Fury became my conscience, and I lost all knowledge of right and wrong.

Before I could stop myself, I leaped over onto her, like a bird learning how to fly, sending Daphne and the chair to the floor. I balled my right fist, leaned it back as far as I could, and with the speed of a race car the first blow went just above her left cheek. And, just in case she was feeling spiritual and wanted to turn the other cheek, I reached back and punched that one too. By the time she could come to grips with the fact that she was getting a butt whooping, I pulled her hair, brought her closer to me, and socked her in the nose so hard blood gushed into my face. While I was at it, I went ahead and pulled a track or two out of her head, and used it to wipe away that fake mole that had once convinced me that she could have really been a twin.

Honey, I beat her like Floyd Mayweather, Jr. beat Juan Manuel Marquez.

With every swing of my arm and every pound of my fist, I released every shred of dismay that I'd bottled inside for so long now.

I beat her for every first lady who had ever had to deal with a Daphne or a Dawn Carlton.

I beat her for every woman who tried to remain classy even amongst women who were constantly trying to pull them out of character.

I beat her for every woman who had lost her man to a Jezebel or a Delilah.

I beat her for every day I felt I had to hold my anger in because I was a first lady.

I beat her until Darvin pulled me off of her.

Epilogue

Michelle

It had been almost a year since the trial was over.

"Daphne Carlton, you are being sentenced to ten years in prison for the attempted murder of Twylah Andrews, and an additional three years for violating the restraining order put in place by Darvin and Michelle Johnson It is my hope and desire that the next time you gain your freedom, you will really be a changed woman, and not just the impersonation of one," Judge Crothers had ordered.

With the slam of the gavel, Darvin and I were on the road to picking up the pieces of our life and starting all over again.

Sitting here on stage at Bethelite brought a smile to my face. I would have never imagined leaving Atlanta and the people at Mount Zion, but after going back and enduring the court battle with Daphne, we felt we needed a change.

Bethelite was that change. Even after a year, they had still not gotten a pastor, and were eager to learn that Darvin had reconsidered.

The people at Mount Zion were devastated at the announcement of our departure. Thousands of tears were shed at the farewell banquet. There were so many memories there, and their faces would never be forgotten. The day that we drove away, I knew that nothing for them would ever be the same.

The move was challenging, but Bethelite had covered all expenses, and had even sent the pastoral aid team to Atlanta to help us pack. They were more than any pastor could ask for.

Overall, we were happy. We were Daphne Carlton–free, and that was the best freedom in the world.

Twylah and her brother, Solomon, were taking care of their mother. She and I had found a way to reconcile, and were on a long journey of trying to rediscover a friendship that we once had.

Chanice was relocating to Baltimore with us. I was relieved to know that she'd wanted to follow us; I certainly didn't want to go through the woes of finding another armor bearer.

DJ was getting bigger by the day. Darvin and I had even discussed adding to the family once we got settled in. As of right now, DJ was a handful by himself.

Today was our installation service. It was something all Baptist churches did to mark the official beginning of a pastor's tenure at a church.

My girl, First Lady Lisa Hodges, was in town with her husband, Charles, and they were our special guests. I was cherishing every moment with her, because I severely missed those Thursday nights with the girls. When I left Atlanta, we'd had one last meeting. Of course, the entire time, the only topic of conversation was about the one thing I'd refused to let them talk about prior to then: the night I beat up Daphne Carlton. I was in no way proud of what I'd done, but at the same time, it sure did feel good. God heavily convicted me about taking vengeance into my own hands, but He'd also forgiven me. And I wouldn't need His forgiveness anymore on that issue, as long as He allowed Daphne Carlton to stay far away from me, my man, and my son.

Life is too short and too precious to worry about facades and saving face. Darvin and I were too busy trying to be the perfect pastor and first lady; we almost lost everything we loved.

It's easy to get caught up in titles, but at the end of the day when you're at home and you're only known for who you are and not what you do, who then are you? You're simply just who you are.

Through it all, I can truly attest to the fact that there's a fine line between being wise as a serpent and humble as a dove. Never again will I be so naive.

Reflecting on that last night with the ladies, I made a mental note to make plans to establish a group here in Baltimore. That support was necessary, and maybe one day my challenge would be starting a global network for first ladies. Lord knows it's needed.

After the service, Lisa pulled me over to the side and into my new office as we waited for our husbands.

"I have something to tell you," she said.

Sensing that something might be wrong, I said, "What is it, girl?"

"I'm pregnant," she said solemnly.

"That's great, Lisa! I'm so happy for you. Even though you and Charles got an army of kids already, I'm still happy for you." I nudged her in the arm.

Lisa was quiet—abnormally quiet. I got the feeling that she wasn't telling everything.

"Are you okay? You're happy, right?"

"Michelle, I'm not pregnant by Charles."

The wind was knocked out of me. I sat down on my couch, for fear of passing out. I gazed up at Lisa, who was still standing. It didn't make sense.

The least likely of any of the pastor's wives in our circle, Lisa had had an affair.

Darvin and Charles walked in, and they both detected immediately the shift in the atmosphere.

Charles looked from me to Lisa. "Who stole y'all's cookies from the cookie jar?"

No, who stole yours?

An excerpt from DiShan Washington's next novel,

The Diary of a Mad First Lady:
The Story of First Lady Lisa Hodges

Chapter One

"Hello, Sister Hodges, how are you doing today?" Mother Askew asked.

"God is good," I replied. What I wanted to do was burst into tears. My life was less than good, and everybody at Pilgrim Baptist Church seemed to make it worse, with the exception of a few people.

"Honey, you got yourself a witness, because God is sho' nuff good! Praise Him!" she shouted as she did a two-step shouting move.

I stood watching her as she danced to the beat of her own music. I looked around and was glad no one was here to stop and watch. Even still, most were accustomed to her "shouting" outbreaks. They normally kept moving on with business as usual.

I touched her on her shoulder to get her attention. At this rate, she would have been doing the holy two-step for another hour.

"Mother Askew, I'm going on to the back now, okay?" I asked in a loud voice. When she was caught up in the spirit, she was also hard of hearing.

"Did you hear me?" I asked again.

She stopped shouting. "Whew. Sorry about that, Sister Hodges. I just had to get my praise on. You know how that is, don't you?" she asked.

I simply smiled. "Yes ma'am. Well, you have yourself a fine day in the Lord."

"You do the same. You tell Reverend I said hello, and give him a big ol' kiss," she said, demonstrating the affectionate gesture to the wind and referring to my husband, Charles. "I just stopped by to drop off his peach pie with Simone."

"Uh-huh, I will," I said, walking away before she had the opportunity to prolong.

I continued my journey down the hall of Pilgrim Baptist Church to my husband's office. Charles had been waiting on a proposal all morning from the real estate investors who wanted to purchase some land that we owned downtown. It had come to our home office, and I decided to stop by his office at the church on my way to volunteer at the nursing home.

I volunteered every Wednesday afternoon, and had been doing so for the last year. I felt some sort of weird connection with older people. Where some didn't understand them or appreciate their wisdom, I cherished it. I never grew tired of listening to their old stories, no matter how many times they told them.

Walking into Charles's office made me wish that I had called prior to stopping by. Sitting on his desk in a much too provocative way was Simone Anderson, his executive assistant. In her early twenties, she was beautiful and sexy in an innocent way; a way that I used to be, but since had lost. And it didn't help that I'd had three kids, all before turning thirty. Some would envy my size ten frame after having that many kids, but that which was a virtue to them was a vice for me.

Charles liked them skinny. He liked them tall. He liked them light-skinned with long hair (real or fake), and he liked them constantly stroking his ego—all of the things that I used to do and possess. Over time, I had gained weight, cut my hair, and had long ago quit stroking his ego.

I found it difficult to love a man that I could never love right. There was always fault found in everything that I did. Nothing was ever good enough. Nothing was ever pleasing to him. It was always this or that. So, one day, I quit trying. I didn't worry about what he thought. It was all about the church anyway. And as long as the parishioners of Pilgrim Baptist were happy, he, too, was happy . . . to a degree.

I walked in as if I had been invited. "Charles, this fax came for you," I said, glaring at Simone.

She didn't even bother to move. One reason was because she was a two-timing, trifling skank, and the other was because she knew that Charles wouldn't make her.

When we'd first gotten married, I used to argue with him all the time about how women would never respect me unless he made them. He had always failed to see my point, so, once again, I gave up on that too.

"Lisa, why didn't you knock before you just burst into my office as if you don't have any home training?" he said to me as if I were just another woman off of the street.

"I didn't think I had to knock on my own husband's door, Charles. Here, I brought this to you," I said, placing the fax on his desk.

He picked it up and looked at it. A smile came to his face, and rightfully so, because the real estate investors were offering us 4.5 million dollars for the acre of land on Piedmont.

"Well, in this case, I will excuse you for barging in. Was there anything else?" he asked, obviously wishing that I would disappear.

I lowered my eyes to the floor. I had grown tired of Charles humiliating me, especially in the company of other people. One day I prayed that God would allow him to feel the hurt that he'd inflicted upon me.

"No. That was it," I said, turning around, walking toward the door.

"And, Lisa?"

I stopped in my tracks, dreading to turn back around and hear what he had to say. It was sure to be an insult.

"Yes, Charles?"

"Will you lock the door on your way out?" he asked. Without giving me a chance to respond, he said, "Thanks. I appreciate it."

I looked from him to Simone. They both disgusted me. If I had time, I would go over there and vomit all over the both of them, but the little old ladies were waiting on me. So, without a word, I walked out and closed the door. If he wanted it locked, he would have to get up off his sorry behind and do it himself. Or send his "kiss-a-tary" to do it; because all she did was kiss his butt.

I walked out onto the massive but empty parking lot. In a few hours, it would be completely packed with cars, everyone trying to get in and hear another one of Charles's animated messages. I rolled my eyes, put on my sunglasses, and pressed the button to unlock the doors to my Suburban. I got inside just as a car drove into the space next to mine.

The Cadillac DTS was black, with black tinted windows, and I couldn't see who was inside. The car looked familiar, as if I'd seen it somewhere before.

A man dressed in a smoky gray Tayion suit and matching gray gators stepped out. I quickly surmised that he must be a pastor, because I'd only seen pastors wearing Tayion suits and expensive gators.

He smiled at me with teeth as white as snow and as straight as a ruler. He had a close-cropped haircut with small, auburn-colored curls that rested neatly on top of his head. And Lord, his eyes; his eyes were a mixture of hazel and gray. And at some point in his life, his momma must have told him that they were his best asset, because when he looked at me, my very soul was pierced. The man was fine, to say the least, and before I knew it, I was sweating bullets.

I rolled down my window. "Are you looking for someone?" I asked.

"You," he replied seductively.

What did he just say? Lord, please help me, Jesus! Did he not see that the sign above the parking space I was sitting in marked FIRST LADY? Nonetheless, I gave him my schoolgirl smile; it was always impressive.

"That's funny, because had I known that, I wouldn't have made myself so hard to find," I flirted.

There wasn't anything wrong with flirting, was there?

He flashed another smile at me. Lord, if he kept doing that, I was going to melt away in front of his eyes.

"First Lady, right?" he asked.

Dang. The sign must have given me away. I hated when people called me out like that, as if to remind me of who I was.

"I prefer Sister Hodges. I don't particularly like the term 'first' because it insinuates that a second, third, or even fourth might follow behind it," I said snappily, because in my case, it did.

"Whoa. Excuse me. I didn't mean any harm. I just didn't know your first name," he said, holding his hands up in defense.

I relaxed a little. "I'm sorry. It's just that . . ." I paused and looked back into his eyes. I didn't know this man, so why was I about to start telling him my business? "Anyway, I'm sorry if I came across the wrong way. I'm not usually like this." I lowered my eyes.

"Look at me," he said sternly. "Hold your head up, because you have no reason to hold it down. You are way too beautiful to not be noticed, and you definitely don't have a reason to apologize to me."

I looked at him. He thought I was beautiful? Charles used to say that, until I no longer fit the mold of what he thought the perfect woman looked like. I was sure this man was only trying to make me feel good. With his good looks, I knew he wasn't running low in the self-esteem department. I bet women threw themselves and everything else at him. Hmph. It was the same with Charles.

"Thank you. Um, obviously you know where you are, because Pilgrim Baptist is not off a main highway, so I'm also going to assume you knew who you came to see," I said as I glanced at my watch. "And I'm almost late for an appointment. You have a good day." I pressed the button that rolled my windows up.

That was a good thing. I needed to roll up that window with him in it. My flirting had gone too far and I could feel it. The sad part about it was I didn't care. It felt good. Too good, actually.

I put my truck in reverse, and the man knocked on my window. I cracked it.

He started laughing. "What? You think I'm going to jump in and get you?"

If he only knew how badly I wanted him to. I wanted him to get me, take me away from this place, and never look back. I sighed. That would never happen.

I let the window down some more. "Sorry. I don't know you."

"What can I do to you in a church parking lot with your husband and one other person inside?" he asked.

I looked over and saw Charles's two-door Jaguar parked next to my truck, and Simone's two-door Mercedes next to his. He had a point.

"I don't know. Like I said, I'm not normally like this. I'm just having a rough day, that's all," I mumbled, head down again.

"Hey, what did I tell you about holding your head down? And the day just got started for it to be bad already," he said. "Let me guess; trouble at the church?"

If he only knew. Then again, it wasn't so much the church as it was the pastor.

"No. Trouble at home," I replied before I'd meant to. Oh, well, he was a complete stranger. The last thing he could do was judge me.

He looked toward the door of the church. "Listen, I can

come back and see Charles at any time. You want to go and grab lunch? It'll be on me," he said reassuringly.

I wished I could.

"No," I said. "I don't think Charles would appreciate that too much. Nor the members of this church, for that matter."

"What about you? What do you want to do? And who cares what the members of this church think? You are a grown woman, and if you want to have a business lunch to talk about business, then that's your prerogative," he said suggestively.

He spoke with a confidence that I could only dream about. I was not that bold.

"You're right. It should be that way, but it's not. But thanks for the offer. Maybe in another life, I'll just have to take you up on it." I smiled weakly.

He put his hand into the truck window and grabbed mine that was resting on the arm rest.

"Look, one lunch isn't going to hurt. You look sad, and all I want to do is try to bring a little sunshine into your life, even if only for one hour."

Lord knows I needed some sunshine. But at what cost? I exhaled over and over. Why was this decision so hard to make? I knew I shouldn't be going to lunch with this man. I knew that I had no business to talk about, and even if that was a good excuse, it wasn't the truth. I couldn't live with myself knowing that I was being deceptive. Besides, I didn't even know his name.

"I'm sorry, Mister . . ." I said, waiting for him to finish the sentence with his name.

"Alex. Alex Mitchell is my name."

"I'm sorry, Alex. I can't do it. Maybe another time," I said.

He released my hand. "Okay, I will accept no this time. I realize that you just met me. But I'm sure I'll be seeing a lot of you, and don't think for one time this will be my last invitation."

He reached into his suit pocket and pulled out a business card.

"Here, take this," he said as he wrote another number on the back. "That's my cell number. Call me anytime, even if you just want to talk."

Like a fool, I took the card. I tried to convince myself that I was only being polite, but I knew that wasn't the case. Maybe not today, but one day, I knew that I would use that number.

He said good-bye and walked to the church. I watched his swagger. He was the kind of man that would get an emotionally bankrupt woman such as me in a whole lot of trouble. If only I had the boldness that Charles had, to do any and everything I wanted to, I would have taken Alex up on that lunch—and maybe a few other things as well. But that was totally out of my character. The furthest I'd ever gone in that direction was today with the flirting, and I felt bad enough about that.

Who was Alex Mitchell? Was he a pastor? Why hadn't I ever heard of him before? Whoever he was, I hoped he wasn't in town to stay. That just might be a problem. A tall, six foot problem.

I finally drove away, but all I could think about was that business card that I had tossed in my purse. It was the forbidden fruit, and I was in the Garden of Eden. I could finally sympathize with Eve.

What the devil was offering looked mighty good to me.

About the Author

DiShan Winters-Washington, affectionately called Lady Di, is a native of Valley, Alabama. She is an author, ghostwriter, playwright, and CEO of Pure Publishing. With a passion for writing since the fifth grade, DiShan have soared to manyheights in the literary world. In 2004, she self-published her first novel, *Up High, Down Low, Too Slow*. In 2007, she met Victoria Christopher Murray, who took a personal interest in assisting her with developing and honing her craft. From this mentorship, the novel, *The Diary of a Mad First Lady* evolved. Lady Di is also a powerful motivational speaker and has conducted and spoke at many women's conferences and events across the Southeast. She has been married since the age of 16 to Pastor Myrondous Washington (Agape Global Church) and they reside in Atlanta, Georgia.

ORDER FORM
URBAN BOOKS, LLC
78 E. Industry Ct
Deer Park, NY 11729

Name: (please print):_____

Address: _____

City/State: _____

Zip: _____

QTY	TITLES	PRICE
	16 ½ On The Block	$14.95
	16 On The Block	$14.95
	Betrayal	$14.95
	Both Sides Of The Fence	$14.95
	Cheesecake And Teardrops	$14.95
	Denim Diaries	$14.95
	Happily Ever Now	$14.95
	Hell Has No Fury	$14.95
	If It Isn't love	$14.95
	Last Breath	$14.95
	Loving Dasia	$14.95
	Say It Ain't So	$14.95

Shipping and Handling - add $3.50 for 1st book then $1.75 for each additional book.

Please send a check payable to:
Urban Books, LLC
Please allow 4 - 6 weeks for delivery

ORDER FORM
URBAN BOOKS, LLC
78 E. Industry Ct
Deer Park, NY 11729

Name: (please print):_____

Address: _____

City/State: _____

Zip: _____

QTY	TITLES	PRICE
	The Cartel	$14.95
	The Cartel#2	$14.95
	The Dopeman's Wife	$14.95
	The Prada Plan	$14.95
	Gunz And Roses	$14.95
	Snow White	$14.95
	A Pimp's Life	$14.95
	Hush	$14.95
	Little Black Girl Lost 1	$14.95
	Little Black Girl Lost 2	$14.95
	Little Black Girl Lost 3	$14.95
	Little Black Girl Lost 4	$14.95

Shipping and Handling - add $3.50 for 1st book then $1.75 for each additional book.

Please send a check payable to:

Urban Books, LLC

Please allow 4 - 6 weeks for delivery

ORDER FORM
URBAN BOOKS, LLC
78 E. Industry Ct
Deer Park, NY 11729

Name: (please print):_____

Address: _____

City/State: _____

Zip: _____

QTY	TITLES	PRICE
	A Man's Worth	$14.95
	Abundant Rain	$14.95
	Battle Of Jericho	$14.95
	By The Grace Of God	$14.95
	Dance Into Destiny	$14.95
	Divorcing The Devil	$14.95
	Forsaken	$14.95
	Grace And Mercy	$14.95
	Guilty & Not Guilty Of Love	$14.95
	His Woman, His Wife His Widow	$14.95
	Illusion	$14.95
	The LoveChild	$14.95

Shipping and Handling - add $3.50 for 1st book then $1.75 for each additional book.
Please send a check payable to:
Urban Books, LLC
Please allow 4 - 6 weeks for delivery

ORDER FORM
URBAN BOOKS, LLC
78 E. Industry Ct
Deer Park, NY 11729

Name: (please print):_____

Address: _____

City/State: _____

Zip: _____

QTY	TITLES	PRICE

Shipping and Handling - add $3.50 for 1st book then $1.75 for each additional book.
Please send a check payable to:
Urban Books, LLC
Please allow 4 - 6 weeks for delivery

Notes